Saving
Tuna Street

"In this difficult world of the shore,
life displays its enormous toughness and vitality…"
—Rachel Carson, *The Edge of the Sea*

Saving
Tuna Street

Nancy Nau Sullivan

Light Messages

Durham, NC

Published 2020, by Light Messages
www.lightmessages.com
Durham, NC 27713 USA
SAN: 920-9298

Paperback ISBN: 978-1-61153-330-9
Ebook ISBN: 978-1-61153-332-3
Library of Congress Control Number: 2019953319

To Charles J. Nau
dear cousin, my friend

One
Forked

OUR STREET. AT LEAST FOR NOW.

Blanche dumped a bucket of water down Tuna Street. She watched the ripples sink into the crushed shell and didn't even glance at the blue waves of the Gulf of Mexico lapping away on the beach. She swung the bucket back and forth furiously.

A rat skittered up a palm tree. All she could think of was Sergi Langstrom.

Something just wasn't right about that guy. He was slick. A Bradley Cooper knockoff without true charm and a carpetbagger, to boot.

"Let's get rid of the non-native flora," he'd told the *Island Times*. "Let's *beautify paradise!*"

"Really! He wants to beautify beauty?" Blanche yelled into the palm trees.

She tossed the bucket end over end, and it landed against a stand of shady Australian pines. The tall, long-needled trees were at the top of Langstrom's hit list of "flora." She yanked the flimsy t-shirt down over her cut-offs and grabbed her bag off the porch. The door stuttered after her as she took the steps two at a time. She had to get to Langstrom.

Blanche hurried toward town, blinded by the sun slanting through the oleander hedges along Gulf Drive. Parrots squawked overhead in the canopy of treetops. She shaded her eyes and sprinted through the winding streets of the island. Her sandals slapped the road, her heart raced to keep up.

She had no idea what she was going to say to Langstrom. But she had to make it clear that he and his bunch of land-developing goons had to go before they turned the island into another magic king-dumb.

She'd get her chance soon enough. The meeting was scheduled to start in minutes. The small white clapboard building was within sight, and cars were pulling in.

She fanned away the humidity that engulfed her like she'd been running in a rain cloud. She caught her breath.

Realtor Bob Blankenship climbed out of his silver Mercedes just as Blanche bent over, hands on her knees, huffing and puffing. Bob's polished wing-tips came into view under her nose. She popped up. His shoulders were the size of an offensive tackle's, but he had the soft brown eyes of a teddy bear.

"Well. Blanche Murninghan!" She got a whiff of something fresh and citrusy.

"Bob!" She plucked at her wilted t-shirt. She wished she'd changed into that newis dress. *Well, too late now.* Her legs were rubbery, her mind worrying over the details of the upcoming meeting.

"You're looking winded!" He laughed and took her arm as they headed toward the Santa Maria Town Hall.

"Winded. Don't I wish that were it."

He shook his head, but he was smiling. "We'll get him. Never knew you to back down."

Bob had just shaved and a nick blossomed below one round dimple in his smile. All white teeth and rosy cheeks. The October afternoon hovered at ninety, but he didn't look it, his silk suit pressed, shirt crisp. He stopped. "Blanche, you got your notebook? You writing this one up?"

"Not this time." She shot him a look. "What are we gonna tell him?"

"To get outta here." He sighed.

"We need more than that."

"Yeah, I know."

It might help if she exposed Langstrom's devastating plans in the *Island Times*. Help what? She'd tried the news-writing approach. She'd written a series of articles about the drug drops at Conchita Beach, and *nada*. Nothing. They were still going on. The police chief was pissed. Blanche had stirred up a lot of talk and trouble. Chief Duncan had told her to lay off and let the authorities work on it. Or else.

Her editor, Clint Wilkinson, had started in: "Now, Blanche..."

She'd stormed out of the newspaper office, leaving a befuddled boss, and headed for the Gulf to cool off. It worked, for a bit, but now she was dealing with one huge writer's block. She'd put her part-time journalism career on hold, consumed with thoughts of Langstrom and his plans. The developer whores were taking over Santa Maria Island.

It stung, like she'd stepped in a thousand sand burrs. Writing them up in the *Island Times* was not going to get rid of them any time soon.

Bob pointed one finger in the air. "We need to keep after them ..."

High heels clicked across the parking lot. Bob's partner, Liza Kramer, hurried toward them in jeweled sandals, her tanned legs glowing. She wore a pink angora shell with a white leather skirt and looked like a freshly decorated cake. She was smiling, of course. Blanche's frustration fizzled. If anyone could lighten the mood, or at least level it, it was Liza.

"You're glowing, girl!" She gave Blanche a big hug.

"*Burning* is more like it." Blanche's face was red hot, her hair stuck to her forehead.

"You *will* say something in that the meeting, won't you?"

"Well, I plan to. If I don't kill the guy first." Blanche bent one leg, then the other, loosening up from her toes to the knot that twisted in her stomach. "Got anything new, Liza?"

"*Lots* of new regs." Liza looked sweet as a cupcake but her brain was prime cut. She held on lightly to Bob's fingers. "I found more on permitting in the coastal zones. There're even more restrictions than we'd figured."

"They'll get those permits over my dead body! Just not gonna happen. They're *dreamin'*." He smiled at her, squeezed her hand. "Liza, once again, you're on top of it."

"Where I like to be!" She bumped him, and his arm encircled her waist.

"Oh, jeez. I'm glad you're so cheery." Blanche forgot her worries for about a second, and then the quaking in her stomach started up again. She wiped the palms of her hands on the back of her shorts. "I don't know. Those people have loads of cash. They'll try to buy their way in."

"They can try all they want," said Bob. "Like I said, they'll pay hell getting the OK for their fancy turrets and whatnot. What they're proposing is a damn theme park. Just won't fly." Strong and sure, that was Bob. Blanche always thought that if he hadn't been a realtor, he would have made a darn good preacher at Palm-a-Soula Baptist Church.

Blanche held back and looked over the crowd while Liza and Bob disappeared through the doors of the town hall. It was a good group, mostly old-timers who loved the place just the way it was. She tried to stay positive, but as the start of the meeting drew closer, the thought of Langstrom's disastrous plan made her crazy. He was going to destroy all of it: the habitat for migrating parrots and butterflies, the historic old clapboard cottages, the bird sanctuary. Presto! The delicate limestone aquifer that was Florida was quickly succumbing to heaps of pink and turquoise stucco—and slime and overflowing septic systems and industry that didn't care. The sleepy manatees would be replaced with boats for the rich—zipping about with perturbing speed along the shoreline and in and out of man-made, stagnant canals. The sea grape and mangroves, home to fish and wildlife, would be gone, or at least cut to smithereens for boat docks and for the sake of a better view. She swiped a hand across her glistening forehead. *He wants to get rid of the non-natives? He's not native. We need to get rid of him.* She had to make a case and hope her words didn't come out like a boiling alphabet soup.

She blinked at the indoor lighting. Bob and Liza stood in the middle of a group of laughing island residents. *Well, that's not surprising.* He was their realtor, and he was also their Little League coach at the community center while Liza worked the phones to raise money for the uniforms. Despite the cheer, the room had the curious air of an inquisition with a little cocktail party thrown in. It was definitely set up for confrontation. She could hear it in the low-key buzz.

The metal folding chairs sat in straight rows on the wide-plank floor—the very floor Blanche had danced upon at age six for ballet lessons. A lot of things had changed in twenty-five years, but not the hall. It was the place of weddings, meetings, plays, and political receptions—some of them contentious gatherings, but nothing like this one. It was now a battlefield.

Blanche waved at Mayor Pat Strall who lumbered to her seat at a long table. She hunched her shoulders at Blanche and looked peeved. It wasn't something she'd done, or said. The mayor was generally peeved. Everybody knew she was not in favor of the land development, but opinion on her views had come up iffy.

She'd made it clear she was fed up with all the wrangling. Now several council members flitted around, waving papers at each other and at the mayor, who shooed them away.

Blanche glanced at the side door. Still no Langstrom. She grabbed a chair.

Becky Sharmette of Island Knitters, Needles, and Knots nudged her arm. "Hear he's a real looker." She winked.

Blanche grimaced.

"Let me tell ya, it's all plenty scary." Becky's expression went from sunny to gloomy. "If those developers get their way, we'll have to go. Just can't afford their houses and those taxes…"

Blanche was visibly alarmed. "Where would you go?"

"Don't know."

"And the business?"

"*Kafoompa.*" Her fingers shot open. "That development would be one big explosion in our faces. Wish Mayor Pat and that bunch could *do* something about it."

Blanche studied the government officials of Santa Maria Island. An ancient air conditioner rattled above the mayor's head and dripped onto her limp pancake of a hat. She inched it off her forehead and fanned herself violently with the night's agenda. She'd told everyone every chance she got that she was ready to throw it in and that she looked forward to assuming her throne (a barstool) at Stinky's, the immensely popular hamburger shack run by her three daughters. It was time for new blood in town.

Blanche slumped—and let her imagination shove her into the rabbit hole of daydreams where she often escaped. She was the new mayor. She saw herself sitting on top of a bulldozer, scooping up these developer hairball types and dumping them at the airport, or worse.

Trouble was, Langstrom was real and not a dream and he was not going back to Chicago. Even if he did, she feared there would be others just like him. He had started something that was going to be pretty darn hard to put a stop to.

She'd tried to avoid him around town, but it had been difficult. He was everywhere: glad-handing at the coffee shop, talking up the land development. Her own newspaper had followed him around to snag some "color." Wade! The reporter was worse than sunburn and a rash to boot, and he was hot on Langstrom's tail. Kissing it.

She shifted on the chair, curling her fingers around the hard edges. Waiting for Langstrom. He was making her sweat. This was something else she loathed about him. A rivulet ran down the back of her thin shirt. She couldn't think of her neighbors, or her cabin on Tuna Street—that glorious pile of logs on the most beautiful stretch of white sand in the world—without the blue eyes of Sergi Langstrom looming into her head like a living nightmare.

One worn Teva flopped up and down from the end of her toe.

A side door banged open, and Blanche jumped. Both sandals slapped the floor. Langstrom walked into the room.

The devil in pinpoint blue oxford.

Two
Turning up the Heat

Smooth and easy, like he owned it. That was Sergi Lackstrom.

Behind him, a short, fussy fellow darted toward Mayor Pat with a stack of posters. She flinched, then removed her hat and wet strings flopped over her eyes. She was spared the initial shock. Blanche caught her breath. They called it The Plan. Blanche called it *hell*.

Langstrom grinned. "Hi, there." The mayor and council members stared at him, wide-eyed.

"*Really?*" Blanche said.

"Fur-ril." Barbara Bennett of Coquina Collections tipped forward in her seat. "Dang. Ain't he the handsome one though," she said in an Irish whisper. The women nodded. *And swooned?*

Blanche couldn't take her eyes off the posters. But then she did.

Langstrom had the loose gait of an athlete. Trim and tall. Cleft in his chin. She imagined him swiveling down a ski slope chipping ice into frosty clouds, smiling with a mouthful of snowy caps. Well, here he was on their bright sunny island, and he could just go back to freakin'…Switzerland?

She mumbled, "I guess you could say that he's not hard to look at. But, I sure hate looking at him." She wished he were ugly. As it was, his boyish good looks would only convince people to run toward him instead of away from him.

He hovered in the front row and lifted Janet Capeheart's fingers like he was asking her to dance. The smile smoothed her cheeks and erased years.

"What is he *doing*?" Blanche hissed. Becky poked her arm.

Rumor had it that Janet's dress shop would likely be the first to go. What could possibly make her so gleeful? Her quaint cottage business—with hummingbirds feeding in the bougainvillea, a wide deck with rockers—would be replaced with a pseudo-Victorian mansion, complete with wraparound gallery. The thought of all those fake curlicues and gingerbread made Blanche gag.

Sergi still held Janet's blue-veined hand. She didn't seem to be thinking about business. Not with that besotted grin.

The room was hot but Blanche was cold. She craned her neck to get a better view. He was fawning over the whole front row. He rolled the sleeves of his fine pinpoint shirt and tucked a hand in the pocket of his pressed khakis. He wore shiny loafers with tassels, no socks.

Blanche gritted her teeth and slumped until she was nearly off the chair.

Langstrom didn't look at the long table where Mayor Pat sputtered: "Who's running for office here?" Blanche could hear her from where she sat.

The mayor hopped to her feet, the gavel waggling in her hand, a menacing look on her face. She opened her mouth but all eyes were on Sergi. He smiled at her. "Thank you, Your Honor, and board members, for giving us this opportunity."

Who is us?

"We certainly have paradise here, don't we?"

We?

The mayor sat down with a loud *whomp.*

"Santa Maria! What a great place!" He fixed them with those ice-blue eyes. "Our beaches, and the sun. *And,* our great restaurants!" He lowered his voice conspiratorially. "Denzel has raved about Banana Cabana!"

"What?" Blanche choked. "He's on speaking terms with Denzel?"

"Who'd a figured." Becky's mouth was open in a dopey smile.

It was true the great movie star had visited Santa Maria and loved the Jamaican cuisine at the Cabana. They loved him. That didn't mean they had to pave the sidewalk with stars.

"It's about time we showed off this beautiful island!" He held up an admonishing index finger. "Now, let's get Denzel and company back here for more of those conch fritters!"

They chuckled and clapped.

Blanche was appalled.

"Before the invitations go out, we have work to do!"

There was that *we* again.

Sergi pointed to the drawing of a huge condo-like structure perched on an easel. It rested among an assortment of fancy watercolors and line drawings with stands of palms and globs of greenery and flowers. He'd spent a fortune on the posters. Money. A flood of it already.

"Just for starters. Here's something along the lines of what we propose...A real beauty." Langstrom tapped the rendering of a house that had crept through the permitting process and gone up almost overnight—a light tan stucco monolith with orange shutters and a green barrel-tiled roof, Tiffany glass and brass coach lamps. It was finished off with white filigreed arches and balconies facing the Gulf. Hideous. At the end of the deck, the builder had attached a purplish-grey guesthouse. Like a wart.

Somehow, the developer had snuck in under the radar and put

up the monstrosity of a model.

It set off Blanche's alarm. She knew the location well. The house, as big as a hotel, was plopped beach side on Sycamore Avenue, cutting off the view for several modest cottages that stretched between Fir and Elm. It put them all in the shade where there had once been sun. And now Langstrom was proposing more of the same—an abominable disconnect from Santa Maria Island. She could only fear what such a plan would do to Tuna Street—if they got their hands on it.

No one moved. It was as if they were hypnotized, watching a dazzling infomercial, or a train wreck from which they could not look away. He smiled, flourishing the pointer like a magic wand.

We are doomed...

"We are prepared," he said, "to offer large sums for your homes." His index finger circled an orange shutter. He drew dollar signs in the air.

"What if we don't want large sums for our homes? How 'bout we like things just the way they are!" It was Jess Blythe, who owned the gas station and was famous for the chicken salad in his deli. "In case you haven't noticed, our island suits us fine, thank you very much."

Langstrom's expression cracked.

Would he dare slice Jess's objection to ribbons?

Jess didn't let him in. "I want to keep my place. Just the way it is." Each word ticked up until he was shouting. He checked his neighbors. They nodded. "I don't get your motivation, unless it's to make money off our backs."

He balled up a fist in his faded baseball cap and tilted back on his heels. His business had grown from a driftwood lean-to into a booming car repair and towing service, and he and his wife, Sue, were not about to let it go. They lived next door in a bright yellow stucco ranch, built in the early '20s, a tangle of purple verbena and firebush blazing up the crushed shell path. The buildings sat right on the edge of Langstrom's first stage of development in the center of Santa Maria.

Now Jess didn't budge. He had a lot to lose, should the plan be approved. He'd be dwarfed by six-story condos and eight-thousand-square-foot houses, cut out of the sun and view in the shadow of monsters. He shifted from one boot to the other.

Langstrom flashed those white teeth again. Blanche was reminded of a shark, the one that snatched a three-year-old in about a foot of water. Tragic. Unexpected.

"Well, I understand," he said. "What did you say your name is, sir?"

"I didn't."

Langstrom put a fist in his chin.

"Name's Jess Blythe."

"Well, Mr. Blythe, let's look on the bright side, why don't we. What's best for everyone? Are you aware of eminent domain and…"

That was as far as he got.

Jess yanked up his jeans with his forearms and gave his baseball cap a whack. "I don't want to hear about your 'eminent domain.' You can put that where the sun don't shine. And don't talk about the bright side of this because there ain't none. You're not very bright if you think tearing down our houses is going to improve paradise."

The grumbling started up. Blanche had the slender hope they might run him out of town right now.

But Sergi's voice dipped. Coaxing. "We don't want to tear down paradise, Mr. Blythe. We want to *grow* it!"

"Huh," said Jess. "I guess we're pretty much all growed up." He plunked the cap back on his unruly hair. "That's what I'm thinkin.'" Sue patted his arm.

Heat crept up Blanche's neck. She sprang from her seat and caught her sandal on the bottom rung of the chair. It clattered out from under her. The chair came to rest on the toes of a startled resident.

"Ouch!" It was Marietta Gantley.

"I'll say," Jess shouted.

Langstrom didn't move, except for one eyebrow.

Three
Hush, Money

"I'm so sorry." Blanche peered at Marietta's foot and recovered her balance. She was already making a mess of it, and she'd lost the thought. She squinted at Langstrom. Hot determination rushed through her veins.

He folded his arms. She caught the hint of a smile.

"Eminent domain can mean only one thing." Her voice screeched. "The rich will benefit. They'll buy up those properties along the beach and get richer in the bargain. And who will benefit then? You, and that bunch of hairballs from Chicago?" She sucked in her breath. She hadn't meant to call them what they were, but she couldn't help herself. Her filter often malfunctioned.

Langstrom grinned, somewhat tightly. Or was that a smirk? "Well, Ms…?

"Murninghan. That's M-U-R-N-I-N-G-H-A-N. Blanche Murninghan, pronounced Monahan, if you wish."

"I wish."

Now what is that supposed to mean? Is he serious? Flirting? Blanche didn't know what to think because rage burned a hole in her brain. Those two little words: *I wish.*

"What is so amusing?"

"Nothing, really, but I understand how you might…"

"Please. Enough with the sales pitch! This plan of yours will kill animals. Trees! Just about everything on this island! Killers, that's what you people are."

What the hell is wrong with me? I can't stop.

Langstrom turned a shade paler. The crowd whispered, and the room closed up around her. She needed to get out of there. Her mind escaped to the sunset at the north point and the manatees at the pier, the circling gulls, and Tuna Street. She wanted the night to end. But she was trapped, and she had put herself right in the middle of it.

"No. That is not our intention, Miss Murninghan. We are *not* killers. Thou shall not kill, nor steal—We won't kill anything, or anyone."

The biblical reference infuriated her. "Yet you want to risk it."

"Improve, not destroy. We want to bring jobs to Santa Maria. Infrastructure. Broader tax base. Large sums for your homes and businesses."

"*Large sums.*" That reference to money again. It sent an odd current through the room. She could feel it like she'd touched the short in her old living room lamp. It took only minutes, and then she realized the horror of it: They were mesmerized at hearing that their property was gold. The murmuring stopped. Silence spun through dead air with not a sound of protest.

Money, especially the doling out of it, made people think about how they could spend it even before it became a reality. She wasn't willing to take Langstrom's word that they would be paid fairly for what they had to give up. She was with Jess on that one. To begin with, she couldn't put a market price on Tuna Street, nor could she endure the cost of losing it.

"Whoa." It was Bob. He was on his feet. Blanche's mind was a jumble, her insides wrung out, but here was Bob. And in her head, she heard her beloved grandmother, Maeve Murninghan of Santa Maria Island—long dead: *Stand up straight, Blanche. Speak your mind.* But her knees wobbled.

Bob gave her a thumbs up and looked around the room. "We have a number of items on this agenda." His hands tamped down the air of contention. "You have a considerable hurdle or two, Mr. Langstrom. We are not likely to back down."

Langstrom ducked his head and rubbed his hands together. Blanche wanted to strangle him right there. "You know, we appreciate your views," he said. "We really do. But let me say, the company will make generous offers to facilitate the removal of dilapidated properties to improve the well-being of the island community."

Dilapidated properties? Whose? Mine? Could he be serious?

"Now let's wait one momentito." It was Bob again. "The plan is ambitious and costly, and devastating to the flora and the fauna." At this, several heads bounced in agreement, mostly because that's what everyone did when Bob spoke. "Do you have state and local permission? You know, it's quite a lengthy and expensive process to get permits to build within the coastal zone. And, normally, you'll only be able to rebuild within the footprint of the buildings you, ahem, destroy."

Blanche's mind was racing. *All he had to do was go to Tallahassee with a ton of money, and he'd get those approvals in a heartbeat.*

"No, we don't have all the permits," Langstrom said quietly. "But we've taken the first step. To get the residents of Santa Maria on board with improvements to their economy." Cool with just a dab of blasé. "And by economy, I mean each and everyone's *personal* economy."

She couldn't hold back.

"Excuse me. Just where is Tuna Street on that board? Is that it? With a different name? Royal Palm Drive? And what about Bertie's house on Tuna next to my cabin, and Jess's place?" Blanche was pointing like crazy. As if the awful green roof and orange shutters on Sycamore Avenue weren't enough, a mall in a weird, complicated design, all fretwork and balustrades, splashed a garish shade of turquoise, cut across the tip of the island and ate up most of the park land.

"By the way, something else is wrong here," she said. "You seem to have forgotten a very important part of Santa Maria. I don't see the pier at all."

Sergi glanced at the drawing and jotted something on a clipboard. He smiled at Blanche. "That pier. Really, so quaint. Maybe a marina instead? With warehousing for boat storage?" He fumbled with the posters and held up a drawing of an elaborate dock with coach lights, a glassed-in restaurant, and Onassis-size yachts.

"I don't believe this." She steadied herself. The murmuring started up again, but no one came forward.

Blanche stumbled into the aisle and headed for the back door, anxious for a breath of air. Suddenly, she was suffocating. She leaned in the door frame, her back to Langstrom and the crowd. Outside, the geckos skittered up the wall, the palms rattled as the wind picked up off the Gulf. She turned toward the breeze and the shelter of the western sky where a patch of fluorescent orange glowed in the dark. It was a relief, knowing that at least no one could take away that sunset and the Gulf of Mexico.

But then she turned back to the disaster. Langstrom leaned against a long folding table, then bounced toward the crowd.

"Hear me out. Please," he said. The buzzing stopped.

"Don't you see what he's doing?" she yelled. She'd been holding her breath, her voice tinny. The back row looked up at her.

"Believe me." Langstrom ignored the outburst. "Santa Maria will be better than ever. We'll plant native species, including live oak and sabal palms. Get rid of those Australian pines." He drew out every word like he was announcing the creation of Eden, the pointer hitting various round dots on the board that Blanche guessed were the "native" plantings.

She was dizzy from the thought of losing the pier, most of the park land, and now this? *How do I defend a tree?* The pines wove a carpet of long needles on the broken shell and hot sand. They whistled and provided shade, and bright green parrots raised a joyous ruckus in the branches in March. Those trees had a life of their own, and they were part of their lives. Langstrom didn't know a thing about them. How could you trust someone who dismissed the trees as a non-native nuisance?

And did he know anything about palms? There were nearly eighty varieties, and the island had quite a number already. Did he know that they bent in hurricanes and popped back up, and that they were amazing transplants? She was not against bringing in more palm trees, but he wanted to make the place look like a Florida postcard. More Fake Florida. Just what Santa Maria Island did not need.

"Hear, hear." It was Bob again. He reached in his pocket and drew out a small piece of paper. A check. "You have some good ideas there, Mr. Langstrom, but I'm afraid these plans for development just don't jibe with our plans for historical preservation. Plain and simple."

He pivoted to the group, showing off the check. "Ten thousand dollars says the park and wetlands at the northern end will not be uprooted, paved over, nor built upon. It's the first donation, and we'll raise more."

Blanche was stunned. Cheers went up around the room. The historical society was coming through.

The handouts fluttered in front of faces, and the buzzing started up again.

Langstrom's pen lifted off the notebook, his expression taut. "You don't say!" He eyed Bob and looked at the clock.

They were already scraping their chairs back. A dozen

residents crowded around Bob. The assistant grabbed a couple of posters, and the mayor looked about to explode.

Langstrom snapped his briefcase closed. "Thanks so much for coming out tonight!" He pointed here and there, and his gaze lingered on Bob. "Hope I can buy you a cup of coffee at Peaches!"

But Bob was surrounded, his large head bent to Janet and Becky.

Confident and peppy, that's Langstrom. Blanche couldn't make his plans go away, but Bob's check was a good start.

She stared at the posters and diagrams, globs of pink, turquoise, and coral. *There should be a revolution, but there's nothing like that. Are they resigned to it?*

Sergi was at the side door, the smile gone. He didn't seem to be paying the slightest bit of attention to them. They could have been telling him their grocery lists from the look of it.

Blanche studied her Tevas but then glanced toward the exit. He gave her a two-finger salute.

What? Victory? The meeting had settled nothing.

She spun around and watched them walk toward the parking lot and down the street. They needed each other if they were to turn things around. She had come in worried yet hopeful and now was about to leave, devastated. She was desperate to know what they were thinking: *Where were the questions? Don't you ask a lot of questions at a town hall meeting?*

Langstrom could not just show up and take their homes. The idea was ludicrous. It wouldn't be possible if people didn't want it. She couldn't imagine they would approve the plan. Some of them had rebuilt after storms many times, the way she and Gran did at the cabin on Tuna Street. They had fought to keep their community together—against water and wind and the endless confusion of the bureaucracies with their new building and zoning requirements. They tried to work within the constraints to preserve tradition. A bunch of developers from Chicago couldn't run over them and change the island into a fake fantasy land.

Or could they?

The night had slipped through their fingers like sand. Many of the shocking posters remained propped on the easels, and Blanche looked around frantically for someone to come and take them down. No one came. Few residents seemed to have concerns and questions, and Blanche had plenty.

Liza hurried over, trailing a cloud of captivating White Rose Musk. She put her arm around Blanche, but she couldn't feel the love, she was so numb. She stared at the fancy boards of dots and squares. Liza didn't say a word as she looked back at Bob, but Blanche said just enough: "No."

Four
A Deadly Purpose

"BOB IS DEAD!"

Liza hit Blanche with this awful news when she walked in the door of Sunny Sands Realty—the morning after the town hall meeting. She'd come to talk with them about Langstrom. They needed to form a plan, settle some loose ends.

Blanche stood in the doorway and stared at Liza. Her mouth open, but nothing came out.

What is she talking about?

Liza was hiccupping and choking through the tears. She lifted her arms and dropped forward on the desk.

Blanche had never seen her so....wild! She had the urge to turn around and run out of there and come back in again. She covered her ears.

"You called me, Liza." She whispered, and her feet began to move.

Blanche managed to lower Liza into the desk chair though it

was difficult to contain her, all silk and tears, shaking and crying up a storm. Her hands flew to her inflamed cheeks. Blanche held on. "Tell me. What are you saying?" Maybe she would take it back. Maybe she'd said Bob was late…not "daid." *Dead*?

The look on her face said it all.

They huddled together, their fingers locked in a desperate tangle. Bob's enormous grey metal desk loomed in the corner of the office. She pictured his wide grin. A lion in a brown suit. She longed for him to walk in and sit down next to them. Tell them it was all a hoax, a prank. A mistake.

Blanche dashed to the cooler for a paper cone of water. She held it under Liza's chin until she took a gulp.

"Oh, my God, I can't believe this is happening," Liza wailed. Her mascara ran, streaking her make-up, and her hair stuck out in every direction. She swiveled from the phone to a pile of notes on a spike, back to a sheaf of manila folders, and then buried her face in the crook of her arm.

"*What* happened?" Blanche nudged her gently. "Tell me. Who told you this, Liza?"

She picked up the phone and stared at it. "I just talked to him, not an hour ago. He was at Peaches getting coffee. And now he's *gone*?" She held the receiver to her cheek as if the last of Bob would spirit himself out of the tiny holes.

Blanche patted Liza's face with a tissue. She couldn't pat this back together. Bob and Liza had been a team. Now it was cut in half? He wasn't coming back?

"No one really knows what happened! It's just impossible. But they found him like that. They couldn't do a thing."

"Who is *they*? They couldn't do *what*? *Where*?"

"He was in his car. At the marina. In the middle of the parking lot. Didn't anyone see him there? Was he having trouble breathing? He must have…" She put one hand on her chest. "I can't imagine the distress. Alone. Dying."

Blanche jumped up and filled another paper cone. She stood

there, hanging on every word, trying to make sense of it, the water running down her arm. It was an odd moment, like being suspended in a balloon or floating in the Gulf miles from shore, with no boat.

"They think he might have had a heart attack, but that can't be. He'd just had a complete check-up, stress test, all of it, last month. He was perfectly healthy, Blanche. I'm telling you, there's no reason for this! He'd even given up hamburgers at Stinky's."

Blanche knew otherwise, but she kept it to herself. He was addicted to Stinky's and the blueberry-nut muffins at Peaches.

"Who found him?"

"Bill Gallit, you know, the new guy who manages the marina. He saw Bob's car, and Bob was just sitting there. Bill walked over to say hello and knew something was wrong. At first, he thought he was sleeping. It must have been right after I talked to him. The coffee was still in the cup holder, untouched. Warm."

Ever the one for details. Each word she said struck a blow. Blanche held on to Liza's fingers.

"Bill tried to get out of there and come tell me himself, but the police were there in two seconds, swarming the place. Shouting. Sirens screeching. I could hardly hear him. He didn't exactly have time to chat."

Blanche's stomach lurched.

"I have to keep the office open." Liza stammered between sobs. She slumped down behind the desk. Her chair spun away and hit the wall. She adjusted her red silk blouse, twisted and tear-stained. At the moment, she didn't look like a real-estate whiz, but she was that rare person who was capable of doing it all. She could crunch interest rates and sales figures better than a Dell.

Now she held back a fresh storm of tears. "I have to watch the phones, but I just don't want to think at all." She stood up. "I have to go over there." She sat down again. "Oh, Blanche, please, will you go?"

"You know I will. Do anything..."

Blanche didn't know what to do, but she had to do something. Liza was her friend, and she had been right there with her after Gran died. Making funeral arrangements. Liza and Blanche—the two of them settled into wicker armchairs on the porch at the cabin, nothing but the geckos running up and down the screens and a bottle of tequila evaporating on the pine table between them. Now here they were again. *About to make funeral arrangements?*

She hated to leave Liza alone. The office, somewhat brightened with wicker and orange floral cushions and a thriving schefflera, was not exactly a comforting place. Overall, it was pretty lonely and grey. Official, like death.

Blanche paced. "Let me make some coffee first." The moment seemed to call for liquids. She checked Bob's desk drawers. He was known to celebrate a closing or two with a toast of fine Irish whiskey. She poked around, and there it was, sloshing around with the pens and paperclips.

Liza was moaning again. Her head on the desk. Blanche busied herself with the booze and the coffee pot.

Then the phone rang. Liza dove for it.

She didn't move. Her face drained of color like someone had let the stopper out.

Oh, this can't be good.

"What're you saying?" Liza's voice cracked, rose an octave. "No, that's not right." Her fingers opened and the receiver clattered to the desk.

Blanche stopped fussing, the bottle of whiskey suspended. She reached for the phone but whoever had called was gone.

"What is it, Liza? Who was that?"

"Bill again. It's Bob. His neck, broken. Or strangled! They think he died. On purpose." Dying "on purpose" seemed to avoid the fact altogether, a denial that Bob had passed away in an untimely, and unthinkable, manner.

"What exactly did he say?"

"He was there when they lifted him out of the car. It looked really bad...." It was all she could manage before she dissolved again.

Blanche blurted out: "What does that mean? *Murder?*" It was too late to take it back. The word shot from her like an arrow and hit the mark. But surely cause of death could not be determined until the medical examiner had a look.

Liza crumpled into the chair.

"Oh, Liza.

Murder is something that is definitely done on purpose. He was sitting in his car...

It doesn't make any sense at all.

Why? Who?"

And why, of all people, Bob?

Five
Say It with Murder

No! THERE WAS NO REASON FOR THIS. Blanche made herself reserve judgment, but her mind was whirling. What reason—the word was related to *rational*—could there be for *murder*? Especially here. Him. Bob was a leader, rallying the preservationists, showing up at every potluck and wedding—a familiar figure in his brown suits. Professional, crisp. Generous.

Blanche had to find Chief Duncan. He wouldn't be able to take it back, and he wouldn't have a reason. After all, he probably wouldn't tell her a damn thing, at least not until Bob's family knew about the death and officials confirmed the circumstances. But Duncan was Blanche's go-to. He was *Duncan*—the law, an island institution, a rock on shifting sand.

Well, that's stretching it. Duncan could be unpredictable, but he was true.

It would be the first murder—if that's what it was—on Santa Maria Island, a place where people left their doors open and bikes unlocked. The safest spot on earth. Residents and snow birds knew each other. No murderers were among them; Blanche was certain of that. They had the occasional burglary and bar fight— even a stabbing or two to punctuate the Fourth of July—mostly tourist related, and few and far between. The worst incident reported lately was an item in the *Island Times* about under-age drinkers caught throwing water balloons on Kumquat Street.

And then there was Conchita Beach. The drug drops—a new turn of events—and, yet, infrequent. Still, they had become a nagging sore spot in this otherwise peaceful corner of the world.

But, *murder? Here?*

Blanche sighed. Deflated, she squeezed Liza's shoulder and set the coffee and water in front of her, and the bottle of whiskey. Liza cried. Blanche wasn't much of a crier. She was more of a rager, and this rage punched about inside her, urging her to find out *what happened.*

She eyed the bottle and took a swig. It burned like holy hell, which was fitting. She was still standing there, one hand on her chest, warm guilt spreading through her for taking up drinking in the morning. That feeling went away, fast. What she wanted to do was sit down with Liza and finish it off.

Liza lifted her head. "Please, Blanche, go. *Now.* You have to see what is going on over there. I just can't imagine. Bobby..."

"I'm going," she said.

Blanche closed her eyes. The perking coffee filled the office with a homey scent. It was small comfort. When she looked around, nothing had changed. There was Liza. The picture of disaster.

She refilled Liza's cup and swept a mess of soggy paper cones and tissues into a wastebasket. She pressed the last tissue into Liza's hand.

"If you could find out *anything,* Blanche..."

"I'll try, but I really hate to leave you here."

Liza shook her head. "I'll be OK." She splashed some whiskey into her coffee.

"I'll get back. Soon," Blanche said. She tried to sound reassuring, but her voice shook.

She slid the bottle closer—after she took another belt. *Oh, God. What am I doing?* She hoped it would be empty when she came back.

"You need some lunch, Liza. I'm going to ask Marge to send over a salad." Tomatoes and cucumbers seemed ordinary, and that's what they needed. Something ordinary. The thought that Bob had been at Peaches right before his death made her wonder if Marge had seen something out of the ordinary. She had to ask.

Liza nodded and slumped over her folded arms, her back erupting with sobs. Blanche gave her one last squeeze. "And I'm going to find Duncan."

She hurried down Marina Drive and dashed into Peaches'. Marge was chopping celery behind the deli counter, her hairnet askew. She drew a knife out of the mayo.

"Girl. What a day." Her face, usually a wreath of smiles, drooped. The news was everywhere in the damp, heavy wind. Everyone on the island knew.

They both looked down the street. People were hurrying toward the marina. Red lights flashed against the blue sky.

"Marge, have you seen Dunc?"

Marge shook her head. "No." She waved the knife and banged it on the counter with an emphatic twang. "I can't believe this, Blanche. Bob was just here picking up coffee. How could this happen?"

Blanch focused on a splat of mayo on the glass cabinet behind Marge's head.

"Oh, God, Marge, I don't know."

"Wish I could go over there. It's a hep-less feeling, ain't it? I got this lunch crew and need to stay put." Tears glistened in her eyes.

"I'm going. Got to find Duncan, but, before that, I want to send a chef's salad over to Liza."

"Of course." Marge looked around like it was the first time she ever saw ham and lettuce.

"Was there anything funny you noticed when Bob came in this morning? Different, maybe? Anyone, but Bob, hanging around over here?" She couldn't say, *before the murder.* It would all come out soon enough. The awful truth.

"No. Seemed kind of usual around here. No one in and out but the regulars." Her gaze wandered, the corners of her mouth quivered.

"How was Bob?"

"He was fine. Busy. Ol' Bob. In a hurry, but always had a good word, ya know." Marge stared at the case stacked with muffins. "He didn't want a blueberry nut today. Was watching the weight and all, he said."

Blanche mulled this bit of information. Bob was not uneasy, or even fearful, moments before his murder. It had to be a surprise. *A terrible, random surprise?*

She laid a ten-dollar bill on the glass deli counter. "Do you think Billy would run that salad over to Liza?"

Marge said, "Done." She chopped and fretted.

"If you think of anything, I mean, about Bob and this morning…Will you give me a buzz? I'd like to let Liza know. Don't know what else to do," Blanche said. "Maybe I can find out something before they move out of there." A thought stabbed her. *Before they move him out of there. Dead.* "I promised Liza."

"Oh, Lord, of course, go on now." With vigor, she resumed piling lettuce, cheese, and ham into a clear plastic container and bagged a saucer-size white macadamia cookie, for good measure. "We'll get these goodies to Liza. Girl's gotta eat."

Six
Disaster on the Double

BLANCHE CROSSED OVER THE DRIVE TOWARD THE MARINA within a couple of blocks of Sunny Sands and Peaches in the island shopping district. The street and the rest of the nearby mall were empty. She hardly recognized the place.

A pall hovered beneath the puffy clouds and blue sky. Bob had been ordering a cup of coffee at his favorite deli, and then he was dead.

What had gone wrong?

For one thing, the town hall meeting had been unsettling, and she wondered about possible connections: that Bob died, or was killed, so soon after the plans were formally unveiled at the meeting. And how about Bob and his check from the historical society? That the two disasters—the meeting and the murder—

occurred back to back struck Blanche as more than just a coincidence.

At the marina, she looked around for Langstrom. He was not circulating in the crowd and promoting the so-called "beautification" plan. *He'd missed an opportunity. What a pity.* Here was a major island event, and, for once, he was not in the middle of it finding a way to use it to his advantage. It was a relief, though a small one, not to lay eyes on him.

She hung back on the edge of the parking lot and tried to think. But all she could do was feel. Bad. The familiar corner, usually jammed with the locals' pick-ups and SUVs, instead looked like a set for a disaster movie. Diesel spewed from the back of one vehicle, grinding away, no driver in sight. A bell dinged over the harbor. The scanners squawked and gulls answered, swooping in from the bay. The police scribbled in note pads and wandered around, united in mayhem and confusion. A lot of them. Force and authority on parade without any apparent purpose and organization.

A red truck with bright gold stripes boxed in Bob's mint-condition Mercedes standing alone. A sad monument to murder.

Blanche's heart stopped. Bob's car was empty. The medical examiner's van pulled away. A white mound visible through the rear windows. It revved tiredly over a low-pitched hum among the bystanders, and Bob was gone. She stumbled toward the van, but it was futile. What was she going to do? Run after the medical examiner and insist on some answers?

She stood at the edge of the lot. It was a strange place to murder someone, in the wide open in the middle of the day. And Bob was such a big guy. Someone strong, efficient and evil, had killed quickly, confident in getting away with it. Or someone who just didn't care about what he, or she, was getting into. But careless murder rarely occurred. Someone cared enough to do it. It was the careless murderer who got caught. Blanche couldn't believe a person like that would be walking around on the island. It had to be a stranger. Everybody else was like family.

Chief Duncan marched along the dock. He was about as easy to wrestle to a standstill as a dirigible, but she was determined to get something out of him. He was one of her main sources at the *Island Times*, and they were fond of trading jokes over awful coffee. A talker, he almost always opened up.

Then she hesitated. Duncan shouted orders into a radio. A harried boat owner gestured to the chief, who shook his head, and yelled back. His voice carried above the noise, an incongruous figure, avuncular and corpulent, in green, against the flashing blue and red lights reflecting off the canal and the bottoms of white sailboats on davits.

She ducked behind a sign advertising charter fishing trips, and when she looked up, he was gone.

How did that happen?

She drew a notebook out of her bag. The blazing blue sky, the salty, musty smell of fish in the harbor, the shouting. *Who what where when why and how.* She wrote fast, with one eye on the parking lot and one on the lookout for Duncan. She'd sort out the scribbling later. When she did find the chief, she'd have some details and context to offer in exchange for information. It was always a give and take with Dunc. Eventually, she'd have to talk to Clint about writing up a piece for the *Times* even though she felt too close to this one.

"What in God's name is going on around here, Blanche?" Melly Ragani popped up beside Blanche. Mel clucked, her hair in wispy disarray, her arms fluffing up and down. "Just *how*. Tell me this is not *true!*"

Blanche shook her head. "Oh, Mel. Did you see Liza?" Mel's real estate office was down the block from Sunny Sands.

"No." Her eyes were misty and round with fright. "The office was dark. I hope she went home to get some rest but I don't know how." Then a surprised look. "Have you been drinking, Blanche?"

"I'll say. I wish we'd finished the whole bottle. Liza and me."

She fished in her bag for gum.

"My goodness, I could certainly use a little something." Mel fanned herself, and they both glanced across the marina at Decoy Duck's, the local watering hole where worries drowned and celebrations skimmed along. The front window with its gold lettering was dark, the pink neon sign turned off.

"Have you heard *anything*, Mel?" She was loath to use the word *murder*. Again. She'd said it once already and regretted giving voice to possibility.

"No. Except for the worst… Killed! Right here in the marina." She screeched. Beads of sweat appeared on her forehead. A whiff of Tabu.

"You heard that? Where?"

"Duncan let it slip. Oh, he was furious. Clapped that big old hand over his pie hole and scooted right off! Never saw our Duncan move that fast."

"Well, that couldn't be a pretty sight." Blanche was stunned at Mel's announcement and relieved he'd disappeared. The irritated Duncan was to be avoided until he calmed down, which was his fairly usual state but probably not now. Not by a long shot.

"Blanche, just tell me. Who would kill our Bobby?"

"No one you or I know. By the way, how would they know Bob was murdered? And know it so soon?"

"Oh, there was no doubt. I saw them take him away, his head rolling to one side. Some signs of a struggle when they lifted him out. Oh, Blanche, I'm telling you it was awful." She stopped. Her hands fluttered to her cheeks. "I have to make that chicken fajita casserole for Liza. Her favorite. I just don't have any idea what else to do." Mel taking care of Liza. It filled Blanche with the tiniest bit of hope. Well-wishers thought of noodles and tortillas at a time like this when the body needed food for the soul. Blanche knew from experience that Mel's casserole would be good for both body and soul.

Mel hurried off, and abruptly turned back, the purple chiffon sailing around her. "Oh, dear. Was about to get in touch with you, Blanche. Some fellow name of Sal came around asking about Tuna Street. Seems he has his eye on property along there."

Blanche froze, if that could be, standing in the ninety-plus-degree heat. "What exactly did he want? What did he say?"

"Why, said he was looking for beachfront. Like they all are. I told him to get lost. Politely, of course. Nothing for sale along there. I know you're not going to give up that cabin. Although, I have to tell you, Blanche, the guy threw out some crazy numbers for a lot or two along there. Over two million."

"Mel, he could offer two million coquinas. Or dollars, or whatever. It's all the same. We're not budging. I'm sure Bertie and the others wouldn't go for it either."

"That's what I told him. But you know the type."

"Yes, I know." Was this a Langstrom lackey? Sal who? "Mel, if you see him again, be firm. Please."

Mel lifted her arms in the voluminous fabric and enveloped her in a hug.

Blanche smiled, but her head was pounding. *Make this stop.*

This Sal business added one more raw nerve to an already frayed bundle. And she didn't know what to tell Liza, who was probably out of her mind. Or, hopefully, passed out with an empty whiskey bottle.

She was numb, but she kept searching the faces, walking around aimlessly. The grieved expressions changed everything. No one was happy. Misery united them. Officer Buck was sitting in his police car with his motor humming, one foot on the ground. She thought of attacking him for news, especially for the whereabouts of the chief.

But then she stopped.

Is it true what they say? The perpetrator hangs around the scene of the crime? Or returns to it?

Blanche's gaze shifted over the crowd. She knew just about everyone in that parking lot. But she did not see the small woman hiding behind the kiosk. If she had, she would have been startled. The dark eyes shone in Blanche's direction. Then the face, oval and smooth as a river stone, turned away from Blanche toward a stranger standing next to a white van. The woman's mouth tightened; her fists clenched. She disappeared.

Seven
Snake in the Van

A COLD WAVE SWEPT OVER BLANCHE, even as she sweat in the glaring heat. It was a strange disassociation, like she was untethered and floating. The whiff of a ghost brushed past. When she looked around, she was alone.

She searched the faces again. Ernie at the IGA, a couple of waiters, Buzz, the manager at the bait and tackle. All long-time residents. Dwayne from the 307 Pine Deli and Wendy from Hairs to You. Michelle from Soap-a-Pooch.

At a murder scene? She knew these people well. All of them.

Except for the fellow standing next to a white van on the edge of the lot.

She didn't recognize him or the van, and his whole getup sent needles down her spine. He was slick, a cagey look about him. He didn't fit. He didn't look delivery, and he didn't look tourist. That was it. That's what threw her off.

He couldn't be a snowbird. Too early for them. Island traffic was up, but the post-hurricane season rush hadn't started yet—not until after November 30. This guy was not here for a frolic on the beach, all alone, lounging with a boot up against the passenger door. He shifted his head from side to side like he had ants running up and down his neck.

Her arms and feet were toasting, and she would just have to take it. She clutched the pen and notebook and kept writing.

She crept over to the shade of an awning at a marina kiosk that sold short walking tours to Gull Egg Key. She stood in the shadow and studied him. He didn't glance her way, and he didn't talk to anyone. He observed. He smoked. She wrote it down: long brown hair pulled back, hooded eyes darting over the crowd. He wore an immaculate white t-shirt and jeans. *One very smooth dude.*

Not a single person in the crowd seemed to notice him.

So maybe I'm nuts.

A few people meandered off and began disappearing into their cars and back to business. But suspicion held her like an anchor, and she had no one to tell.

She was alone with him.

Would anyone think this odd? Much less, would anyone hear me out?

Duncan was still MIA. Some of the officers were trying to keep the last of the onlookers at bay. Most weren't sticking around. Doors slammed. Officer Buck put two feet on the ground but that was as far as he got. He never looked up, and then he tucked back into the patrol car and drove away.

Her mind raced. She dropped back, and wrote furiously.

He was young, probably in his late twenties. Short, five foot eight, maybe, not more than 150 pounds. Easily, he pushed off the van with a boot, swung his arms, sinewy with muscle. A tattoo? A vine of thorns, or letters? He was wiry but his movements were graceful. Careful.

He opened the passenger door, reached in the glove box, and pulled out a pack of smokes. He tamped it against the palm of his hand, unwrapped it, and rolled the pack into a shirt sleeve after he withdrew a cigarette. He rubbed his forearm, shifted from one boot to the other, and still, he gazed at the crowd. Smoke curled from the cigarette in his fingers. He walked around the front of the van, each boot landing hard and sure.

She looked down at the scribbled mess in her notebook. *You never know when a mess will come in handy.*

The guy was rubbing his arm again. The tattoo of … a snake? The boots with silver buckles. The dent in the side of the van, the skull and flag on the rear window.

She needed his license number. The description alone wouldn't get it. Who would believe her without that number? *Who is going to believe me anyway?*

She bent to her pages. A loud splat—the thrust of an engine—drew her attention, and she looked up just as the van roared out of the parking lot. He'd been lounging around a minute before. Now he was gone. *Just like that.* She sprinted from her hiding place, but she couldn't make out the license number. Tires skidded around the curve toward the bridge. Soon all she saw was a white speck against the blue water of the bay. She tripped in her sandals and again made a mental note about her deficient wardrobe. She needed those running shoes.

She looked down at the tire marks he left. Wide bald tires and a wiggle in the sand. She wrote a few more words, thumbed through the two pages of detailed scribbling that she could barely read, and she started filling in her notes. She was disappointed that it was all she had, but baking in the sun had not been a complete bust. She had a very good description and a buzzing in her brain that said something wasn't right about the guy and the van.

She was still flipping through the pages when she saw it. The sun glinted off the crushed shell and sand at her feet. A piece of cellophane.

She picked it up using the tips of her nails and hesitated, held it up to the light. Fresh and new. Of course, that's all she could tell, but the thought struck: *Oh, my. Fingerprints?* She placed the cellophane carefully in a tissue and put it in a side pocket of her bag. She turned back to search the ground for cigarette butts. There wasn't a single one. *What? Field stripping his cigarettes and pocketing the butts? Like the military. They don't leave a trace.*

But he had dropped that cellophane. It was something. Blanche pushed the damp curls off her forehead, and wondered. It didn't hurt to wonder.

She'd show Duncan the *evidence*. The thought of it made her wince. She'd have to face the gruff old police chief without the license number. If he scoffed, she'd have to go to plan B. *What's Plan A?* With Duncan, it was hard to plan anything. All she had was a tiny piece of cellophane and a description. And not much else.

Bob's Mercedes was still parked in the lot between white lines. There it sat, and the loss hit her again. The car was a large, boxy model, polished and shiny, in top shape—old-school vintage with a touch of class. One more thing that reminded her of Bob. It just wasn't fair, and she began to miss him all over again.

Yellow police tape flapped in the breeze. Two officers chatted, their backs to her. She lifted the tape gingerly, bracing for a reprimand from at least one of them. She was, in fact, breaching a crime scene. But the cops ignored her. She peeked inside the car, and, sure enough, the coffee was in the holder. Undisturbed, with the lid on it. Bob's tie, a blue silk with tiny fish, was on the passenger seat, bunched and wrinkled. Bob wouldn't have been caught dead without his tie. He wouldn't have removed it... willingly. He sometimes even wore one when he coached Little League. *Why was the tie wadded up, thrown aside on the seat like that?*

There were indications that his neck had been broken. Someone strong had gotten to him. Or someone just awfully good at killing. And somehow that tie had been removed.

Lost in thought, she didn't hear the grunting at first—like an old motor being dragged over concrete. Jess Blythe's work boots stuck out from under the rear bumper of the Mercedes. "Drat this tow!"

"Hey, Jess!" She bent down to take a look. He slid out from under the car. "Blanche!" He dropped the wrench into his bag, sat back on his haunches. "Stinks, don't it."

"I'll say."

"Who'd want to kill our Bobby?" There it was again. That's how they all thought of him: "Our Bobby." The island stuck together, thick as a patch of mangrove, reliable as the sunset.

"Jess, I don't have any idea. I just saw Liza. She's torn up. It makes me sick." Blanche peered into the car window again, stood back with her hands on her waist. "So, why do you suppose his tie is on the seat. Can't imagine Bob would take it off."

"I haven't got one idea."

"I'm stunned."

"That about says it." He was still sitting back on his heels, squinting up at her. He took off his hat and slapped it over his knee.

"Were you here when they took him away?"

"Yeah, but they whisked him out of here pretty fast. Looked like there'd been a struggle 'cause that shirt was mighty rumpled. That sure ain't Bob. I didn't see much more than that."

"I hope he gave whoever did this a good one." Maybe he'd left a mark. She was thinking skin under the finger nails, a hair left behind. *Something* left behind.

"You betcha." As if he read her mind, he added, "They went over this here car worsin' you do on a dog with ticks, and that investigator is comin' around again to bag some things. Hope they find somethin'."

Blanche went off to peek again. Jess said, "They gets pinchy when you stands too close now. They says to me, be quick. Not to touch nothin', 'cept under."

"Got it."

She backed away. A couple more notes on the pad. The coffee cup, the tie, nothing much else. No stains, tools, ropes. Nothing. The back seat was clean. It must have happened from the back seat. The guy hiding, reaching up and forward. Or just getting into the Mercedes casually, greeting Bob. Bob, so friendly, wondering, what property the guy was interested in seeing. And then, whammo!

She held the notebook over her eyes, crouched down out of the officers' sight. Jess finished the clanging and wrenching, and it jangled a string of thoughts that popped and scattered. First, this business with Langstrom, then the murder. Now the stranger and the white van. Her fingers sifted through the broken shell, her knees weak and wobbly.

She longed to put it all back together and make it right again. She needed solid facts. Maybe she had at least one or two, the guy, the cellophane—maybe not. She had this, and an awful feeling, this uncanny sense of connection and absolutely not one iota of proof. Facts and feelings.

Jess was standing now, wiping the grease off his hands. Blanche brushed her shorts off. She stood, scanning the parking lot one more time. "Jess, you notice any strangers around here?"

"Nope." He jammed his cap down squarely, picked up his bag. "Not really. It's all pretty strange though."

"Hmmm. You didn't notice a guy and a white van? Didn't seem to fit?"

"Why, Blanche, there's so much comin' and goin', who'd know? An awful lot of white vans out there." He mumbled, shuffling up to the rear door of his truck. He shook his head. "Why you ask?"

"Oh, I don't know. I saw this guy…"

"Oh, Blanche, now, you let Duncan and the boys take care of all that. That business of lookin' here and yonder."

Blanche smiled. "I hear you, Jess, but you know, I'm just asking. You know me."

"I sure do. We can't know where all this is headed, but I can say this, Blanche, and you hear me good. You take care now. I mean it."

"I will, Jess. You, too."

She watched him hoist his tools into the cab, mumbling to himself, and slam the door.

Blanche's stomach growled. She was disgusted—and starving. The whiskey had been a bad idea. She was sweating like crazy and in need of food and shelter. Naturally, she thought of Cap, grilling fish and frying potatoes, but, best of all, they would talk. If anyone could bring some calm and perspective to the day, it would be Cap. Surely, he'd know about Bob because he stopped by the police station almost every day to gossip and see Aloysius Duncan and bring him soup, or something more nutritious than his usual diet of pizza and Chinese.

She didn't have one worthwhile thing to report to Liza. What could she tell her? *I just saw the murderer driving away in a white van!* Blanche was loath to offer some half-baked theory and risk further upsetting her. Wouldn't do any good to go blabbing about a guy and a white van because he had now dissolved into a sea of white vans cruising around Florida. He and his license number were long gone, and the more she thought about it, the less likely it seemed anything would come of trying to find him. Unless he showed up again. *Oh, what if he shows up!*

Her sandals dragged across the lot. An investigator arrived, snapping on the gloves, frowning in Blanche's direction. Jess sat in his cab, the motor running. She waved, listlessly. She couldn't believe it. She'd started the day angry over the planned destruction of the island, and now she was sadder than hell.

How are we going to fix this?

We can't get Bob back. That's really the worst of it.

She was afraid to think of how it would end—and what needed to happen to end it.

Eight
Lost and Sort of Found

THE OFFICE OF SUNNY SANDS REALTY WAS DARK when Blanche peeked through the blinds on the French doors. She hoped Liza had gone home to sleep. She'd left a note taped to the glass: "Be back later." Better later than sooner. She'd need a lot of rest to get through this mess.

Blanche dropped by the police station. She was eager to test her suspicions on the chief, and at once reluctant. He always greeted her with eyes like BBs. She wanted to get into "context" about the sighting of the guy and the van, and she hoped he'd calmed down some. She only half expected him to be there. He was not.

Pennington sat at the information desk. "Gone, Blanche," he said. "Official business at county."

"Meaning…?"

"Meaning business, and not yours."

"Really."

He hardly looked up from his Sudoku. "Sorry, Blanche. Orders. Got to keep it all on the down low."

It was deadly calm in the large, open police station—as if the world did not know Santa Maria had been turned upside down. Pennington bent his head over the crumpled newspaper. Down low, Blanche noticed. Her eyes blazed onto the puzzle in front of him, hoping to ignite the damn newspaper under his nose.

"Don't know when he's coming back, Blanche."

"Well, thanks a bunch." She turned on her heel and walked out.

She didn't really care about Pennington's rudeness. She was used to it. A bit of friction between the press and the police lingered over every conversation. Blanche was nosy, and persistent, and Duncan put up with it. The police had other fish to fry, sometimes, literally. Once Blanche tracked the boys to the Starfish landing dock where they were smoking mullet and grilling whitefish. It was a Monday, and the business of policing was on hold, as usual.

They could not afford that now. She worried that Duncan might not pursue back-up in the investigation. He was deliberate, but the murder was bigger than Santa Maria. She reasoned that he couldn't keep it to himself. He needed a wider net. Blanche prayed county was leaning on him. In any event, she'd be leaning on him soon enough.

Cappy's back door was open when Blanche walked in and yelled:

"YOOOOOHOOOO."

There was no answer.

Where is everybody today? The emptiness swept over her again. She shook it off. She was starving.

She stuck her head in the kitchen. If he'd been there, he'd have greeted her in his apron, wringing a dish towel, a big smile on his face as wrinkly as the bark of an oak. He was usually at the stove, if he wasn't on the water. But the familiar aromas did not welcome her. No olive oil and garlic simmering in the iron skillet, bread baking, potatoes frying in onion. The kitchen was dim in the shadow of a thick stand of palm trees.

He should have been there. He went fishing around five o'clock almost every morning, and they had a lunch of whatever he caught—lately grouper or red snapper. He didn't like to eat alone, and Blanche was only too happy to diminish Cappy's loneliness by eating his food. He was a great cook, and she was not.

She'd been starving, but she also needed to talk. Blanche stood in the doorway. If she couldn't have the Cappers, at least she could have this refuge. For now. Her eyes adjusted to the dim light after her run through the blazing island sun. It filtered through the open windows and washed the cupboards, walls, and hardwood floor in mellow gold. Outside, the palms crackled, doves scurried and cooed on the broken shell. She dropped into an old maple armchair with blue canvas cushions and hugged an embroidered pillow. She started to drift off, and almost let herself go. She was tempted.

Back here at Cap's, she was close to Gran….Gran, who had brought Blanche home at age five after the car accident that killed her mother, Rose. She never knew her father; her mother hardly knew her father although Gran said they'd been madly in love. He was shipped out. They'd never gotten around to getting married before he was killed on a rice paddy in Southeast Asia.

On her deathbed, Gran had made Cappy swear that he would keep an eye on Blanche, which at one time had annoyed her to no end. That phase of antsy adolescence was long past. Cappy had become a grandfather, mother, father, grandmother, and best friend. He was set in his ways, and she was, too, but she couldn't think of a time when they didn't have each other. She bounced her ideas and plans, her loves and disappointments, off the Cappers—

Donald Nicholas Reid but nicknamed the Caps for his collection of hats and caps accumulated during his travels from the Gulf to the Galapagos. He'd met Gran fifty years ago after traveling the world and finally settling on Santa Maria where he opened up a small charter line and fished off the island. They'd been devoted to each other and at once fiercely independent, and Blanche and her cousin, Jack, had thrived growing up in their care.

How Blanche missed Gran! At least she had Cappy. Somewhere. Where?

No telling where he'd gotten himself off to, but she had a sudden longing to see him, and Jack. She needed her family. So much had happened in a day, she'd hardly thought of the love and support she had in her life.

Blanche shook off the daydreams and wandered through the organized chaos of the kitchen. Tangled herbs cluttered a shelf, the pungent bay and thyme mixed with sweet gardenia at the window. Copper cooking pots of every size hung from the rack over the counter. Jars of tomatoes, peaches, and pickles he'd put up himself, towers of limes, lemons, and oranges, all were within easy reach. She pushed the rattan stools back in order.

He'd left a grapefruit with eyes and a mouth made of whole cloves. The smiling Buddha sat on a nest of waxy leaves. The note said, "Hi, Blanche."

She burst out laughing. He still surprised her, and it never got old.

She wrote him a note and tore the page out of her notebook: *See you tonight, and thanks for the cheery greeting.* She couldn't bring herself to mention the terrible morning.

She stuck the message under a refrigerator magnet. It occurred to her that the islanders rarely locked their doors. Now maybe they should. Cappy's door had been unlocked. Reminder: Get extra keys. Tell Cappy to lock his doors. She had a queasy feeling that the world of Santa Maria was changing, and not for the better.

If she didn't eat something soon, she was sure to faint dead away. She reached for the fridge. Cap was always a step ahead of her. He'd left a plate with Blanche's name on it—grouper, sautéed, and topped with grapes, mango, and raspberries. She felt better just looking at it.

She sat down at the counter and ate the whole thing, cold, probably not out of the Gulf a day. She added to the note: *PS, Delicioso! We have to talk. XXX B.*

Revived over lunch, Blanche rinsed the dish and headed out the back door, the screen door flapping after her. She hurried down the drive to the cabin.

The beach was calling. But first, she had to call Jack.

She couldn't wait to get hold of him. If she could. Getting his attention was a bit like stepping on a rolling wave. After all, how much help could he be in making the week stop spinning out of control?

She picked up the pace. The sun descended behind the tops of the pine trees. Her sandals crunched the shell path, and the gulls cawed. It was the only sound at the quiet north end as she took the steps two at a time and dashed for the phone.

Jack. He had to know the awful news. He had to get back soon.

Nine

Just Ask Jack

HE WAS ONLY A FLIGHT AWAY, BUT A FLIGHT AWAY from *where*? Chicago? Texas? He'd always had a sense of adventure, and that had led him to travel, and, finally, into business in transport. He'd started as a truck driver in college, and now he owned a division of a trucking company with a conglomerate in Chicago. But he always found his way back home on Tuna Street. He was long overdue for one such visit.

He surprised her when he answered on the first ring. She sat down on the porch bench and stared off at the Gulf.

"Jack! Where are you?"

"Don't I get a 'Hi, I love you and miss you' first?"

"Hi. I *do* love you and miss you." She chuckled at the sound of his voice. "Now, tell me where you are."

"I'm in Shit-cago. In traffic."

"Well, glad I got you."

"You got me, Bang. For about one minute." He'd nicknamed

her "Bang" when he was a toddler because he couldn't pronounce Blanche. The name stuck, and it suited her off-the-hip nature.

She heard the blaring in the background. He was driving around, dodging buses and taxis. Cursing. Punching the buttons on the radio. Eating.

"We have a mess here," she said. "It's bad news. You better pull over."

"Was just about to call you. I know."

"You know? What?"

"Bob Blankenship's been murdered. Jeez. I heard. Blanche, it's terrible."

"That's what they're saying. *Murder.* It's not official yet, just happened this morning. But it's not looking good. At all. How did you hear about it?"

"I have ways."

"Well, OK, You have ways....*What ways?*"

Honking. Chewing. "I follow the news."

"*Really?*" This was too confounding to pick apart in a minute or two. "When do you think you can come down here? How soon?"

"Don't know. But, soon. Promise." A bus revved up, the traffic exploded in her ear. "Wish I could get out of here right now... *dammit...* How's Liza?"

"Not good. Please, Jack. We need to talk."

"The thing is..."

"I have a feeling, I know it's not much, but I have a feeling that the murder is connected to that other business. You know, those Chicago developers who were nosing around here on the island."

"What? Come on, B."

"No, seriously. It's been growing on me. First this developer—Sergi Langstrom—shows up with all his posters and ideas. Then we have this meeting and Bob is murdered. Back to back. Bob didn't want Langstrom and that bunch on the island, Jack. They're gonna bring in the bulldozers."

"*Bang!*"

"You're in Chicago. Will you please look into this? You know people up there. See what you can find out about Sergi Langstrom. Ask around." Jack was oddly silent. She waited, for about two seconds. "Are you there? Jack? Listen to me."

"Uhhhh. Ask around about what? 'Hey, did you murder Bob Blankenship?' That kind of thing?" It was a response full of crumbs and slurps. "Sure. Right on."

"Some help you are. Of course not. Just ask around, find out if there is any connection between Bob and Langstrom. *Anything*. He's slick. A damn hairball."

"Really? That's pretty harsh. And crazy. But I'll see what I can do, just to prove how crazy you are. In the meantime, may I emphasize, let Duncan do his work. *Stay out of it.*"

She ignored the staying-out part. She didn't want to hear it. "Promise, Jack. Nothing's right about all this business, I'm telling you. It's all wrong."

"No, it's not right, but forget the theories. The authorities, Blanche. Remember, that's their job, not yours."

It was a clipped response, but she dug in. "I've got a job here, too, Jack. I have to do something. You know what this has done to Liza? To everybody? Bob was....more than just Bob."

"Don't you think I know that, B?" His voice softened, then blended into the screaming traffic. "He was an uncle, a dad when we didn't have one. He helped me get my first set of wheels, and he did a lot of other stuff for us, and for everybody. But this business with the murder. It's just real bad." Tires squealed. Jack yelled over the noise. "I really have to go. We'll talk later this week. Really miss you. I'll get down there...Soon."

Blanche held the phone away from her head. "Jack? When *exactly* can you come down here?"

He was gone. She flung the phone on the table. Connections were notorious on the island, but really? He wanted her out of it? Just like that?

He *could* help. He would. She had to believe it. He was in Chicago, but at heart he was an island boy. He loved Santa Maria Island, and Blanche. They had grown up together on Tuna Street, their quirky little stretch of shell and sand on the beachfront between Spring and Palm. Their cabin sat among a few old frame and log houses, this year, about 150 feet from the Gulf. And then there were the times the waves lapped at their door.

Gran left the cabin to the two of them. She'd taken on both of them after his mother ran off, and his father, another Jack in a long line of elusive Jacks, went missing for years. Presumed dead. Blanche's Jack was the brother she never had. But sometimes he could be so...removed. Elusive, and unpredictable as his father and grandfather. He wasn't inclined to check out Langstrom and that bunch. So she would *make* him do it.

Blanche sat there, stewing. She looked around the cabin. Which part was Jack's? The porch? The empty wicker chair across from her? The matching table—where she and Liza had shared more than one tequila? The extra bedroom in the back with a mango tree that dropped fruit bombs onto the roof? His "alarm clock," he would say.

Next to that tree, protected from the salt, orange hibiscus and flaming mandevilla edged the patio where hummingbirds darted about. In the front, sabal palms and sea grape, pines and bushes full of red berries grew out of the shell and sand dunes. Yellow and purple beach flowers twined through the snake grass and sea oats under the Australian pines, and farther out, the white frill of waves rushed the beach.

She stood up, stretched, and then took off over the pine needles toward the shoreline, determined to clear her head. She was bound to dump her frustration with Jack, her disappointment over the land development, and her terrible feeling of loss. If anything could fix her, it was the beach.

Sandpipers skittered in the foam. Balls of it broke away and flew across the sand like little round ghosts. The clouds towered, closing off the sun, then opened their huge white doors.

I wish he were here. I could make him see... See what? I can't even see any of it clearly myself.

Blanche muttered as she walked along, off into the world inside her head. Talking to herself was like having a tiny counselor between her ears.

Many times, he'd said, "Bang, I'm going to call the mental hospital on you."

He didn't turn her in. They were a team. They hid out in the dune grass—from the ghosts of pirates and Indians—and climbed palm trees for coconuts and the mango tree to the top where the fruit was sweetest. Gran told them stories about the Miccosukee who lived on Gull Egg Key, and Jack became obsessed with exploring the tiny key off the north end of Santa Maria. He swam out into the Gulf until he was a dot on the waves, and he went alone. She was not thrilled at the prospect of meeting sharks and jellyfish in the dark water. She was always relieved when he made it back—with more ghost stories.

They were afraid sometimes, but youth was in their favor. They were always able to run, climb, or swim out of their fear. They abandoned all fear and sense when they snuck away from Dunc, Cap, and Gran and built their clandestine camps along the beach. Their hideouts of sea oats and palms promptly blew away. They always rebuilt.

Blanche realized Jack had changed. Lately, they had grown apart, and given their terse conversation on the phone, she had a feeling he would be the uncooperative Jack. If he didn't show soon, she'd bug him until he did. This, he expected.

He knew something about the troubles on the island. She sensed it. He'd always been curious, and that would never change. She hoped, with just the right amount of nagging, she could get him to come up with *something*. She wasn't going to back off.

Ten
The Burning Bridge

IT WAS FOUR O'CLOCK. THE WATER WAS WARM and the sand cool and plush as wet suede under her feet as the sun shot a path across the Gulf toward the shore. The gulls circled in a frenzy—their happy hour—squawking in a terrific cacophony of bird talk before flying off to their nests. It was a signal to the last of the sunbathers to unfold themselves from their beach chairs and disappear with their novels and coolers. They'd be back for the sunset, but for now, it was the best time of the day. The cooling off. Quiet, and deserted.

She splashed along the same daily route, but every day was different. The only predictable thing was how it made her feel, and that was good. She welcomed this separation from reality. She was small, and everything else that was ever disappointing or troubling was small here, too, in comparison to what she saw on the vast and beautiful beach.

Blanche looked back at the cabin, and at the other cottages, with bright red-orange windows that reflected the flaming sun. On fire. Blanche shuddered. Destruction in Technicolor. She couldn't get away from it. They were drowning in a sea of change. The animals were disappearing, the asphalt prevented water filtration to the aquifer, beach refurbishment was turning the shore to concrete, traffic clogged the roads and the air. Real Florida had been paved, clipped, pruned, and sodded over. It was losing all its character.

Again she thought of Langstrom. Whatever happened, that team of bandits couldn't take the beach away from them. Or could they? Footage right on the edge of the water—and twenty feet inland—was already public domain, but what good would it be if they couldn't get to it? If there were no place to park their cars and bikes? The developers would restrict the right of way. Their gates would limit access to those who couldn't afford beach-front property. Blanche thought of all those condos on Lone Shark Key just south of Santa Maria. The island was so narrow, Cap had thrown a baseball across it from the bay to Gulf. Developers had sucked it up, like a noodle, and then greed was pushing them north to Santa Maria.

Bob had fought to preserve Santa Maria Island. Now he was dead.

Blanche picked up the pace, and she could sense she was not alone. Stingrays and sharks were close to shore, and, this year, trouble in the person of Sergi Langstrom—a shark if she ever saw one. What would Gran have said? Blanche didn't need to close her eyes to picture her grandmother, her cloud of white hair and fierce green eyes. Her anger rare and spectacular. ... *Open yer mouth and tell all ya know.* She was gone, but she was always there.

Gull Egg Key rose up out of the Gulf beyond the tip of the island. On the beach just ahead, the pedestrian bridge and sandy park came into view—the park that Bob had worked to preserve as a refuge, and Langstrom was planning to whack away.

Her feet pounded the sand through the tide pools. It normally thrilled her, approaching the north end of the island, where the bay met the Gulf and the Sunlight Skyway far off in the distance formed a metal-concrete rainbow to Tampa. Approaching the tip was like walking off the edge of the world. Now she looked up again and wondered what she was walking into.

Men in long pants, vests and hats, milled back and forth on the small wooden bridge. It was an odd sight, so late in the day at this time of year. They wielded equipment, lines and tripods, and poles, such as those used for tents at weddings, but this was no party.

She wanted to avoid this business, but she aimed for the bridge anyway. It was part of her routine to cross it from the beach, and she didn't want to cut short the second leg of her walk back from the north end of the island. The display of flowers, rattling palms, bright birds that sputtered out of hedges. Jacaranda and trumpet vine, oleander and rose bushes blazed, and the orange and lemon trees bloomed with tiny green marbles that would turn to fruit by Christmas.

She ignored the buzzing in her brain.

She kept an eye ahead. Most of the men drifted off. All except for one person. It made her anxious, an emotion that was appearing with maddening frequency. She tried to control it, use it to push her. She walked faster still, eager to work off the fluttering in her stomach. The long-needled pines swayed in the breeze—the ones that Langstrom wanted to rip out. Her anger spiked. She was so distracted she didn't see the broken conch hidden in an ebbing wave. She tripped and nicked her toe on the sharp edge of the shell. Blood trickled from her foot, but she kept walking through the salty water. A thin red stream ribboned away.

She couldn't mistake the blue shirt. That lanky stroll. It was Langstrom at the head of that group. She could hear him shouting directions, his voice a loud baritone. That, and the shrieking of gulls. He pointed to a couple of trucks parked at the end of the street leading to the beach. She watched him pace along the arc of the bridge. Blanche's heart sank. Her toe throbbed, but she shook off the pain.

He had his back to her, partly hidden behind a clump of sea oats. She could still get away, but she couldn't deny the urge to confront him. The last of the workmen shouted and lugged away the equipment. Doors slammed. He was not going with them. Curiosity now propelled her over the sand. She had to get it over with.

Her legs were stiff, but she set her shoulders and trudged on, the anxiety expanding inside her. She wanted to talk to him again, and at once she dreaded it. The town hall meeting had ended in a battle of nerves, and not a single point of contention had been settled. Langstrom had clearly been under the impression that he was going ahead with the development plans. *The nerve.* She damn well wanted to learn more about what they had in mind, and cut them off. And yet, she couldn't stand to face him. She wanted to walk past him and get home—to the home that he wanted to destroy. He was worse than a hurricane; he had intention, while nature did not.

Then, he was steps away.

"Hi," he said, thrusting his hand toward her. She hesitated. He waited until Blanche reached for him. So sure that she would. She felt positively ill. Her stomach was churning, and she hoped it would be quiet. She bit her tongue.

His mouth curled into a slow smile.

She still held his hand. His grip was strong, and it anchored her to the spot. His eyes were even more startling blue up close, and friendly. "Hello," she said. So loud she surprised herself. The word dropped like a stone.

She stepped back, away from his aura of self-confidence and control, but it was no good. His looks added to her confusion. The sky seemed sharper, the pines greener, her mood not so bleak. The shadow on his chin, the wave in his hair gave him a careless, rugged look.

I need to get off this bridge.

"Remember me?" His face was close to hers, his expression almost yearning.

She caught herself. "Yes, I remember you."

"I hope there's no hard feelings." He scanned the waterline that ran like a silver thread sewing the sky to the Gulf. "It really is a beautiful place, isn't it?"

"Yes, it is beautiful. Just the way it is."

He studied her. Forehead a spray of light freckles, black eyebrows sheltering deep green eyes. She didn't turn away from the horizon. She made him see it for what it was: the real beauty of it. She wanted him to understand how strongly she meant what she said.

"Your foot. It's bleeding," he said, already reaching into a pocket. He pulled out a folded square of linen.

Blanche put the offending toe behind her leg. She was mortified. "It's nothing. I stepped on a shell."

"But look." The toe was indeed making a small, red pool in the white sand. Langstrom bent down to dab her foot with the cloth. Blanche stood there frozen, unable to move.

"Thanks. That's very kind. *Doctor.*"

Langstrom looked up at her, smile brilliant white. "Ha, doctor! I did think about medical school at one time, but I decided on law."

"Yes, I know." She yanked her foot from his grip. The handkerchief had worked fine. "It was a clumsy thing to do, step on a shell. I usually look where I'm going."

"Really? Well, I guess you should. I'm sure you didn't do it on purpose." That was an odd thing to say—on purpose. Harm sometimes arrived out of nowhere, for no apparent reason, and sometimes it arrived on purpose, like murder.

She stepped back but he hovered over her. He was tall, and he still managed to be inches from her nose. "You better get some antibiotic cream and a clean bandage on that toe. You wouldn't want to lose it. It's a nice toe."

This is absurd, Blanche thought. Yesterday I wanted to kill him, and today we're all cozy.

"I've saved your toe and all, and we haven't even met, formally, Blanche M-u-r-n-i-n-g-h-a-n. I'm Sergi Langstrom." Once more the hand shot out and grazed Blanche's arm. "Hello. Again."

He remembered how to spell her name when most of the world did not. "I know who you are," she said. Blanche didn't want to sound so cold, but that was how she felt and she had difficulty hiding it. It was something she needed to work on when the occasion called for it—like now. She looked him in the eye. "And, yes, I'm Blanche Murninghan of Tuna Street and the Santa Maria *Preservation* Association."

"Yes. Blanche." She could see the town hall meeting reeling through his head and a switch of gears. "That's curious. I've never met anyone named Blanche."

"My mother had a crush on Marlon Brando."

Why did I say that?

Her mother, long dead of the accident that Blanche survived, liked the name because it sounded clean and classic in one short sound bite. That was what Gran had told her.

Sergi was laughing, sort of a private, thoughtful laugh. "Well, I don't know. You look more like a Stella. Stellar. Doesn't that have to do with stars?"

"I suppose so," Blanche said, a little miffed he'd laughed at her name. "What kind of a name is Sergi." Sergi wasn't an all-American moniker but, indeed, sounded rather strange and, Blanche hesitated to say it, Communist.

"I'm half Italian and half Swedish. Don't ask me how that ever happened." He had that laugh again that seemed to come up from his toes and right out the top of his head. He leaned close to her, and she could see the hair on his chest.

I really have to get out of here. "I have to leave."

"Really? Don't want to chat?"

"I have to go." Blanche turned to walk off the bridge and then stopped. She wanted to know more, to satisfy that urge that wouldn't go away.

"Where were you this morning?"

"Why?"

Blanche tried to decide what to make of him. Was he being coy? Why didn't he answer the question? It really was none of her business for one thing, and besides, what could he possibly think she was driving at?

She didn't care. That irritation began again. Something didn't add up about Langstrom, and all those plans for the land development, and then Bob's murder. He was everywhere, and he didn't seem to know there had been a death—on purpose—on the island.

"Because they say Bob Blankenship was murdered. They found him at the marina in his car."

Sergi hesitated. He didn't look very surprised, nor sad, at the news. He just resumed his study of the skyline with an expression that said this bit of information was not of particular interest. He could turn one expression off and another one on at will.

"Well, you don't look too broken up about it," she said. "Where were you anyway?"

"I'm very sorry," he said.

"Well, where..."

"What a sad thing to happen." His face was in the shadow of a pine tree, his shoulder angled toward her. Blanche could feel the breeze lift the hair on the back of her neck.

"We need to find out who did this. What could possibly be the motive? Who would murder Bob?" She could feel the desperation in her voice, almost pleading.

"I have no idea."

"Well, somebody does."

"I suppose you're right." His tone clipped, he looked at his watch. No one wore a watch on Santa Maria. "I have to go. It's really getting late."

He turned and hurried down the far side of the bridge toward a black Escalade, its silver rims glinting in the sun.

"Do something about that toe," he said over his shoulder, smiling back at her. "See you soon."

She almost said—*I hope not.* But that wouldn't have been quite true. Blanche wanted to see him again. What was she thinking? She had questions. A lot of them.

For one thing, who was this Sal character? And did Sergi know anything about him? Was Sergi sending emissaries door to door to entice property owners to give up their homes? She almost ran after him, but stopped. She wanted answers, and, at the same time, nothing more to do with Langstrom. That was impossible because she needed him. She didn't trust her feelings. They got her into trouble. She had to be cool, and that was so un-Blanche.

She steeled herself and dashed off the bridge. Langstrom knew more than he let on. And so did Jack. She had to get both of them to tell what they knew. She needed to tie up the loose ends whatever it took. They both had to come clean, and then Sergi had to go.

Eleven
They Stop at Nothing

It was almost seven o'clock when Blanche cruised into Cappy's driveway—more like lurched as the Taurus had developed a reluctance to change gears. It was a good thing she mostly walked around the island, but every once in a while she had to get the wheels out to see if they still turned.

The lights were on in Cap's house hidden in the palms and dune grass. She followed the curving shell path to a parking spot off the deck of his kitchen. She hoped it wasn't too late to get some dinner out of him, and she knew it wasn't. She could count on finding him at the stove. He enjoyed the evening for puttering, just like Blanche did. The bonus was that his puttering included cooking. Hers mostly involved wrestling with a stuck window or a stack of short story ideas and cleaning up fronds and weeds around the cabin. Her treat was hanging out in Cap's kitchen.

The Taurus stuttered, and stopped. The back door popped open, and Cappy yelled: "YOOOOHOOOO."

"YOOOHOOOOO yourself," she yelled back. "Whatcha got?" She leaped out of the car and into a hug. She put her hands on his shoulders, startled at how bony and thin he was getting. He seemed to be shrinking, his hair finer and whiter. His eyes cloudier. Even bluer? And sad. Yes, she was sad, too.

They would talk about it. Bury that sadness for now. She wanted to protect him from *murder* and all the rest of it.

"Stone crab today. Season just opened up." He squeezed her fingers and guided her toward the door. "Heck of a day." He shook his head. Bad news was all over this island. Blanche sighed and followed him into the house.

Steam from the huge metal pot lifted into the yellow light from a small lamp. Pungent bay seasoning filled the warm, damp air. She shut her eyes tight to savor the moment. Stone crab season— October to May—was one of their favorites.

He'd trap each crab, remove one claw, and return it to the Gulf to skitter off and grow it back. Her mouth watered, but somewhat guiltily, as the thought struck her that Cap could get more than twenty dollars a pound at the IGA for stone crab this size. This dinner was meant to cover a multitude of woes.

Cap busied himself at the pot, heaping crab claws onto a platter. He poured melted butter into a white cup and arranged lemon wedges in a bowl.

He turned to her, wagged a finger. "You need to eat. Bet you been running around all day."

"Well, I had that delicious grouper lunch…"

"Oh, that little sliver."

She smiled at him, cocked her head. "Then, we talk?"

She scooted up to the orange Formica counter that ran the length of the kitchen, one eye on Cap. He set out a plastic bib, utensils, and paper napkins and slid the crab claws, fried potatoes, and coleslaw close to her. The claws were plump, the shells a beautiful cream and rose color with black tips. Blanche cracked one open and dug out the white meat.

He clacked the spoon on the edge of a large pot of simmering soup. Lentils, she guessed, and like a band leader, he used another hand to stir the fried potatoes in the back. Blanche stopped shoveling and dipping and chomping. "Cappy, come on. Have some of these. They're the best! *You're* the best!"

But appreciation for stone crab only went so far.

He clattered over the stove a bit more—Cappy's way of dispensing with the malingering darkness. Blanche's stomach tightened. Everybody knew about the murder. Everybody was deeply affected, except Langstrom, it seemed. Standing on that bridge, he had disturbed her with his indifference, an attitude that irritated her, grated on her, urged her to find out what was going on behind that smile.

She moved the broken shells around on her plate. "You thinking about the horrible morning? I am, too." The spoon clicked emphatically into its porcelain rest on the stove top. "Caps?"

"Oh, Blanche." He smiled, shaking his head.

She thought of the guy and the white van, and now she wasn't so sure if that was a good idea to bring it up. Surely not from the look on Cap's face.

His rounded shoulders slumped in the worn flannel shirt. It had been eighty-four degrees today, but he needed to warm his old bones.

"Cappers, come on over here. Let's talk about it."

"You've been asking questions, haven't you?" He blurted it out. "About Bob? There's not a thing you can do about that. And this plan for the development at the north end?" He spoke softly. "They say it's going to happen. There's nothing anyone can do. Things happen. Sometimes, bad things, but we have to move on."

"Cappy, please. You know what they're trying to do. I have to ask questions."

"And what good will that do? They can do whatever they want.

They've got deep pockets. You mustn't get involved. Please, stay out of it."

"Well, they are not going to get away with murder. Literally." She leaped off the stool and pounded the counter. "I'll be damned if they'll get away with killing Bob, if that's what they did. I have to follow through on this, Cap."

"Now settle down, Blanche."

"I can't. I feel like someone is slowly squeezing me to death."

"I know, girl." He touched her hand. "It's too close to home."

"Speaking of which. Some guy has been nosing around Tuna Street, looking for property. Mel told me."

"Tuna? There's nothing for sale over there."

"I'll say."

"Unless…" He stood perfectly still, and studied her. "Blanche, maybe you should consider it. Now, don't get het up." The look on her face sent him back to the stove to clatter away. He was silent while her cheeks grew redder, eyes blazing.

"Cap, we're not going there, and if that guy shows up again, I'll…." She pounded her fist again. He jumped.

"Great," he muttered. He stirred, and she attacked the last bit of crab meat in a black tip. Finally, he turned and smiled, his eyes lit with concern. "I'm thinking. About lemonade. When all you have is a huge pile of lemons. I know you don't want to hear it, but you should at least think about it. Maybe someday. You could get a nice settlement for the cabin, and you could travel, or take time to write that book. Or do whatever you want to do. Just get away from all this for a while."

"You want to get rid of me." She gave him a sly look.

"Now, Blanche…You can stay here whenever you like. You know that."

He was still smiling, and she didn't want to argue with him. That would be stupid. He only had her best interests, and had his. She knew this even while her heart was on fire.

The dinner had been delicious, but she was worn down. She

looked at Cappy and wondered where the strength came from.

Twelve
See How They Run

SHE PILED THE JAGGED MESS OF CRAB SHELLS ON THE PLATTER and wiped the butter off her chin. She felt sluggish and fought it. She shook herself, then went after Cap and gave him a hug.

"I'm sorry, Cap. It's just that….You know what I want to do? I want to stay right where I am." She couldn't be upset with him. There was no future in it. She'd learned the hard way to let Cappy have his *say*—even though he wouldn't have his way.

He shook his head and went back to stirring the lentils. He had more on his mind. She could see it like she was watching wheels turn in a clock. And she wished he'd get on with it. He turned sharply and stared at her.

"What is it, Cap?" She braced herself.

"For one thing, Bob."

"Yes. Someone killed him, and it is terrible."

"I'm afraid it goes further than that."

"What do you mean?"

"It's not going to stop. Think about it. He didn't want the destruction of the island any more than you do, and he got murdered because of it. At least that's the theory." He measured the words. "I didn't want to mention it, but I should. I got back early to the dock and saw Duncan. He'd been talking to Liza."

Liza! What did Liza know? Blanche needed to get over to Sunny Sands.

"What'd they say?"

"Bob talked with those developers, and he didn't like what they were up to. Liza's got something on that. But it just doesn't make sense. He set up that preservation group for improvements at the park near the point. Didn't that come up at that meeting? I hear he even produced a check for playground equipment, and he had the backing of the state historical people. He was against that turquoise and pink mall. Would've wiped out most of the park land. Don't you see?"

"Now he's dead."

She *really* wished she could get hold of Liza. And Duncan. The sooner the better. And that would have to be after the memorial service, probably the first of several.

He reached across the counter and took her hand. His fingers were smooth as a new leaf. "Why do I have to walk you through this?" His eyes were pleading.

"Please, Cap. Don't be worried. I see you are, but don't be," she said. She could understand it, but she was pulled in another direction.

She ransacked her brain for a new topic.

The guy and the van. Not now.

"It'll take some time to resolve this mess. We've got a lot of digging to do."

"*We?* No. *They*, Blanche! Leave it to the authorities. I'm saying, Bob was against it, and he ended up dead."

Cappy picked up her plate, opened the lid on the trash can, and dumped the empty crab claws. He looked up at Blanche. She could see it coming. "You know what I'm going to say, Blanche. I worry more than ever with you over there on the beach by yourself."

"Oh, Cap. Here we go again."

"Wish you'd find a nice fella. Ain't too many around here, but I know there's some lucky guy out there for you. Just waiting. Now, if you sell that cabin…"

"Cap, that is not going to happen." They all wanted her out of her beloved cabin. For very different reasons, to be sure. But it irked Blanche—She did not want to leave her home. Not to the goons with two million dollars, or anyone.

She jumped off the stool and went around the counter. "And, besides, I have a nice fella." She gently reached up to his shoulders, her hands settling on the knobby bones under the flannel. "You know what Gran used to say, 'Shut up about that fella stuff already. That'll come.' I can just hear her."

"Maeve did not like complications. Or meddling." He bent his head and chuckled. "She'd say, 'Leave it alone, Cap.' But I can't leave you alone, my Blanche." The blue eyes misted over.

"I don't want you to."

He headed to the fridge. "Now, how about key lime pie? That should fix everything." He swirled whipped cream on top of the green mousse and set it in front of Blanche. A proper deflection from Santa Maria, murder capital, and Blanche's non-existent love life. She pushed away troublesome thoughts—including those of persistent snowbirds pecking at her property on Tuna Street—and replaced them with pie.

She enjoyed every bite, but it couldn't make her forget that change was in the air. One thing was for certain: the end of things. Cappy reminded her of that. He was concerned about her and the cabin and her future, but he reassured her that she would always have a place in his heart and in his home. Blanche looked at his sturdy back as he moved across the counter from stove to sink. He was aging, to be sure, but he appeared to be indestructible.

Blanche tried to convince herself of that while she knew the truth. One day he'd be gone, too. Yet, he looked out for her with an urgency that made Blanche think Gran had appeared to him that morning to tell him to watch over her granddaughter. Gran was always there even when she wasn't.

She wanted to stay in the moment. *Their* moment. "You know," Blanche said, holding up a fork full of pie, "all is not lost. Not yet anyway. Bob helped the association file for preservation status. Those hairballs can't tear down a single stick if we get the state historical designation. I'm thinking, it would be nice to get a petition going and name that park on the north point after him. What do you think? Blankenship Beach?"

Cap had been pensively drying the same bowl for a full minute. He nodded in agreement.

Blanche leaned over the counter. "And, we probably should be extra careful in those meetings. Not let Langstrom get hold of that plan for historical status. They know Bob had that check, and that's all. He and that bunch don't know all we're up to, so let's not stir it up. They could head off the whole park project. They have bags of money, and I'm afraid of what they can throw at all the work we've done on preservation."

"They don't know Santa Maria, or what they're getting into," said Cap. "'Just keep a low profile on this. That business with the historical society might be enough to hold them off, and you're making headway there. In the meantime, stay out of that murder business. More trouble is brewing. I just know it."

"My God, Caps."

"Like I said, Blanche, I know you've been asking questions, and you have to stop." He stacked a few dishes and flapped the wet dish towel on the counter. "Promise me, Blanche."

"Who's going to bother about me? I haven't done anything. I'm just a reporter, walking the beach. Maybe a bit nosy…"

"You've drawn attention. You ask questions. It's just your nature, and let's not forget, it's your job."

"I hear you."

He smiled ruefully and patted her hand, the one that didn't have fingers crossed behind her back.

She was sorry she'd gone off like that. But now it was time. She couldn't hold back anymore. Not from Cap. "I came by earlier today. I wanted to talk to you about something." She took a deep breath. "I haven't seen Duncan yet, or said anything to anyone about this. I wanted to tell you, I saw a guy and a white van, hanging around in the parking lot right after Bob was killed. I got the description. He looked pretty fishy is all I can say. I have to tell the chief."

Cap seemed to consider this bit of news. "It was probably Omar delivering chum for those crazy shark hunters. You know they take those bloody fish guts out into the Gulf and see what they can scare up."

Blanche was relieved at his response even though it had to do with sharks. "Don't think so. Omar drives a black jeep, and I never saw this guy and his white van."

Cappy's face was hard to read. She hesitated, bit her tongue. Her timing never felt right.

She tried to appear nonchalant and avoid a contentious discussion about the stranger. She leaned forward on the stool and bent over the pie. "Caps, this is great. Did you make it yourself, graham cracker crust and all?"

"Well," said Cappy. He shook his head, his mind clearly not on pie. "You have to get to Duncan with this. Soon. Before things get too cold. As far as I know, the chief and the lot of them haven't got any idea who's involved in this mess. There's a lot of ideas floating around out there and nothing of substance."

Blanche nodded, relieved he didn't take off on the guy and the van.

Maybe I'm way off.

"We'll talk more about this in the morning," Cappy said. "Maybe you ought to stay here tonight."

Her resolve returned. She carried her plate to the sink, scrubbed it, and went back to the counter. "Caps, I'll be fine."

"You know what I mean. Don't think I like the idea of you by yourself, is all."

"The Belsons are coming back from Canada next door, and Bertie will be on the other side soon. She may be back already. It's not like I'm alone over there."

"Just the same. I don't think we can be too careful."

"That's why I came over here. I wanted the hell scared out of me. I'm sorry I said anything about the guy and the van." Then she was sorry she brought it up again. "And, Cap, please, keep this door locked—I have a key. It was open earlier today when I came by."

He looked weary. She was sad for him. For everybody.

"Yes, I will," he said. "And you make sure that phone is working. Follow up with Duncan as soon as possible with the description of that fella, and keep out of it. Nothing's the same around here anymore. Something's been broken."

Thirteen
Rest in Pieces

IT WAS ONLY A COUPLE DAYS AFTER THE MURDER, and Santa Maria Island was about to kick off the first of several memorials to celebrate Bob's life. He'd been an island savior and supporter, and most of the residents were just short of seeking canonization for their beloved Bobby.

Blanche arrived early at St. Joseph Church, ready to pay tribute to Bob and to keep a look out for his killer. Well, she wasn't sure she'd see the killer, but her antennae were up. She was anxious and uncomfortable, the navy blue, polka-dot dress a bit scratchy and the high heel sandals a sort of torture.

She could see the top of Bob's sister's head and the Ex's hat from where she sat in the back of the church. It was hot in there, and Bob was destined for colder climes. His family planned to take him back to Potosi, Michigan, although he'd been part of Santa Maria for more than thirty years. Most everyone on the island didn't agree with the removal of Bob from the area, especially

Liza, who carried on at the ceremony and could not be consoled. Bob probably wouldn't have liked the idea of leaving Florida either. But the Ex and his sister—joined at the hip in quilting and in lamenting Bob's adventurous ways—were the sober deciders. The two, and the body, would be on the first flight northward after the autopsy and memorials.

Bob's sister was a timid woman but she stepped up and objected to an autopsy—"Bob is dead. R.I.P.," she said. "What's done is done." The authorities had insisted. They had to "verify" the strangulation complete with broken neck—euphemism for murder—and that Bob had truly not suffered some other demise.

What? Accidental strangulation in the front seat of one's car? Sometimes police work baffled Blanche. Well, most of the time it did.

The autopsy was necessary CYA (cover your ass). The women were all for propriety, and agreed. But they wanted to leave the island as soon as possible. They had never cared much for the "humidity," or for Liza, whom they agreed was, indeed, a "presence."

Blanche scanned the crowd. She wanted to honor Bob, and vindicate her suspicions. She was dying for the lanky guy with the slick hair and tattoos to show. She couldn't pin a thing on him, but the needles in her brain would not go away. *Sometimes the perpetrator returns to the scene. What prurience, what evil. What if...*

It was a peculiar obsession, casing the church, searching faces, but that was just fine. She didn't care how it looked. One could never be too watchful. The authorities should be searching the crowd for a suspect, just as she was doing. Duncan and the officers were there, but they didn't appear to be attending in an official capacity. She'd overheard Duncan out front talking about a three-foot grouper he caught off Dave White's charter. Now he seemed as out of place in that pew as a manatee in a bath tub. But he was here, and this time, she wouldn't let him get too far.

She finally decided the guy from the white van was nowhere in sight and probably was not going to show. That loose end was still flapping in the unknown.

All the while she listened to the service, she hoped Bob could see—from wherever he hovered—the outfit Liza wore to his memorial service: He would have approved. He liked her "flare," he called it, which at the ceremony included leopard high heels, a black lace sheath and veil to match, with feathers. The dangling glitter at her ears added to her sparkle, which could not be dimmed despite the pall of tragedy. Liza must have gone through a box of Kleenex.

The Blankenships, fortunately, were at a safe distance in the pews at the other side of the church. The Ex sat ramrod straight in the first row, a tiny black pill box atop her head. She hadn't moved an inch since the ceremony began, no doubt anxious to get out of there and into the skies. With Bob aboard.

The word around town was that Sunny Sands would go on the market, and Liza would be left without a job. Bob and Liza had never gotten around to firming up the real estate partnership. Murder happens. But it was common knowledge that they were working on a relationship, both business and personal. They had planned to wait until Liza got her broker's license.

Even so, Blanche wasn't too worried about Liza. She surely would land on her own two high-heeled feet and shine in the real estate world on her own, with or without Sunny Sands.

Blanche just didn't want Liza to leave. Liza was a friend, and an island leader. Enough was lost already, or slipping away. Liza *had* to stay. Liza had a knack. She could carry on. She would step into Bob's shoes though the thought of it was amusing to Blanche. Liza's triple-A, size six, wearing Bob's enormous wing-tips. But, yes, Liza *had* to stay. It made Blanche cold to think it, but Liza might lure the rat out of the cracks, the one who did this awful thing to Bobby. The thought of catching this person, or persons, made Blanche grind her teeth with anticipation. Whoever did this to Bob was sure to circle around again. They would get him. Or them.

The investigation grew colder by the moment. She'd finally gotten Duncan on the phone, and he'd said he'd see her after the memorial service.

Blanche caught his eye and waved discreetly. He nodded. He'd taken his time answering Blanche's calls, but he hadn't missed Bob's celebration—in fact, the church was bursting at the seams. They missed their "Bobby," as the blue and white satin banner across a heart-shaped spray of red roses referred to him—compliments of the staff at Sunny Sands Realty (Liza).

Fourteen
A Shot at the Chief

CHIEF DUNCAN WAS SITTING BEHIND HIS LARGE GREY METAL desk, sheaves of paper obliterating the surface. The place smelled like burnt coffee and grease, or ink—not unlike the newspaper office, which gave Blanche a pang of comfort. Duncan's green polyester uniform shirt was too tight, and so were his pants. He gave the appearance of being crammed into a job that somehow didn't fit his nature. But he still managed to separate the demands of policing from his easygoing personality, and finally leave the pressure of the work load at the office. He was a typical Florida guy, normally laid back, born and bred in the sunny ways of the South, but it seemed as if this murder had sent him over the edge.

"I need retirement," he said to Blanche, without preamble. He scooted away a pile of papers in front of him. "Real retirement."

"Not now," she said. "We have to figure out why Bob was murdered, and who did it."

"We?" Chief Duncan had known Blanche since first grade, and

he still looked at her like she had peanut butter and jelly on her face.

"I wish your Gran could see you now."

"I wish I could see her, too. She'd have a thing or two to say about all this awful business. And she might have an idea or two about how to clean up the mess. Bob's murder. Unforgivable. And what's up with these Chicago types trying to take over the island. I could lose Tuna Street. We're all on the losing end of this." Blanche felt herself lapsing back into the police beat for the *Island Times*. It was like slipping on a pair of comfortable old shoes. She collapsed into a chair next to his desk, her eyes averted and studying the overflowing desk and waste basket.

"Oh, goodness, girlie. One thing at a time."

"Well, I'm not here to waste your time though it is always nice to see you, and chat." It was good to butter him on all sides, like a Parker House roll, before she bit into him.

He looked up and smiled. He loved her lop-sided grin.

She stood up and leaned on the desk. "I saw something. *Someone*. In that parking lot the day Bob was murdered."

Duncan had eyebrows like caterpillars and now they jumped. "And who would that be?"

"A guy and a white van. Not far from Bob's Mercedes, about one hour after the murder, I'd say, noon-ish." The who, what, where, when. But no why, or how.

"That right?" He tilted back in the metal armchair, thumbs in his waist band. With Blanche, it was always the questions. And no answers. "There are about a million guys and white vans in Florida, give or take. Can you be a little more specific? Why this guy?" He waved at Blanche and the world, in general. She sat, knees crossed. She had a hankering for her notebook. She looked Duncan in the eye.

"Because I know. I've got this radar." Duncan knew all about Blanche's radar. It had worked many times, especially when she had a lead on a good story. But he had a soft spot for Blanche, and he'd loved Maeve. He'd taught Jack to throw a mean splitter—alongside Bob.

"Blanche, this ain't *Star Trek*. I need a little more than that."

"Wish'd I'd gotten that license number. But all the same I wrote down a very good description." At that, she reached in her bag and pulled out her notebook and began to wilt at the thought, *Yes, there are a million guys and white vans, but this one was different. Somehow.* "Something just wasn't right about him. That's what I'm saying. He didn't seem to know anyone, or connect. He didn't talk to anyone. He just hung around after the murder. Scoping it out. Then I found a piece of cellophane on the ground that I'm positive he threw away."

"Really! Well, maybe we can pick him up for littering—as well as loitering."

At that she pulled out a small plastic bag.

Duncan put on his reading glasses. "What's that supposed to be? A plastic bag. Of air?"

Blanche shook it gently. "I hope it's something. It's the cellophane from that guy's cigarette wrapper. I don't have a license number. But this might help."

Duncan's face, as large as a pie plate, studied her, one eyebrow raised. Deflated, she wondered why he'd even consider the flimsy evidence.

"We'll tag it." He reached for the bag.

"He shot out of that parking lot like he had a rocket booster on his van. That sort of did it for me."

Duncan hesitated. She could see his brain cells clacking together, like dice. Would he roll them? "It needs follow-up, Blanche. It does. Lemme have that description again." He held up the bag. "And we'll print this for sure."

He flipped open one of the notebooks scattered about his desk and squinted at his writing as Blanche dictated the particulars she'd written down. She had the sudden urge to push him along, a frustration overwhelming her that was almost palpable. He seemed tired. Now was not the time to be tired.

Blanche itched for more activity, and the police station did not have the flavor of an active murder investigation. A clerk shuffled around the office, slapping papers into folders and taking his time to answer the phone. Business as usual at the Santa Maria police station was pretty dull, but Bob's murder had foisted a new cast on the policing of the island. *Business should be picking up around here.* The bulletin board over Duncan's desk had several menus and a baseball schedule pinned to it, but the white board did have a fresh list of officers from all over the county. The wheels were turning, geared to island time, chugging and grinding, like they needed a good shot of WD-40.

"I'll be back soon," said Blanche, "with more details. You'll let me know what you find out, won't you?"

His bland expression said neither yes, nor no.

"Say, chief, I hear you talked with Liza. About a connection between the developers and Bob?"

"You heard that, did ya? Lots of talk going around. I'll say that. But we have nothing firm. Just talk, for now."

Ah, Dunc, lots of talk and no action? But she smiled. He was one big old sweetheart, basically.

His eyes were clear, and concerned. "I do thank you for stopping by. You be careful while you're out and about. And let me know if you see that fella again." He grunted and his head went back to the paperwork, fingers like bratwurst wrapped around his coffee cup. He sighed.

Blanche hesitated in the doorway. She turned back to him. "Chief!"

Duncan jumped. "For lord's sake, Blanche, what is it now?"

"I just thought of something." Duncan was visibly wary. Blanche's thinking was an energy field into which one stepped carefully.

She couldn't figure why it struck her so hard, but it did. The guy and the white van again. "He was rubbing his arm."

"So? I'm just not getting it, Blanche. This about the guy at the scene? The cigarette wrapper, the white van, the rubbing of the arm. These things do not exactly add up to murder suspect."

"Maybe not. But why was he rubbing his arm? And he kept at it. Do you think something, or someone, scratched him?"

"Blanche, there are bugs, you know."

"Not so many. Not now." It was true. Santa Maria was a bird sanctuary and birds loved bugs.

She could see, in her mind's eye, the smoke curling from the cigarette in that guy's fingers, the hand passing over his forearm. More than once. "And check out Bob's tie. It was on the front seat. Bobby would not remove his tie like that and just wad it up on the seat. Before he was murdered?" Blanche still hadn't moved a hair out of the doorway. "Maybe something's on that tie? And maybe something's on that cigarette wrapper."

Duncan lips moved, but nothing came out except, "hurump." He moved a stack of papers, the pen hovered over it. "Goodbye, Blanche." He sighed, and the pen began jabbing the paperwork.

Blanche started across the parking lot where Bob had died, and Santa Maria had changed forever. She hoped to heaven the chief was all over it, and that he wasn't just humoring her. She wanted to help. Flashes of the town hall meeting, then the murder, hounded her. Urged her to keep digging. These events had left her on edge and with nowhere to go but deeper.

Fifteen
Pandora in the House

Murder on the island was more unsettling than a hurricane—the prospect of which added to the jitters. Hurricane Wilma had been brewing off the coast of Africa in the Atlantic, and would soon be flying across the ocean and threatening the Gulf coast. The projections were notoriously inaccurate, despite the use of computers and the lucky guesses of storm-team meteorologists, but, still, the islanders listened with their ears to the sand while they kept their eyes on the tube. Hurricanes could be devastating, even when they didn't directly hit the island. They churned through the Gulf of Mexico leaving a wake of damage, pushing the rising water ashore and slamming property. Beach furniture and trees flew around in high winds, once landing a baby carriage in a palm tree on Tuna Street.

A hurricane was not completely unexpected this time of year, but it was most unwelcome. What they needed to do was rebuild sanity. They did not need more destruction of any sort.

Blanche put her worries about the weather aside. *Not now.* If Wilma were to be a bother, she'd give them plenty of warning before she washed over Santa Maria and wreaked havoc. She hoped Wilma had the decency to do that.

In the meantime, Blanche hurried off to see Liza.

Liza sat behind the desk, the phone propped on her shoulder as she talked and took notes. She looked up when Blanche walked in the door. She held up two fingers and wiggled them. Blanche marveled at her friend, who seemed to have rebounded. The blond curls were tamed, makeup fresh, and her grey pencil skirt and medallion-print silk blouse were straight out of a Sarasota boutique. One taupe patent leather heel dangled from her foot. Liza had a way of covering the gamut of fashion, and the profession. She ruled it all. She'd ended up teaching one of her real estate classes after she told the instructor she just loved the "software." He thought she'd said "underwear" probably because his mind was elsewhere.

Blanche landed in a nearby chair and put one foot on the waste basket. Liza appeared to have entered the angry mode, leaving the grief-stricken sobbing phase behind. She stabbed at the note pad and knit her eyebrows. She squeezed the pen until it broke in half, and then she threw it against the wall.

Blanche couldn't decide if this were progress. She peeked at Liza's scrawl but it was hard to read upside down. She made up her mind to be patient, which involved grinding her teeth. They should have been stumps by now.

At least Liza had been busy around the office. She'd re-organized the file cabinets, pushed her desk closer to the window next to an azalea Blanche had given her. And she was working. A lot. The calendar had a number of appointments and open houses penciled in—a duty Mrs. Blankenship had given up because those Sunday afternoons conflicted with her quilting bees. She had never been one for the real estate game. Her father had owned a grocery store, and she'd hoped Bob would have been more interested in tomatoes and peaches—and not the Liza variety.

Bob's corner remained untouched. A brown suit jacket hung over the back of his chair. If only jackets could talk. Blanche thought she could almost hear him: "Now, you listen to Liza... She can melt the frost off of a Michigan buyer, point out the obvious advantages of having a small kitchen or tiny bathroom. Less cleaning, especially when you've come all the way down here to rest! Why, Liza can pin a sale on a northern donkey faster than anyone."

The voice in her head faded. Bob was gone and he wasn't coming back. The finality of it hit her all over again.

Liza held up a perfectly manicured index finger and mouthed, "One more sec."

She grabbed a pen and took notes furiously, punctuating aloud as she wrote, words like... permit... Langstrom... email. Whatever was happening on the phone had something to do with the whole mess.

Liza slammed down the receiver. Blanche flinched.

"Ouch," she said. She was developing a strong allergy to phone calls. Lately, they'd been worse than hives.

"I knew it." Liza stared back at her friend, her hand still on the receiver, which, miraculously, was in one piece.

"Well, that was one hell of a conversation."

"I think I've opened Pandora's box of....snakes and *worms!*"

"Do tell!"

Liza stood up and put her hands on her hips. She seemed about to explode, and then she did. "I traced some of Bob's phone calls and the notes he made. I think he might have been onto that Langstrom. That blue-eyed, carpet-bagging, deep-dish-pizza-eating son of a bitch."

"*Really?*" Blanche bounced out of her chair. "But pizza?"

"I love pizza. I love you," she sank back down. "Thanks for

coming over, Blanche."

"What's going on?"

"Those dweebs in Tallahassee. That's what's going on." She leaped up and started pacing. "They won't tell me much, but apparently Bob found out that Langstrom was paying off someone to demolish the park and cottages on the north end. For starters. This bit of information turned up in the latest emails, and I confirmed it. I told Duncan right away. He didn't seem too interested but he did say he'd get back to me."

Liza leaned over the desk. "And get this. Langstrom called and asked me to list that awful orange and green colossus on Sycamore they built on spec. Can you believe it? The nerve. Mel can have it, or it can fall down into a pile of multi-colored trash. Wish Wilma would take it with her."

"So that's what you were talking to Duncan about. I mean, the emails, not that awful place on Sycamore." Both feet hit the floor.

"Yes, of course. Blanche, we need to get after this. There is a connection between Bob and Langstrom. Bob *knew* he was crooked."

She picked up the pen, and Blanche ducked. She was stunned. Her ears were ringing.

"We have to do *something* about this right now, but I'm not sure what," Liza said. "Those developers are moving fast. It's almost a done deal where that park is supposed to be. You were right about the group on the bridge. Those shady bastards were up there surveying the point!"

She wilted back into her desk chair. Blanche planted two fists on the desk and leaned over.

"This couldn't be better that he showed himself for the damn hairball he is."

She smiled at Blanche, her voice a whisper. "It's just so depressing. I feel like I'm slogging through a mile-high sand dune over here."

"That would be difficult given your choice of footwear."

"Ha!"

"Slogging. One high heel and one sandal at a time." Blanche looked back at Bob's computer and thought of the clues that might be revealed there. Liza circled the office again.

"The smooth delivery." She slapped those slim hips. "Their promises to dole out a fortune for the homes. Their plan stinks, and it's all for that corporation, not for the island. And Bobby knew it."

Her red-tipped fingers went to her cheeks. Blanche expected waterworks, but instead she saw grit. Liza went to the cooler and gulped a paper cone of water. They were both on the same track: the money trail. Bribes and lies littered the way.

Blanche could hear Gran now: *Money. Nothing. But. Trouble.* Nature is what lasted, and its profusion was glorious on Santa Maria Island. The combination of money and nature was oil and water. It just didn't mix.

"Liza, they'd love it if we rolled over. But we won't."

"We need to dig into those emails, Blanche. We can get back to Duncan soon enough. But for now, we have to do this." She turned to Blanche, pleading. "He doesn't have the personnel over there, or the will, it seems. He's dillydallying with county now. I can't wait a minute longer."

Blanche kept hearing—*let Duncan do it, stay out of it.* She pushed the words out of her head. "It's pretty clear Langstrom's going to stick around. We don't have a choice. And that's a good thing. We'll *make* it a good thing."

Liza nodded, twisting a handful of curls into a bun. She stuck a pencil in it.

"I hate to say it," said Blanche. "I can't stop thinking about *him.*"

"Oh, jeez, not *him.* What are you saying, girl? Those dimples and blue eyes don't fool you."

"That's not it. There's just no peace. The thought of him ruining the island, and that he could have murdered Bob. Or know who did." There was the "m" word again. She shuddered. "He'd been so concerned when I cut my toe. So earnest. That day I met him on the bridge he looked me right in the eye, and I almost believed him."

"Well, he's a liar. And a conniver. We know that. I don't think we can believe a thing he says." Liza glanced again at the computer.

"I'm going to have to meet him again, and the next time, I'm not going to let him off. He has to own up."

They heard thunder and moved to the window. A line of silver-rimmed black clouds rolled over a ten-foot-high sand dollar on the roof line of the gift shop; and to the north, a blue sky still. "Wow, look at that," said Liza.

"Just what we don't need. More bad weather."

Blanche said, "Let me get over to the cabin and lock it down. I'll be back as soon as I can."

"I'll be ready."

Blanche was becoming averse to surprises, natural and otherwise. Lately, none of them had been good. But, now, another was just around the corner.

Sixteen
Jack Be Quick

BLANCHE HEADED DOWN GULF DRIVE TOWARD TUNA. She had to get back to Sunny Sands. But now, she'd have to put it off a bit. A powder blue Cadillac convertible was parked in front of the cabin. *Look what's blown in from the North.* He wasn't in the car. Keys were in the ignition, top down. No sign of Jack.

She knew where she'd find him—in the water. He had to be part fish, and Blanche still had trouble imagining him in the big city. "It's a living, Blanche," he'd told her. "A good one, and it lets me get down here whenever I can." Where he got the wheels when he'd suddenly appear, she never could figure. He had connections. She just wished he'd use them for more than a car rental.

He was wading in the Gulf, wearing expensive pants, probably part of a fine light-wool suit. Blanche sighed. He had a key. He could have gotten into the cabin to put on some shorts.

She came up behind him and threw her arms around his back. He must have heard her tromping over the sand because in an instant he scooped her up, and Blanche found herself in about three feet of water, the waves splashing them both. Jack laughed. "Jeez, it's like bathwater. How you doin', Bang!"

He splashed her again, and Blanche gave in. "Now look at what you've done to my outfit," she yelled.

"Some outfit. Where'd you go? Goodwill?"

She flopped about, trying to gain footing—his foot—to pull him under. He was quick. He splatted a wave at her. But she caught him off guard, grabbed one slippery ankle, and he went down. The two of them were soaking wet and right back where they were twenty-five years before, two kids splashing around at the beach.

"B, let's swim out."

"You're crazy. Look at the sky. Didn't you hear a hurricane is coming?"

"It's not here yet, won't be for at least a day or so." The water was lightly capped, the blue sky streaked white to the north, the bottle-green Gulf capped in silver to the south. Blanche thought of the day they'd almost drowned, the current between the point and Gull Egg Key deceptively calm.

"Jack, remember that day we swam out to the key? Thank God I talked you into a life jacket."

"Yeah, and I had to pay you a dollar. I still can't figure that one out," he said. His shirt was plastered to his chest, his tie ruined, the trousers now rolled up and hopeless. "Oh, damn, my wallet." He pulled it out of his pants pocket and squeezed the salt water out of the leather.

"No harm done. It's all plastic."

"Except for the picture of your mom." They both stood up. Jack opened the wallet and carefully removed the photo of Rose Murninghan—Blanche's mother, Jack's aunt. Rose had cared for Jack like a son when his mother disappeared—"with the circus," his dad always said. They knew it wasn't true, but the family mystery was never solved, and Rose and Maeve took care of Jack until he was eight. Until her accident.

The Jacks. The story was never resolved. Jack's dad had been in the merchant marine and was gone for most of the time. And then he all but disappeared; last the young Jack heard, his father was in Polynesia working in import-export. Jack Senior, Maeve's brother, was a pirate of sorts who finally never made it back from sea. His was a nebulous occupation, maybe fishing, maybe guiding fishing charters. Maybe making deliveries he shouldn't be making. Maeve had always been vague on the subject of the Jacks. She would tousle Jack III's black curly hair and say, "Maybe we finally got it right."

She was devoted to Blanche and Jack III and forgave them everything—their truancy, beer drinking, and swimming in dangerous current. Duncan had rousted them more than once from their hideouts along the beach and from the neighbors' pools. "Stick together. And when you make mistakes, make them right," she'd say. She didn't dwell on the past.

But Maeve did look back to a time she had her beloved daughter, Rose. "An angel. That's what she is," said Maeve, who never got over Rose's death in that senseless car wreck. She kept her memory alive. It was about the only concession she made to the past.

Jack held up the damp picture of Rose in one hand, and with the other, pulled Blanche into a hug.

They looked at Rose's black curly hair, her laughing eyes, and the wide smile. It was the same photo that Blanche hung on the wall next to the fireplace. Next to a painting of a Miccosukee chief, the origin of which was never completely clear to Blanche. Gran would get uncharacteristically misty over that picture, and Blanche didn't push it. Gran told them fragments of stories, but the truth remained buried in the lore of Santa Maria, and in the dunes and grasses of the keys along the coast. Blanche always wondered, *why?*

She looked at the photo of her mother. "You still carry her."

"Wouldn't be without her. Neither would you."

"I always feel she's around. Somewhere, watching. Maeve, too."

"And the Jacks?"

"Oh, God, I hope not."

"Maeve's probably working some magic juju right now. Somehow setting them straight." She looked up at a bright cloud so like her grandmother's fluffy white hair and imagined her lining up all three Jacks. *What would she say? Would she ask, Where have you been in all this?*

Jack waved the photo in front of Blanche. "Earth calling." He shook the picture of Rose in the humid Gulf air. "She'd understand. This mess we're in. They all would, really, and they'd have our back. Now, let's get dry and drink some cold wet beer."

He held Rose next to Blanche's face. "Twins."

Jack and Blanche raced up the beach toward the cabin, Jack slightly in the lead. They carried pounds of sand in their pockets but happiness lifted their spirits. They were back at the cabin together. Rose ran along with them, just like they knew she always would.

Seventeen
Hot Words, Cold Beer

"'THIS MESS WE'RE IN.' YOU SAID IT."

"Murder. Hairballs. You're the one saying it, Blanche."

"It *is* a mess. You won't believe all that's happened." She was bursting to tell him the whole story. Confide in him, just like the old days—when they hung out in the dunes, smoking and drinking orange soda, sometimes with booze they'd stolen from Gran or Cappy. Such times they never held secrets from one another.

But times were different.

Jack slumped in a wicker arm chair on the porch. He'd changed out of the wet trousers into old board shorts from high school. Times were different but he didn't look it. He was tall and lean, a broad-shouldered athlete nearing forty who hadn't lost his easy gait and casual grace. "This about the murder? And the development? You going to harp at me about how Chicago is destroying Santa Maria? Are you serious, Bang?"

"Keep an open mind. Please." She'd wrapped herself in a towel and sunk into a chair opposite Jack. On the table between them he'd placed a bucket of Modelos on ice. "I just want things back the way they were."

"That's a big fat laugh. Nothing stays the same." He opened a beer with his teeth.

"*Really*, Jack? We'll need to fix your teeth along with everything else."

He grinned. "Tell me." So she did.

She went over details of the murder—and the appearance of the guy and the white van, Cappy's warning, and Chief Duncan's lackadaisical reaction. It felt like just the beginning of a horror story.

Jack's eyes got wider, but he waited until she finished. He was chewing it.

With a deep sigh, she stopped just short of bringing up Langstrom.

But she couldn't avoid him. He was like an itch she couldn't get at, and always there.

"Jack, you know Sergi Langstrom, don't you?"

"Is that a statement of fact, or a question?"

"Come on, Jack."

"Know him? I know of him."

"What do you mean by that?"

"Yeah, I've run across him. You did mention him in that phone call. Remember? And I know that meeting at the town hall didn't go well. A lot of what you just told me lines up with what I heard from Ben and Josh."

"From Manatee High?"

"They would be the ones. The murder, et cetera, is discussed far and wide. Except for this business about the guy and the van.

Really, B? Do you have any idea how many guys with white vans there are in Florida?"

"I know, I know. But this was different. He didn't seem to fit. He was creepy."

"Have you been to the The Drift recently? Plenty of island creepy there in various stages of dress and drink."

"I guess. But who in the hell would kill Bob?"

"You got me. He was our rock." Jack tipped his beer and shook his head. "To Bob."

Blanche drew her knees up. Easy and nonchalant. "So, what's the word on Langstrom?" She bit her tongue, and leveled her gaze at him. She'd take the gamble he knew more than what he was letting on.

He seemed to measure the question. "Those development folks, including Langstrom, are involved somehow with my new trucking business, and they're re-thinking their strategy down here. Brecksall and Lam. Their corporation has tentacles. I'm trying to stay out of it, but I don't know if I'll be able to entirely."

It was as if he'd dropped a bomb in her lap. He knew Sergi Langstrom from his business dealings? His *new* business?

Well, welcome to the small world of the United States, from Chicago to Florida.

"Don't stay out of it." She stood and faced Jack. "You have to get in it, and find out all you can about him. He's shady as hell. The changes he and that bunch want are not good."

He stood up, tipped the beer bottle back. "Come on, B. Don't start. You're making assumptions. *Leaping* to conclusions is more like it." He walked toward the end of the porch and looked out through the pines toward the Gulf, a sadness in his eyes. "It's complicated. And I don't know what's going to happen. I just know, I miss you, I miss it. Santa Maria. But in the end, I don't know what we can do. About any of it."

"Don't say that. We have to figure this out." She didn't quash the desperate tone. "We need specifics. You've got to help, Jack." She thought of Liza, but he couldn't help there. Liza's information was gold and she didn't want to spend it. She'd keep those revelations about the emails and notes quiet until they knew more.

"Wish I could." He still didn't look at her.

"We've got another meeting coming up. What do you think? Will Langstrom blow it? Give himself away?"

"I don't see that happening. The guy's got millions behind him, Blanche. That's what I'm saying."

He clamped his mouth shut and dropped into the chair. Blanche walked back to the kitchen in a zombie state. Her thoughts were making her brain numb and her feet like bricks. She brought out Jess's chicken salad from the deli and lit a few candles, hoping to shed some light. Jack eyed the chicken. He was ravenous. He gulped down another beer.

Blanche had to dig more out of him, but she waited. She sighed. Some things never changed. If you put a dead horse in front of him, he'd eat the whole thing. With barbecue sauce on it. She hadn't finished half her beer. She couldn't eat. She willed herself to be patient, and calm. It would be the only way to get to him. Then he looked up. He couldn't avoid Blanche's scrutiny.

"You should probably listen to Cappy," he said. "Stay out of this, Bang. Keep a low profile." Even as he said it, he knew he was talking to air.

"Everybody wants me to go away. Keep out of it," she said. "I can't let it go. For one thing, we're not only talking about losing the island. We've lost Bob. You know, *Bob*. Come on, Jack. This can't all be happening."

"Well, it is happening. Bad shit happens. That was also one of Gran's favorite expressions. We just have to deal with it best we can."

"You told me Langstrom and that bunch are part of your Chicago conglomerate. Why can't you have some influence there?'"

"They are in a whole other division. I'm new. I don't know if I can change things."

"You could. If you gave a damn." She leaned on the table, her arms taut as boards. She wasn't being fair, or calm, but she couldn't shut her mouth. She stood at her full height of just over five feet and stared a hole through him.

Jack lounged in the armchair, gazing out at the water. Jack was being Jack. He could be as stubborn and independent as Blanche, but they were two halves of one whole. They finished each other's sentences and laughed at the same jokes. They were as close to being brother and sister as any two could be, but just like many siblings, nowhere was it more apparent that two who are most alike can also be most opposed. They had their own opinions, and they fought. Loudly.

"Jack!" Her face was beet red, fists clenched. She flopped back down. "I've been counting on you. Maybe you can't stop the development. But, then, maybe you can do *something*. You have to ask around! Please?"

He forced a smile. "Blanche, how many ways do I have to say it. It's not our business, at least this murder investigation isn't. And as for the development, I don't know. Let's see how this plays out. We keep going at the same two problems, and we're getting nowhere. Really, neither one is our worry right now."

"You can't just go back to Chicago like nothing is happening down here."

"Calm down. I only care about you. The cabin could blow away, and one day it probably will, but I don't want you to be in danger. Yes, Bob is dead. That is bad, really bad, and the only thing you need to do right now is take care of yourself. I can't make it any clearer than that."

"Jack, why are you here?"

"That seems like a fair enough question. I normally don't just show up in the Gulf to dunk my favorite cousin, and then piss her off." He was usually pretty good at diffusing a difficult situation with that crooked smile, and he knew it.

"Yeah, well, *why*? I'm awfully glad you are here."

"I'm here to see you. You called. Remember? I'm sorry I missed the memorial, but I couldn't get away."

"Langstrom. Chicago. And? Out with it."

"Jeez, you are a regular Rottweiler."

"That so."

"I hesitate to say it, Bang. You probably won't like it."

"Try me."

He drew a breath, put his hands flat on the table. "This Sergi Langstrom. I more than ran across him. I have met him. I've sort of dealt with him." Jack looked sheepish.

It was a relief to get somewhere, probably far from the truth, but at least he'd pulled the web a little tighter. "Join the fan club. Who hasn't run across him? He's everywhere, and he means to take over. I even met him on the bridge at the beach, and he bandaged my toe."

"Hmm. I can't imagine how all that went down, but OK."

She stood up. "You know he wants to destroy the island."

Jack pushed his chair back and looked Blanche squarely in the eye. "That's not exactly the case, B. You have to trust me on this."

"What are you talking about? I saw the plans, and so did everyone else in that meeting last week. He means to build a mall and take out all the streets and houses. Then he and his bunch will go after the rest of the island and there won't be a pine tree or a bird left around here. And, again, I just can't get it out of my head that there is some connection between the murder and Langstrom."

"Bang, that is preposterous." He avoided her beseeching look. "Langstrom may be here now, but he works in Chicago, and Bob was here. I don't think there's any connection. And why do you keep insisting? You don't have a single link between the two."

"They knew each other, and Liza's got proof. Maybe Langstrom didn't do it himself. Maybe he and that bunch he's hooked up with hired someone to get rid of Bob."

"Oh, great. Your feelings and murder and real estate development? Damn, Blanche, you just aren't making any sense. And what kind of proof does Liza have? Bob knew him. So. What."

"I know. It sounds crazy. But I'm going to do this. I'm getting back to Liza, and we're going to look into this. Together."

"*How?* With your detective license?"

"Very funny." She didn't see anything funny in this. She was fuming.

Jack glared at her. He was tall, and his size would have been intimidating to anyone but Blanche. She still liked to remind him that once she'd beaten him in arm wrestling.

"B. Please." Now his tone was gentle. He reached for Blanche and pulled her ear, a signal they had that all was right with the world. *Their* world.

She jerked away, her teeth digging into her lower lip, and threw herself back down in the chair. Jack paced up and down the porch.

"All I can say is that I know a little about the guy, and I don't think it is going to be as bad as all that. He's definitely not a murderer, so just drop it. And, in just the little we've met, I started to think that he genuinely wants to work with us on the development. I hate to bring it up. But that's it. That's all I can say."

"Don't even put Langstrom and genuine in the same sentence. Except to say he's a genuine phony."

"Genuine phony. Really."

"You know what I mean."

"No, I don't, and there's no proof of what you say, Blanche."

"We'll see. If everything is so great, why do you all keep telling me to back off? What harm is there in asking a few questions?" She drew her legs up under her, and curled into a ball. She looked like a bun with a burned top. She was beyond disappointed, and now she was getting angrier by the minute. Every day seemed to end the same way, and it wasn't getting any better.

"It's the murder. Why take the chance?" In the low light, he seemed to be fading away.

"I'm begging you."

"We'll talk. You know that. Let's wait until we know more. But right now we know zilch."

She needed sleep. She'd talk to him in the morning. The only thing she knew for sure was that she was not going to back off. Ever. Except now, to go to bed. *Get some wits about me,* as Gran would say. It was one of the wisest decisions she'd made all day.

"Your room is made up, towels in the closet." She jumped up and pushed the wicker chair out of her way, almost toppling it over. She put her hands on her hips and blew out the candles, leaving them almost totally in the dark. "Good night."

When Blanche got up the next morning, the sun was shining, which it usually did before a hurricane, and Jack was gone. He'd left a note on the dining room table: *PLEASE, listen to me. Be careful, and just leave it alone. I love you. Jack.*

Eighteen
Murmurs on the Storm

IT WAS NOT A GOOD WAY TO START THE DAY, but there it was. Her plea for help seemed to go nowhere, except out the door with Jack. Gone. She was just going to have to dig in by herself. With Liza. Of course, they would take all the care in the world finding out more about that scoundrel, Langstrom, and his plans for the island. Sooner or later, Jack was going to have to face the situation. *He admitted he knew Langstrom!*

It was early, too early in the day for a walk, but it would be good to pound away her frustration and sort out her thoughts. The Gulf was cool and inviting, the air wet and heavy and unusually hot and humid for an October morning, the summer heat lingering. She started down the steps, then retraced back to the porch, and sat down. She'd be drenched by the time she got back from the beach. She didn't have time for a walk. She had hurricane prep to do around the cabin before she went to Liza's, but in the meantime, she was a pot ready to boil. The stillness hovered as they waited for Wilma.

She closed her eyes, a breeze riffling overhead. She needed to think, get back to normal. But she was beginning to wonder.... *Normal? What the hell is that?* That next town hall meeting was coming up, and they weren't prepared. They needed to get into that computer and those notes and see what was up. They needed ammunition.

She went into the kitchen for a third cup of coffee, dropped a couple ice cubes in it and a huge dollop of sugar—procrastinating her tie-down efforts before the storm. She grabbed the radio and clicked on to the country station. She wallowed in the music, the fiddles and sad stories. She always listened to the whole story— about the guy who was young and then old, the loves lost, the drunks, and dirt on the boots.

"Why do you listen to that stuff? All they do is complain," Jack would say.

"Maybe. But the people are *real*."

He hated it. If he were here, he'd grab the radio and turn it off. And then she'd turn it back on and so it would go with them. The thought made her chuckle. He liked *real*, too. She missed him and wished he'd stay around, for once.

She looked out the window south through the pines. She switched off the radio and turned on the small black and white television on the kitchen counter. It blasted details of the approaching hurricane, which was taking her time, like a large, grey, meandering beast.

Blanche wished it would come and go. Get it over with. There hadn't been a devastating storm in years, not since Richard hurled himself out of the Gulf and turned most of the island upside down. They never knew what hit them. They rebuilt, just like they always did following a natural disaster. It was the man-made disaster that was most disturbing.

She went out on the porch and stared, transfixed, as the sky reshaped itself—dividing grey to the south and blue to the north. How precisely Wilma painted it. So neat, and balanced. Maybe that's what they needed: a hurricane to bring them back in balance. In stormy times, they pulled together, and Blanche, in her own peculiar island-girl fashion, looked forward to the power of nature, awe-inspiring and commanding respect. The storm could also be counted on to give the place a good power wash. Wipe it clean. Shake some of those dead branches and mangos and coconuts out of the treetops. If she busied herself welcoming Wilma, she wouldn't think about Bob, Jack, Sergi, and the rest of it.

Trouble was when the wind died down, there would be another mess to clean up. And Jack, and his heal-dragging, to deal with.

She moved the plastic chairs off the patio and looked for other potential missiles. Garbage cans went into the shed. She rolled the heavy wooden shutters down over the windows. They kept the cabin tight in high winds. But it wasn't so much the wind; it was the water. When the hurricane blew through the Gulf, the water pushed farther onto shore at high tide and a wall of it had fearsome strength. Eventually, it percolated down into the great limestone aquifer under Florida, but, now, with less frequency. The increasing amount of asphalt slowed percolation. The water lingered, and pooled, causing damage to the landscape (and animals), foundations, and cars. The mosquitoes loved it. The situation was not going to improve—not with *the plan* looming.

Blanche sighed, twisting the edge of her t-shirt into a knot. She'd have to move off the beach, and stay over at Cappy's. *That'll make him happy. Safe from the storm and murderers.*

She looked around the cabin, ran her fingers over the old cedar door jam, tucked some cushions in a wooden chest. Seventy-five years, and counting, built in the early '20s when the island was settled. Log and frame, with a screened porch across the front, it had seen many storms wash through the front door. After a bad one, the soaked floor boards popped up into hills of wet slats. It took a week for the old wood to dry out and flatten back down, helped along gently with a hammer. There wasn't a single surface that hadn't gotten a good beating in a storm. It was the trade-off for living on the Gulf.

By necessity, the interior was furnished simply and defied the water. The sofa, chairs, and an old dining table stood off the floor on wooden legs. The walls and furnishings had wavy white watermarks, one for each storm it had withstood. They matched the inked lines in the door frame that dated Blanche's growth to just over five two, Jack past six feet. She couldn't say the cabin wasn't family.

Cap's place offered a bit more protection. His old house's foundation was elevated a couple of cinder blocks off the ground so the Gulf flowed right under it. Agnes of '72 had not damaged Cap's nor Blanche's too badly, but that storm had truly left her mark. Regulations after Agnes mandated that all housing be built fourteen feet off the ground. The rule produced a scattering of "bird houses" throughout the island, which was fitting given that Santa Maria was a bird sanctuary.

She was hurrying, and thinking about what to tie down, what to throw out, and where to look for the key to the shed when she saw Bertie coming around the stand of pines that divided their property. "You're back!" yelled Blanche over the rising wind. She ran to hug her old friend.

"Yeah. What great timing," said Bertie. "Murder. Hurricane. Sergi Langstrom. Why stay away?"

"Oh, Bert!" She held Bert's shoulders and looked into those eyes peeping out of her soft, pink face, and then she hugged her again. "So you know about Bob."

Bertie's smile crumpled. "Hope Duncan is making a miracle happen. Whoever would do such a thing?" A gust of wind blew off the Gulf and carried a funnel of sand toward them.

"There you have it. It's in the wind. We don't know, but we have to find out." They fell silent, except for the whistling in the pines. The opaque sky was mashed potatoes, the waves bottle green with frothy caps.

"How have you been, Bert? How was the drive?"

"Can't complain." She sighed. "Actually, never felt better, except for the hitches in my gitalong. Lord, what's this world coming to?"

She fussed around in a shopping bag. "Got somethin' here." She handed Blanche a loaf of cinnamon apple bread, fresh from the Alachua bakery. Bertie always passed through the northern Florida town on her trip back from Michigan, and she never forgot to pick up the treat. The Upper Peninsula was already feeling the onset of winter, so she timed her arrival on the island to get out of the cold.

Blanche took the bread and held it to her nose, grateful for the scent of cinnamon and nutmeg. "Thank you! Come on. Let's toast some and have a quick cup of tea."

"Can't right now. But I'll take a rain check. Literally." Bertie looked at the southern sky. "Besides I don't think this is a good time for a tea party, girl."

Blanche laughed. "Guess you're right."

Alberta Van Satter was one of the staunch, some said stupid, who held her ground in a storm, as had her mother before her. The Van Satter cottage was cypress, weathered to iron like Blanche's, and had a tight attic and heavy shutters with wide slats that rolled down from under the eaves. She'd cultivated thick sea oats and snake grass and sabal palms facing the Gulf for protection. The cinder block foundation stood two feet off the beach. Bertie would tie herself to a beam before she'd move out.

"Say." Bertie planted her frayed Keds about a foot apart. "I saw Jack pull out of here early this morning. He sure did have a look on him. Like a cow shite on a frosty morn."

As peeved as she was, Blanche laughed. It was a perfect

description of the scowl Jack might wear, especially early in the morning. "We had it out, you could say. He doesn't want to get involved, and he doesn't want me to get involved. In the murder investigation, or the development plans." They migrated toward the cement bench between their properties and sat down. Two gulls on the beach.

"Involved? I'd say you're mighty involved. The both of you. Got Gulf water in your veins and sand in your shoes. Forever."

"I know, Bert. But he says, let Duncan figure it out. That's only right. But Liza and I can't sit still on this." Blanche shifted on the bench, sand needling her ankles. "I've got to get back over there."

"Liza." Bertie groaned. She had babysat for Liza. "My little blond sweetheart."

Blanche put her arm around Bertie's wide shoulders and squeezed. "She would love to see you, Bert. She is pretty broken up."

"We talked. Still can't believe what I was hearing. Is there anything new?"

"Not yet, but we are getting after it."

Bertie took Blanche's hand. "And how are you holding up? Cap? The job at the paper? And this awful plan for developing the island!"

"We're getting along, but listen to this one. Mel says this guy was over here looking at Tuna Street. He wants to buy beachfront, and he was pestering Mel to come up with something."

"The damn pluck. I'm not going. Bet you're not either."

"Bert, it makes me nervous, this development plan, the pressure to sell. To leave. I can't." Her chin dropped, shoulders slumped.

"Land sakes! I'm getting so bad," Bert said. "Remembered the bread but not this other. Forgot to tell you what I heard out front here on the beach. Real late. After I pulled in. Swear it was right out there." Bertie pointed across the sheets of white sand whipping in the wind. "Real strange."

Blanche looked across the dunes in front, the sea grass doing a dance in the breeze. "What?"

"Moaning, or singing. Or something."

"Probably the wind. Listen to that." Blanche peered up at the tops of the whistling pines and out at the advancing waves.

"No, I know the wind. This was different. It was almost a chant. You haven't seen anything, or anyone, strange hereabouts?"

"No, Bert." She thought about the guy in the white van. He certainly was strange, but he wouldn't be out there whistling and chanting.

Ridiculous.

"Well, keep an eye out. Whoever's out there is going to get a good wash. Soon." Ghostly clouds blew up heading north.

"I wouldn't be surprised," said Blanche. "But, really, I'm sick of surprises."

They stood up. Bertie stretched. "I hear ya. But I think we're in for it."

The storm was coming. Fear nagged Blanche, but she pushed it aside for now.

She finished up quickly, threw a garbage bag over the television in the kitchen, rolled up the sisal rug, and flung it onto the sofa. The poster of Native Americans dancing and cooking fish next to their chickee had begun to curl, and, sadly, the storm would likely finish off the feast. Again, she thought of Gran and her stories about the Indians. Something had never been settled there, and the wind did nothing but stir the notion. Of ghosts and legacy? Of stories still to be told?

She snapped out of it, brought in the last of the lawn chairs, broom and buckets from outside, and she fastened the last of the shutters. The Taurus was crammed into the shed, and good luck there. She loved that car, but insurance would never cover it. She picked up a small bag full of clothing and a couple of books.

The rest was up to Wilma and her powerful lungs.

Blanche looked up into the pines, like soldiers, holding the sand in place around the cabin. She couldn't stand the thought that someone wanted to kill them. The whistling high in the branches turned to a roar, and then retreated, the eddies of wind from the hurricane not far off. The treetops swayed and snapped, and then went silent.

Surely that's what Bert was talking about. The sounds of the trees. What else could it be?

She walked out of the porch and over the carpet of pine needles. In the south, faint traces of rain striped the sky, from the clouds down to the Gulf. The grey sky moved northward, eating up the blue horizon.

Blanche turned to look back at the cabin, its logs interspersed with white stucco, its flat roof. The dark windows carved out of the logs. Eyes shut.

She waved at Bertie who stood on her deck looking out at the beach. She gave a thumbs up and folded her arms. The waves were closer now, roiling off the shore.

Blanche adjusted her bag. She was happy Bert was back, and it was good to know her old friend was holding down the beach.

Blanche's feet pounded the road back to Liza. White blossoms swirled like snow, the palms crackled. She would *not* lose the cabin in this hurricane; the islanders would not lose their home. She refused to give in to the possibility. And somehow if they did, it would be better than losing it to Sergi Langstrom.

Cappy warned her, and she tried to listen. He was philosophical about changes, resigned to them, but try as she might, she couldn't go there. The changes meant loss, and she wouldn't accept it. But she couldn't deny his words.

Cappy lived in the present, and he saw possibility in the future. She needed to be more open, to accept some things, and if she didn't, she would be closed to possibility, and opportunity. She'd be stupid not to listen to the Cappers.

But, in the end, it was not enough. They had come this far, and there was nothing to do but keep going. She would never give up the cabin. And they were damn well going to find out who killed Bob.

She slowed down and walked down the misty road. The island seemed deserted. Lightening cracked the sky and a roll of thunder followed, clouds raced over the tops of palm trees. The trees glistened, the flowers shone with wet brilliance, and bright petals blew around like confetti at a wild party. Her hair, eyelashes, face were damp. She was nearly soaked to the bone, and that was fine. She turned into the storm. It gathered strength, and she headed into it.

Nineteen
Hurricane Party

BLANCHE BENT TO TIGHTEN THE STRAP ON HER SANDAL. Still no running shoes. She had no interest in shopping and even less in rummaging through her closets. She wore the same t-shirt, rinsed and dried, and now more wilted and damper than ever. Liza had called. "I have a mess of stuff here, Blanche. Come over right away. Please. The hell with the storm."

The timing was not good for detective work. But Blanche and Liza were of one mind: Make the most of a rainy day while the island hunkered down and before Wilma had her way with the utility poles.

The pines whistled; the Gulf roared. She loved the sun, but something about a good storm zapped her to the ends of her nerves. The wind abated and then started up again, fresh and terrifying. A scent of salt and fury in the air.

One neighbor was packing up to leave the island, but most of them didn't see the point. Like Blanche. They had short memories and were willing to live with a beauty that would throw a tantrum once in a while. They would tie down like they always did and get through this one, and then another and another.

Cappy was expecting her later, but for now, Liza. She had news.

Blanche dashed across the parking lot, the backpack slapping her hip, just as a blast of rain and wind rattled the front door of Sunny Sands. Liza scurried past the window with a batch of papers. She seemed to ignore the palm trees bending outside her door, the boats tossing up and down like toys in the marina. The island floated in a cloud of mist. The first bands of the storm had arrived.

"Wow. Am I glad to see you," said Liza.

"Same here, girl." Blanche started to hug Liza and thought better of it. She dropped her wet bag in a corner.

A small television screen sputtered with flashes of white and green. A forecaster danced around, pointing to Wilma approaching from the south. The island appeared to be clear except for a darting weather pattern.

Liza finished pushing chairs and coat racks and wastebaskets into a closet, but she left the bare bones for them to sit on—and the computer against the far wall. She stacked some papers into a cardboard box as she clicked around the desk in her high heels, waving a cigarette. Liza reached for a hug, despite the rain cloud Blanche was wearing. She hoped it would put out the cigarette.

"What's with the cigarette?" Blanche was a reformed smoker. She'd never seen Liza with a cigarette.

Liza looked at the Marlboro Light like it was a foreign object. "I don't know. Haven't had one in years." She took a drag and made a face. "Tastes terrible. But I'm accepting the abnormal. Helps me cope."

Again Blanche heard Gran. *This too shall pass.*

Liza tossed the last of the manuals, nudged a chair against the wall.

"Can I help?" She was anxious to see what Liza had in store

and less inclined to rearrange the office.

"Oh, honey. I'm about done here. They say this storm won't be too bad, but you never know. You can't count on anything these days," said Liza. She moved the azalea and a potted orchid away from the window.

"True. Is everything good at your condo? All tight over there?" Liza's condo at Westbay Moorings was only two blocks away. Blanche peered out the window at the pathway disappearing in the rain.

"All set. Calvin has the shutters down, outdoor stuff in the storage shed. Thanks for worrying." Liza had not forgotten her White Rose Musk and the curling iron. She dressed for every occasion, even for Wilma. She wore a tight purple top and black stretchy pants, a moon on one thigh, the sun on another. "He's going to come by later and walk me over."

"I'm dying to hear what you found."

Liza gave Blanche a sly look. "It's good, Blanche. Real good. Or real bad, depending on whose point of view." She clicked over to a recessed counter and small fridge. "We have some digging and sorting to get to. And some drinking and eating. How about we have ourselves a little hurricane party while we plan what to do with Sergi!" She stopped abruptly, one hand on hip, one eyebrow lost in a curl. She waved the cigarette and sprinkled ash in her hair.

Liza spread a lacy napkin on top of the desk. Blanche was starving, and, drat, if she hadn't forgotten Bert's cinnamon bread! She started opening an assortment of deli cartons packed with pink and white seafood. "Crab Louie! Bet Marge made this."

"Sure did. She had to close up early, and I was only too happy to take it off her hands."

Blanche fluffed the ash out of Liza's curls. She kicked off her wet sneakers and curled up on the chair.

The cigarette dangled from Liza's glossy lips. Blanche shook her head. But the smell of burning tobacco was nostalgic, tugging at her willpower. *What if I just give up?*

Blanche had seen some mania in her day, and Liza was a maniac. She yanked a chair closer to the desk. She dragged on the last of the cigarette and sizzled it out in the dregs of her coffee in a foam cup.

"Here's to the storms in life." She jammed the corkscrew into the top of a bottle of La Crema, not bothering to remove the foil.

Blanche held out a plastic wine glass. "To the end of them. Especially the murd… bad stuff."

Liza poured the chardonnay. Almost to the top. She took a sip, and lit another cigarette. "Come on now. Perk up. We need our strength."

Liza only picked at the seafood salad, but Blanche demolished hers. Margie's homemade Thousand Island Dressing was delicious, the crab, plump and sweet. They sipped and the storm rattled away. But then Liza was up again. She crunched the cartons to a pulp and flicked open a garbage bag. "Now, you know what we need? Emails for dessert. Got some sweet ones!" she said. "To go with another bottle of wine." She paused in her circuit around the room. She looked across the street to Decoy Duck's Package Liquors, but the lights were out. "Oh, well."

Blanche was a little fuzzy around the edges. She needed a water layer to dilute the booze, so she went to the cooler. She brought a cone of water to Liza, who seated herself at the silent gray computer. A doorway in the dark.

Liza plugged in Bob's username and password. "Makes me feel he's still here. Sort of. I just can't give him up." She leaned in and began clicking away through the pages of Bob's emails. There were hundreds.

"When I go in there, I can almost hear him." She looked near tears. "He always had such a good sense of things. What would he do with this?"

Blanche would never know. It was up to them now.

Liza's forehead creased with concentration. "We know for sure

Bob did not back that development. He wouldn't cooperate with them. We can start there. At square one."

"Whatcha got?" Blanche pulled a chair around next to Liza. A sign clattered past the window and flew across the parking lot to nowhere. They hunched over the screen as Bob's email popped into view.

"Oh, yeah. This is going to take some sorting, Blanche. And connecting, one thing to another. I don't feel much like a detective, but this'll do." Liza looked less like a detective and more like central casting. But she had a pen stuck behind her ear, the computer up. She waved at a stack of notebooks. "We need to cross-reference these emails. And I have notes Bob wrote about appointments and phone calls. I put them in a separate box."

All Blanche could think was this: Evidence. In black and white. On paper. "Did you hear phone conversations, too?" She was positively gleeful.

"I did. Trying to think." She looked again at the rattling windows. One high heel hit the ground.

"Phone conversations?"

"Yeah. Now let me see…" Liza pushed away from the desk. She went to a tiny alcove that served as a kitchenette and produced a bottle of Irish whiskey and two glasses. "Sometimes I think better when I drink. I need to maintain an altered sense of reality."

"Reality could use a little bending." Blanche poured.

Liza plopped a crate of papers on the desk. "Let's have a look here. I need to check something. Something he wrote in one of these emails. I told Duncan about this. Haven't heard a word."

Duncan was plodding along, the definition of the wheels of justice grinding slowly. Maybe he knew more than was advertised, but he seemed unwilling to share it.

They hadn't heard from Langstrom in a while. He seemed to have gone underground since the town hall meeting. Another was scheduled soon, but first they needed to get their act together. Blanche was leery about which boot the developer would kick them with next. They needed to kick back. The developers had a plan, and Blanche and the residents didn't. Sometimes Blanche woke up in the middle of the night and felt like she was suffocating, helpless to do anything about it.

She looked over at Liza and hope niggled in the pit of her stomach. Just maybe they had something here. Finally.

Twenty
Digging for Gold

BLANCHE PICKED UP A MARKER AND DREW A WEB on Liza's whiteboard. She began outlining what they knew so far. She stuck bubbles of names and bits of information on the board. Bob. Murder. Langstrom. The plan. They needed more names, dates, times, and places. It was all somehow connected, but she fought to reserve judgment. She didn't have any idea how it all fit together. But as a visual person, Blanche could see that the web was starting to make some sense already. All she had to do was turn into Spider Woman and leap from one point to the next. And save the town.

The computer cast an eerie glow in the nearly dark office. Some light filtered through the wooden slats. Wilma thumped and cracked outside.

They raced against the storm. They still had electricity, but one well-aimed palm frond would end it. They'd be sitting in the dark, probably for a day or more. They needed a head start before fresh hell broke loose.

Liza swiveled back to the whiskey. She poured two more fingers into each glass. Blanche shrugged. "Drown the shamrock." And she tossed it back. Liza took a sip and set the glass down with an emphatic clink.

Blanche's throat burned but it was a false sense of warmth. The adrenaline and whiskey did not mix well.

"Look at these emails," Liza muttered. "Where do we go from here?"

"Back to the beginning?" Blanche stared at the web, her mind wandering. *How would I look in a blue and red suit with no hair?*

"A lot of this mail is related to those calls." Liza sipped again, her lips puckered. "I hate to think back. It must have been the beginning of a very bad time for him. It seems the phone conversations got worse. Sort of testy, and threatening. That would be about three months ago."

Blanche noted the call pattern on the board. "We need to check the notes and see who he was talking with."

"It's here. Somewhere." She scrolled through some pages. "I told Dunc about it, but he seemed so distracted."

Blanche drew a large green circle for Chief Duncan and connected him to the early warning. He had his own special bubble in the web. "Duncan. You gotta love him. Mostly."

"Well, I don't want to wait on him. Acted like I didn't know what I was talking about." She waved at the computer. Big mistake for Duncan. They both meant to pursue this to the ends of the earth.

"I hear you. But if we find anything, we should bring it to him."

"He's checking with county." Liza rolled her eyes.

"You said you shared some with him? How much? There's a ton of stuff here."

"I just couldn't get into it, at first. I was so angry, and sad." Liza frowned. "It was so ugly—the calls especially. Bobby had put his foot down about that development. Fortunately, he dated some of this, and I have notes on my calendar. Let's put up what we can." She pointed to the board.

Blanche paged through one of the notebooks, but it wasn't making much sense. "Who was calling here? Looks like this happened a little closer to the meeting."

"Some outfit in Boiling Brook, or something like that. Up in Chicago."

"Bolingbrook?"

"Yes, that's it."

"No name there." Liza slumped and stared at the screen.

The sky was nearly black and the wind blew branches against the windows. Blanche cringed. They still had power.

"The flurry began about June, I'd say. Maybe later. He'd get angry—I never saw him so angry." Liza took another swig of the whiskey. Blanche carefully moved the bottle to the floor. "Here, look at this, Blanche."

The email read:

"Mr. Blankenship, it will not benefit your business interests, nor those of the community of Santa Maria Island, to obstruct the plans that Brecksall-Lam is proposing for the northern quadrant of the island in question…"

With that, Blanche felt her stomach lurch. "What? Liza, that's the name of the headquarters for Jack's new trucking business." She made a special bubble for Brecksall-Lam. "Why didn't he…. well, elaborate?"

"Now why would he do that? I don't think he has any idea about the extent of this."

"Oh, I don't know. Maybe not, but I do remember hearing about these people. Jack's been working for them for months now." Blanche stared at the screen. No answers popped out at her. "You know Jack. He wouldn't report back. He's still vague on details about the new business no matter how much I press."

"Blanche, you have to press. Jack is such a sweetheart, you just know he'd like to help."

"Humf. Sweetheart."

Liza looked quizzical. And Blanche wondered about this new business of his. *What are we supposed to do with this piece of news?* She considered the various bubbles of calls, names, and notes.

"All I can tell you is that Jack had the small freight office set up in San Antonio, and another in Chicago, and he kept getting more calls for cross-country work. I think Lam wanted to sell his part of the trucking division, and Jack heard about it through his connections and jumped in." Blanche sat back in her chair. "He was cagey, all right."

He had to have had some idea about the trouble on the island and a possible link to his business. He seemed to have eyes everywhere, and here was proof of it. Tenuous, but a connection nonetheless.

Be careful, he'd said.

Blanche felt betrayed, and she couldn't help it. Was he lying to her? Or protecting her? Or both?

"Call Jack and find out what's going on. Really, Blanche. You know he'd want to help. This is his home, and I'm sure he'd clear up some of this. He's right in the middle of it," she said.

"I've tried to get after him. But he's not very receptive. And he certainly has not been cooperative. We talked about Langstrom. Jack said he knew him. Said to stay out of it. The usual."

"The usual doesn't get it. This business with those developers was building. Bobby had some cranks, and he could get riled up on the phone. At first, I thought that's all it was. I didn't see trouble coming. This Brecksall-Lam outfit went right over my head."

Liza turned back to the screen and scrolled down through the emails. "Here's another: *Brecksall-Lam is prepared to draw up an offer to purchase certain parcels of land, which will be used to build the mall, tentatively named Silver Shells Emporium, between Hibiscus Drive and Gulf Avenue. We anticipate your cooperation, as arrangements have been settled in your favor. In the unlikely event essential cooperative efforts are not in place by October 1, representatives of Brecksall-Lam will find it necessary to seek appropriate action through their agents."*

"Appropriate action! Yeah, right," said Liza. "There's nothing appropriate about any of this."

Now Blanche had bullet points to go with the bubbles, and her hands were shaking. She stood back and looked at the web of deceit. *Oh, what a tangled web we weave, when first we practice to deceive…* Gran again.

Liza stared at the computer. "What bullshit." She took a sip of whiskey and reached absently for her cigarettes. They both hovered over the screen.

"They moved fast," said Blanche. "But this is weird. Why would they be making 'arrangements' with Bob? What is that supposed to mean? Bob was against the development."

"He was against it. I know he was. He shouted at that phone, something about not wanting any 'arrangements.' That they had come up with them at the last minute. He told them, most emphatically, that their plans, such as they were, would *not* be in the interests of the island. An original deal was supposed to include the kids' park and the nature preserve, but Bob wasn't buying their version. They never came through like they said they would. They had another agenda. A takeover."

"Money. Somehow they got to him with cash, but he didn't want it. He didn't like their terms."

Liza pushed off the desk. "Yeah. They did make some donations. He asked me to make the deposits to a special account: SMI Parks-Preserve, it's called. Actually, I made a couple deposits of just under $10,000 each over a month or so. They had to be broken up into smaller amounts so there wouldn't be suspicion about the origin of the money. In any event, Bob didn't want any complications, or questions. He said the money was for charity, plain and simple, for the park and the kids. I know that for sure because I heard him talking to the commissioner and to the pastor at St. Joseph's, telling them about the improvement fund and plans for the sports teams. That money is sitting in that fund."

Blanche stopped scribbling dollar signs and connecting Bob and the "arrangements." She stepped back. "My God. The check Bob produced at the meeting! *They* donated all that money?"

"No. That check was money Bob raised through the historical society and from residuals on sales from Sunny Sands. That money was one hundred percent Bob. But this other is not. Brecksall-Lam made donations, and they lied about what they wanted to do with the north end. They weren't planning parks and playground equipment. I'll bet Bob was backing out, trying to return their money." Liza drained the last of her whiskey. "Something went wrong."

"A *lot* went wrong."

The two looked around the office, from the whiteboard to the pile of notebooks, and back to the computer screen.

Liza sat still as stone, but her wheels were going around. Blanche hurried over to the kitchenette and put a filter in the basket of the coffee maker.

"Liza, did you ever see a guy and a white van hanging around the marina? Parked in the lot? Someone who seemed new around here?"

Her gaze broke, she turned to Blanche. "I see a lot of delivery trucks. Pete's Restaurant is near there, but I haven't noticed anything, or anyone, new."

"Strange." Blanche measured out the French roast.

"Why do you ask?"

"I really didn't want to bring it up, not yet, anyway. But this guy. He was definitely not a tourist or a snowbird. He looked so out of place, and suspicious. Hanging around, watching everybody at the marina. You know, that day."

"Put him in a bubble, Blanche. Even if he doesn't pan out, at least we have him up there where we can check on him."

Lulled by the whiskey, suspended in the storm, they studied

the tangle of information spread over the whiteboard. It was not a pretty picture.

"Bob, it seems, was a victim of corporate manipulation, to put it mildly. But what was behind the donations? And what went wrong?"

"Pretty simple." Liza banged her fists on the table top. "He just wasn't buying it. He resisted their plans, and they *killed him*."

Blanche handed Liza a box of tissues and a cup of black coffee. "It's awful, and it's weird. But somehow, at this point, I feel kind of relieved, Liza. They are not going to get away with it."

Liza's eyes were blazing. "It's dangerous, B." She leafed through pages and checked Blanche's board. She stacked the notes and notebooks, copies of emails, in chronology.

"Jack certainly has some explaining to do, whether he likes it or not," Blanche muttered.

"In the meantime, here we have it. Evidence." Liza pressed the print button on the computer, and out came dozens more emails. She pushed the desks together and spread the print-outs of emails, calendars, and notes and shuffled them in order. Blanche taped computer paper together, drew lines and notes, and kept filling in the board with details. They worked through the afternoon, oblivious to the dark outside while the office burned bright.

They had proof that Bob was operating outside the lines, and someone was out to get him. A. Smith in accounting signed some of the emails. It didn't add up to a hit on Bob, but the recalcitrant exchanges were linked to Brecksall-Lam—and, unfortunately, to Jack, too. The question presented another disturbing twist. Blanche couldn't deny that Jack was involved in the mess. But how? And how deep?

"It helps that Jack knows the territory," said Liza.

"Helps or hurts. Who knows at this point? Could be bad. I'm mad as hell he didn't level with me. Instead, he just tells me to be nice and go away. Like the whole thing is just going to go away." That was exactly the problem. Way too much was going away.

Twenty-One
Jack Be Very Nimble

"DAMMIT, JACK. DON'T TELL ME TO BE CAREFUL, and don't tell me to stay out of it again. I saw the emails from Brecksall-Lam. And I want to know how, exactly, you're connected to these people." Blanche was standing on what was left of her porch and yelling into her land line that for some reason still worked.

"You don't have to yell. I can hear you perfectly. Unfortunately."

She was too upset to let him try and calm her down. She felt betrayed by her only living relative, and her house was nearly destroyed as a result of Wilma blowing past the island. There had not been a direct hit, but in her ramble through the Gulf, the hurricane had blown out most of the southwest corner of the cabin. The second floor was cantilevered over the screened-in porch, which was mostly devoid of screen. Bertie had weathered Wilma, and she had gone on a road trip to visit her sister in Homosassa. In fact, most of the Santa Maria beach front had withstood the storm pretty well, except for Blanche's old cabin.

She looked around at the destruction. Everything was going to hell, but to Blanche hell was not a permanent residence. This could be fixed. Blanche was determined to pull herself out of this one, too.

"Well, if you can hear me perfectly, why don't you answer me? What is going on, Jack?"

"Look, I'll be back down there next week. We'll talk about it when I see you, and by then I'll know more. I don't want you to talk to anyone about those emails, and tell Liza not to say anything either. Bob's dead, and that's awful, but let's hope to God that's the end of it. And, Bang, dammit all, I told you to stay out of it. Let me find out more about Langstrom's dealings with Brecksall-Lam. I'm not sure how much the business is tied up in the mess, but I'll see what I can do and let you know."

"Liza's already gone to Duncan with some stuff—mostly emails she found in Bob's computer. You're going to have some explaining to do. Fair warning."

"Oh, swell."

Blanche could practically see him raking through that thick, dark hair.

"Jack, are you OK? This doesn't sound good. What have you gotten yourself into?"

"I'm fine. But I really have to look into Brecksall and Lam's history. I should have done more of that before I bought in, but there just wasn't time. They've got it all, Blanche—trucking, legal, food, imports. I let the lawyers handle it because I was so busy. I finally signed the paperwork."

"You wanted to do that months ago. What happened?"

"I tried. Had a lawyer on it and everything. Kept getting postponements. There was so much paperwork, and then along the way, plenty of screw-ups. I need this trucking line, Blanche, and I was pretty desperate, but transport across state lines involves a lot of bullshit."

Amos Wiley, construction genius and hurricane doctor, pulled up in his truck next to the cabin. He started whistling and dragging boards out of the back bed.

"Gotta go, Jack. And you better be here next week like you promised. Or else."

"Or else what, Bang? You're a trip."

"No, you're the one with the trip. Here. Next week."

"I'll try. Remember what I told you. Serious…."

"Again. No. It's too late."

Blanche threw down the phone and the broom, then kicked a pile of fronds she'd piled neatly and then decided to punish instead. The wind had gone, the water had receded, and she'd swept most of the sand out of the cabin. The condition inside on the first floor was another matter. The floor boards had buckled into small wet hills and seaweed decorated the furniture.

Amos lugged two-by-fours across the sand. He waved and set about propping up the second story so it wouldn't fall down into the porch. Oddly enough, as in most hurricanes, much of the infrastructure in the cabin was intact. The wiring worked. Sand was mounded around the plumbing in the ground floor bathroom, but the toilet flushed. She had to deal with the goofy-looking wavy boards until they dried out. It wasn't the first time; she hoped it wouldn't be the last. Many hurricanes had come and gone and tried to blow it all away. They'd failed so far.

Twenty-Two
The Gulf Is a Hungry Ghost

BLANCHE PICKED UP THE PHONE, DUSTED IT OFF, and put it gently back in the cradle. Guiltily. She couldn't seem to slip the anger that burst out of her. But she knew the antidote of the moment was Amos.

She walked over to the corner of the porch. He was looking up and down at the ravaged cabin. "Don't you wonder where it all goes?" He smiled at Blanche and looked out over the shining Gulf that belied the recent storm. The sun was brilliant on the water, and the sky was sapphire blue.

"Only God knows."

"And Neptune."

Amos began fitting the uprights under the porch ceiling. He never looked like he was about to build a house, always dressed in lightly starched shirts and dark jeans. But he was a busy, hands-on contractor who had built the best houses on the island. Lately, he'd turned to rehabbing because most of the island was built up and out to the edges of the water, and Amos would not cram another house, even when permitted to do so, into one more fifty-foot-wide lot. With setbacks on either side, that kind of construction required ridiculously narrow houses with living room in front, kitchen in the middle and bedrooms in the back, all of it on stilts fourteen feet off the ground. The railroad flats of the island where there were no railroads. He'd been "footed" to death, sideways and back to front, kicked in the rear by all the zoning restrictions and the ever-present demand to build on every inch of beachfront footage. Now he did what he wanted to do, and it was all quality—mostly restoration and the occasional grand home inland.

One good thing about the hurricane: She would get to see a lot of Amos. It was like he was part of the family; Gran had had a soft spot for him. He came over after every storm and often on Sundays for Gran's cherry pie. He had a ton of gossip—and he was supremely adept at putting houses back together after a storm.

Blanche righted an overturned Adirondack chair. "Want a chocolate sundae?"

"Well, one thing at a time." He was grinning. He tapped a board into place. "I have to go to the truck, but I'll be right back. Put some peanuts on that sundae if you got 'em."

Blanche scooped ice cream into bowls and drowned it in chocolate sauce. Fortunately, she had red-skinned peanuts in the freezer—to complete the Tin Roof sundaes. She carried them out to the porch and set them down on the table. She retrieved the chair cushions for the Adirondacks, one of them dragged off the beach where Wilma had deposited it in a dune. It would take her weeks of sweeping, pounding, and cleaning, once Amos got the structure back in shape. She yanked at one of the flapping screen panels and secured it against a nail.

Amos dug into the sundae. "The best, as always, Blanche. Thanks! How you been?"

"Except for Wilma, and the murder, and those plans that Langstrom is talking about, I've been just peachy. How about you?"

"The murder. How could it happen?"

"To Bob? I just don't know."

"Well, I hear Dunc has his hands full on this one."

Blanche wanted to share her theory, and Liza's find, but decided to turn her filter on. For once. Land development was Amos's bailiwick, and any light he could shine there would help in the long run.

"Langstrom. What do you think, Amos?"

He gulped the last spoonful. "Don't want anything to do with him. Those people don't know what they're doing."

"I wish you'd tell them that. They can't do this to the island. They want the cottages, the park, the rest of the north end."

"They got a fight on their hands. They also got money." It was a bitter message to swallow with all that ice cream.

"Do you know anything about their plans? Aren't you able to file objections to permits? You know all the ins and outs of coastal building. You have friends in Tallahassee. Can't you stall that Chicago bunch?" She didn't want to mention the business with Jack. She was worried that he was in trouble and talking about it to Amos would just give it life.

"Whoa, Blanche. I'm quite the little guy when it comes to these guys. Like the St. Bellamy Corp. They've all but destroyed the Panhandle, the east coast, and they're working their way through the state. At this point, we really don't know what these Chicago folks are up to."

Amos looked at the corner of the porch. He pointed with his spoon. "Blanche, I have to tell you, you have other worries. More immediate. The town will condemn this place if it's more than fifty percent destroyed. I'm just giving you a heads-up."

"It's not half gone. The plumbing and wiring all work. Most of it is standing. Want to look around?" She jumped up eagerly.

"It's not what I have to say about it. The inspectors will tell you the second floor is uninhabitable, and it is. You can't go up there. It isn't safe. You better go to Cappy's for now."

"But you can fix it, can't you? You always have before."

"Of course, I'm going to try. But things are different now, and it has to do with money. A lot of it. You have a prime piece of beach here, and I know you want to hold on to it." He looked out at the water and back at Blanche. "I have to say, I've never seen anything like it. If you can see a dot of water from a spot of land, they want to build on it, and they don't give a hoot about restrictions and permits. They want weird staircases that spiral up to the roofs." He shook his head. "They get too many margaritas in them, and then the little kids climbing… I don't know where this is headed, but it's not good."

Blanche frowned. "How can they get these permits? I thought you had to rebuild within the foot print if it's a teardown."

"They're buying off inspectors and officials left and right. They say they aren't, that it's special permitting, but they are making up more permits than anyone knows what to do with."

"Which reminds me. Mel told me some guy came asking her about property on Tuna Street." A floorboard from the second story creaked, broke off, and plunked onto the beach in front of them. She felt like she'd lost a limb. "Oh, wow. I need my house back."

Amos took Blanche by the arm and guided her away from the corner.

"Have you heard of this guy, Amos. A Sal someone?"

"No, haven't heard of that one. One of many. There's only so much beachfront, and it seems they'll stop at nothing."

"They'll get caught and the market will collapse right on top of their heads."

"Maybe. In the meantime, enjoy the cabin after we get this mess cleaned up and hope for the best. Walk the beach. Don't think about the rest. What good will it do?"

"I'll try." She studied the corner. "You'll try, too?"

Amos grinned. "You know me. Every wall and door knob I put in feels like mine. I'll get to it, and soon. Before those goons come around. You don't want to be out of code, especially when that talk starts up at the next town hall meeting. The hurricane put a damper on that business for a bit, but they'll be back, and I don't like the sounds they're making."

"What about them, Amos? Really. They've dreamed up a fantasy land. What can we *do*?"

"We have to stall them, and we have to do what we can to prevent the permitting. I don't know if it'll work, but the island will never be the same if we don't. And it's not so much the ugly, commercial, cookie-cutter look of their plans. It's just not good for the environment. Too much, too crowded. It's just plain unnatural."

She and Amos looked out over Tuna Street at the white sand and turquoise water. Even with the devastation of the cabin, with the porch open to the breeze, it was paradise. The yellow beach flowers, revived and soaking up the sun, the palms and grasses glistening.

"What if I just left it open like this?" Blanche looked over the exposed porch, a few steps up from the crushed shell.

"Ha! Sometimes I wonder if you're a girl or a gull."

"Bird brain, maybe. I swear Langstrom and this murder are making me crazy."

Amos gathered up a couple of tools. "Blanche. It'll work out. It has to. Hang in there."

He added fuel to the notion that they wanted Bob out of the way. They were out there, and they were doing their worst.

"And Bob," said Amos. "He groused about those plans. The word is they left no room for the park and no way to handle all that traffic and asphalt. The kicker is most of the islanders wouldn't be able to afford the housing they propose, and the property taxes. They'll have to leave the island. No wonder Tallahassee is on board with the permitting. More money for the man. It's getting to be one big sewer up there."

"So you think these hairballs had something to do with the murder?"

"Hairballs! Ha! Like something the cat upchucked on the carpet?"

"Yes."

"That's sort of a leap. For a cat or anyone." He laughed, then frowned. "Hate to put words to it, Blanche. But if it's true, that they killed Bob, it'll come out. Just you wait. Duncan may be slow, but he's plenty het up about this. He won't let it go."

She smiled. "And I won't either."

Twenty-Three
The Girl with the Black Jewels

AMOS PROMISED BLANCHE HE'D BE BACK SOON with an estimate—and some tools to secure the windows and doors. She was an adept handy woman, and she could do a bit of fixing up herself, but she needed help with the heavy lifting.

Fortunately, Gran had left Blanche in a position to pay for repairs. Even so, the flood insurance skyrocketed every year. If Gran hadn't taken care of covering that cost, the bill to fix the cabin would have been out of control. It appeared that Amos would need nearly $20,000 in materials alone to put the porch and the second floor back in order. He'd save Blanche a considerable amount on the labor.

The place definitely was not habitable. She had to move out until the work was finished, and that was clear after a peek at the top floor. After Amos left, she ventured up the stairs to have a look. She stopped when the old cedar boards creaked a warning. The sky opened up through a hole in the roof. She mentally cranked in another $5,000 for roof repairs.

She gazed longingly at the bookcase and bureau from where she perched at the top step. She dared not enter her own bedroom. It looked damp in there, books curling, the pages flipping in the breeze. Clothes were strewn around. Her bed was neatly made, and soaked. She wanted her things, but she would just have to do with what she scrounged downstairs.

Her displacement wouldn't be forever. But, in the back of her mind, was the nagging thought that maybe this was it. Wilma had done her worst, and Langstrom, or that Sal, would come in behind her and clean up.

Blanche called Cappy. He didn't answer, so she left a message. He would be happy to have her back at his place, and she'd be happy, too. She loved hanging out with him, listening to stories about island history. They drank tea at his kitchen table and sat at the bar eating the catch of the day. Cappy always had potatoes hot and ready—in soup, simmering, fried or baked—a bite of his Irish ancestry, he'd say.

Blanche picked up the empty bowls before the ants got the last of the chocolate sauce. She turned toward the kitchen, and stopped. A spoon clattered to the porch floor. Someone, or something, was crying. She heard it coming from somewhere out in front of the cabin. Whatever it was, it started to wail. Higher and higher until it was almost singing. It wasn't a bird, or any animal. The sound was human.

She dropped the bowls on the table and walked off the porch toward the beach. The high-pitched cries were coming from a hollow in the dunes.

The cry changed into a song and reached a crescendo, like a rainbow picking up colors after a rain. Someone was out there in the sea grass singing a tune with the birds and the waves.

Bertie had been right. There was a presence on the beach. She'd heard it, too.

Blanche crept over the sand, trying not to make a sound. She was barefoot but withstood the pine berries and broken shell. Sand had blown up during the storm, creating small hillocks of soft powder, and she stepped from one to the next.

Now she could see through the low brush: A woman was sitting in a dip between two small dunes. Her hands were in the air as in an offering, the singsong mesmerizing. She had her back to Blanche, and all she could see was the woman's black gleaming hair, plaited in a long braid. Her t-shirt was ripped and thin as tissue. The bones of her shoulder blades were small golden wings. She sat cross-legged, wearing short faded red pants, and her knees were polished brown knobs.

The girl turned. Maybe it was a girl. She had an ageless glow, her skin smooth as stone. The eyes, like black jewels, had the quality of someone who had seen more than her years.

"I hear you," she said.

"Well, I see you."

The girl put her hands on the ground and leapt up. Blanche stepped back. She was about the same height as Blanche. Her eyes were almond-shaped, lifted at the corners under perfectly arched brows. She had the aura of a blackbird, and she moved as quickly. She took hold of Blanche's hand. "Strength," she said.

Blanche didn't know what she was talking about. Was this advice or warning? Whatever it was, she didn't feel any stronger than five minutes ago, or five days ago, for that matter, and lately she'd had a spell or two of feeling, quite frankly, pretty weak. Was the girl also going to tell her to be careful? That piece of advice was getting to be a drag. Blanche withdrew her hand from the girl's grasp.

"What are you doing here?" Blanche's voice was accusatory. She hadn't meant that tone, but this odd appearance—added to the rest of the week—was pushing her to the edge. She was inclined to help the girl, if necessary, but she didn't welcome the added confusion.

"I live here," the girl said.

"No, you don't. I live here."

The girl laughed. "No, no, I don't mean the house. It looks like a fine house, and now you practically have the pines in it with the porch gone. The trees are home."

Blanche didn't know whether to feel relieved, or tell her to leave. It was getting late, and she'd left a message with Cappy that she would be back soon, plus, she wanted to check in with Liza. Now this strange girl.

Blanche had to leave, and all the while she was curious. She softened her tone. "Look, can I help you? Do you need to call someone? Where are you staying?"

"That's many questions, and none of them are important. You do not need to help me. I'd like to help you." With that, the girl sat down on the sand. She pointed to a spot next to her. Blanche couldn't see any harm in that, and now her curiosity had doubled. She sat down.

"Stop thinking," the girl said. "Listen to the pines, the waves, and the gulls. You are forgetting to listen. You will close your eyes." The girl had closed her eyes and put her hands in her lap. She was sitting cross-legged again.

Blanche knelt next to the girl. She should have been annoyed at the odd, staccato commands, but she wasn't. The girl had made a fine suggestion. Blanche loved her trees and birds and beach. This girl was not telling her to do something she didn't want to do. Blanche closed her eyes to view it all with her ears. She heard the sounds like she hadn't heard them in a long time. The girl started singing in an even high tone. All Blanche could think of was wind in the dune grass, touching the waves, bending the beach flowers to the sand. The images went through her head like in a kaleidoscope.

She kept her eyes closed. Ever since Gran died, she'd become more and more withdrawn, like a curtain was closing. Now it was opening, and she felt a burst of reasons why she loved being right here and nowhere else. Gran—and Cap—had always lived in the present, and it was something Blanche had great difficulty doing.

She didn't want the moment to end, but it would. It always did.

Blanche opened her eyes, and the girl was gone. She had not heard anything, not a sound of movement or footsteps. She definitely needed practice listening. The girl had simply vanished. And in her absence, Blanche felt a strange calm, now tied to resolve she'd always had and lately lost. She closed her eyes again, and the waves broke, then receded, rolling toward the beach and then back, pulling and pushing. Strong and never stopping.

Blanche could smell something like lemons and flowers that was sweet and tart at once. Had she been dreaming? No, she had not. There was an indentation in the sand where the girl had sat. Small pyramids of sand that the girl had scooped into piles were left where she'd been sitting.

She crept around the scrub palm and snake grass looking for the girl. But there was no other sign of her. No camp or hideout, dug in or contrived from palm fronds. No clothing, no food. She had simply vanished.

The girl was strange, indeed. Where had she come from, and what did she mean about listening?

Blanche looked out at the clear line of turquoise that blended into a blue sky. It was her beach but not the same. Someone else had been there who seemed to know it as well as she did and in ways that Blanche rarely considered.

Blanche didn't even know the girl's name, but she felt she knew her. "Girl," she yelled. She stood on the sand under the pines and looked up and down the shoreline. "Girl!" But she was gone.

She'd be back. Blanche was sure of it.

Jack had been so right about those ghosts. How could she know they were real? Until now.

Twenty-Four
Believe in Ghosts

CAPPY WAS SORTING FISHING TACKLE ON HIS CARPORT when Blanche drove up. She jumped out of the car and landed in a pile of rubber worms and feathered flies. Fishing line wrapped around one ankle. Blanche bent to extricate herself and made it worse.

He clipped the line, and chuckled. "Catch of the day. On my carport."

"I'm sorry, Cappers. I'm not looking where I'm going."

"Don't make a habit of it."

"Did you get my message? Amos came over, and he says I can't stay in the cabin. Second floor's hanging over the porch, and he probably can't fix it for a few weeks. All right if I have my room back?"

"Of course," he said. He ratcheted up, back and legs creaking like an old machine, and stacked the last of his fishing equipment in the tackle boxes. He peered at the angry red mark the fishing line left on Blanche's leg and shook his head. She rubbed it. He looked her in the eye. "What are you so fired up about? You're hopping around like a toad on a hot pan."

"You won't believe it."

"Really." He held the screen door and waved her inside.

Blanche perched on one of the counter stools. He made himself some tea and opened a Corona for Blanche.

"So." He folded his arms and leaned back against the counter. That was the thing about Cappy. He always had some time, and he listened. He did give out his share of free advice, but not without the listening first.

"It's crazy. I met a mermaid or an Indian princess, or a phantom. Or somebody! Right there on the beach in front of the cabin."

"You don't say."

"She was real, Caps. This *girl*. She was chanting and sitting in the sea grass in the dunes. We talked for a while, listened to the birds and waves, but then she up and disappeared. Just like that. It was eerie."

Cappy's mug of tea stopped midway to his lips. "That reminds me of a story I heard from Maeve years ago. I think she was sitting on that very stool. Maeve, not the Indian princess."

"An Indian princess?"

"Yes, a story about one," he said. "What did the girl look like?"

"Eyes like black jewels. She was very small and raggedy dressed."

"Brown skinned?"

"Gold, and her hair, black and shiny."

"Well, she's no mermaid." He mused, smiled and glanced at the sun streaking through the window. "I wonder." Cappy took out a bunch of lettuce and commenced chopping. He seemed to think more clearly when he was fishing or cooking, and he always produced good results under both circumstances.

"What are you wondering?" Blanche leaned on the edge of the counter, a thrill went through her. "Caps, this girl wanted to tell me something. More than just to listen to birds."

"Could be. If that's true, she'll be back. Keep an eye out. I haven't seen any Native Americans around here for years, but they're here. In all parts. She may be Miccosukee."

"What makes you say that?"

He pushed the cutting board aside. "The chanting, for one thing. And the listening. You said she talked about listening to the trees and wind. And those eyes. Just from your description, it makes me think of the Miccosukee chief who used to come through here when Maeve's mother ran the rest stop. I'll bet anything your mystery girl is somehow related to that chief and his people. Why else would she be here? And why is she taking an interest in you? I hope she comes back."

A wave of history washed over her, and she had no idea why. The connection was visceral.

"Gran mentioned a chief but never told me the whole story." She whispered, and Cap leaned forward. "She'd get misty so I didn't push."

"Yeah, well, she didn't tell you everything. How could she? Besides, your great grandmother and the chief spent time together, and that's something Maeve probably wasn't too happy about."

"Why?"

Cap didn't answer for a bit. "It's a long time ago now." He rested an arm on the counter top. "Maeve was left alone a lot when she was growing up. She took on responsibility at the store at a young age, and then she took in you and Jack. She had a lot going on. And she had a big heart."

Blanche tried to imagine Gran as a child, talking to the leader of local Native Americans. "Gran," said Blanche. The name alone brought comfort. Cappy's expression was far away, and she pulled him back. "Come on, Cappers."

"There's an old island story that comes from the Miccosukee who used to live near Tampa. Some came here to the island, but it's been decades since we've seen the tribe, and a very long time since we saw the chief around here. The Native Americans have married and assimilated, but the customs and traditions, and the stories, still hang on.

"I've got a story for you. A good one. Not sure how it relates to your girl with the black jewel eyes, but it just might." He teased, all the while he peeled and sliced and dropped half a dozen potatoes into sizzling olive oil, grated a pile of cheese, and prepared a large bowl of arugula, avocado, and jicama. "You really want to hear that old stuff?"

Blanche propped her elbows on the bar, ready to practice listening.

Twenty-Five
Well, Once Upon a Time...

"THERE WAS A SMALL BAND OF ROVING MICCOSUKEE who settled in the sand dunes on Gull Egg Key, which as you know is now uninhabitable except for short walking tours. The water had overtaken most of the island but at one time it was like a stepping stone from Tampa to Santa Maria Island, and stopover for the Miccosukee. It was the perfect place to rest between the large mainland where they gathered mangoes, bananas, and coconuts and Santa Maria where they camped when the hurricanes came and washed over Gull Egg. It was an ideal life," Cappy began.

"The Miccosukee are a nomadic mix of southern Native American tribes who fled to the southern tip of Florida after the Spanish invaded Florida in the mid-sixteenth century. The natives were a handsome, talented lot and masters of living off the land

and inventing ways to survive. They fled to the Everglades ahead of the Spanish and disappeared onto the hummocks—those tiny islands you see today where the white pelicans roost. The Spanish struggled in the chase, but they could not catch up. Most of those hummocks in the River of Grass are barely more than mounds of sand. Nothing grows on them but scrub, and they are great hiding places, unsuitable to foreign invaders.

"The tribes were able to divide and conquer, something that Caesar and Alexander the Great and later Napoleon mastered. The practice was cultivated among the Miccosukee who were survivors. And conquerors. The Spanish were never able to subdue them.

"The Indians vanished into the Everglades and other parts of Florida, living off the fish, alligator, snakes, and fruit. And they used everything they caught or harvested—skins for clothing, coconut shells for bowls, fish bones for utensils, shells and shark teeth for arrow heads, palm for shelter. Because the diet was so fresh and healthy, they grew strong and lived long lives, that is, if they could stay away from the Spanish who carried the insidious weapon of disease."

Blanche knew some the Native American history, but Cappy filled in the blanks. "What about Gull Egg?"

"I'm getting to that." Cappy's clock was set on island time; he didn't know the definition of hurry. Blanche sipped her beer.

"The Miccosukee worked and rested on Gull Egg. Half the year the heavy rain and hurricanes stayed away, so in the late fall and into early spring they planted and the harvest ripened fast. The small island had oaks and palms, kumquats and temples, and hibiscus for tea. The natives had taken care to insulate themselves in small huts and even plant gardens of flowers and keep pets of rabbits, lizards, and cats. They made clothing from woven plant fiber. They were among the first to grow oranges and lemons on the barrier islands after the Spanish brought citrus plants to Florida around 1500.

"And, so. It's hard to keep a good thing a secret, and the Spanish and English settlers who had moved to Tampa and were developing the area came upon Gull Egg Key.

"One morning, the Miccosukee chief was paddling along in the Gulf, and a small ship of Tampa Bay buccaneers, of sorts, followed him. He must have known they were tracking him and to throw them off, he didn't return to Gull Egg; he went instead to the northern point of Santa Maria Island. That's probably how the island first came to be settled. The whole area was overlooked for a time. Until the chief ventured off in his canoe.

"One cloudy night, he returned to Gull Egg and moved his tribe off the key, hoping to avoid discovery. They didn't get far. A terrible storm blew up and the canoes got caught in the current where the Gulf and bay meet. Most of the tribe capsized and perished, including his son, but the chief managed to save his wife and two of his children and some of the other natives. He took the survivors back to Gull Egg, and they recovered amid the oaks and palms.

"The trees, especially the mangrove, were particularly holy to the natives because they afforded protection, shade, fire wood, and beauty. After the disaster, when the growth was scarce, it became even more sacred. The chief carved the names of the lost natives on the trunks of the trees. With time, the names grew into the bark, the shapes curving and widening, the edges smoothing, as they became part of the trees. The chief and the other natives believed the lost members of the tribe talked and sang to them when the wind blew through the treetops. They would sit for hours and listen, and they learned chants to answer the singing in the trees. They had come to feel together again with those sisters and brothers they'd lost but now found in the comfort of the trees.

"Then one time near hurricane season, the chief led the tribe off the island for safer parts inland. They boarded canoes and headed south on a hunt toward the Everglades for food. They didn't stay long; the weather was hot and the hurricanes had been silent, so the journey was calm and rewarding. They pulled rafts of alligator and croc skins and fruit with them. They were content.

"Until they arrived back at Gull Egg. Something was different. The island looked barren, open. That was it. Many of the trees were gone! They could hear the chopping. They crept closer to the devastating sound, and there they found men cutting down their trees.

"The chief and the others ran at them, trying to knock them off with blows and weapons, but the chopping continued. The chief could not communicate to the destroyers to stop, he could only cry out loud in anguish at the destruction and the monuments that had stood in honor of the tribe. Then he walked slowly up to the tallest tree, the one that had his son's name carved deeply into the bark. He stood next to the tree and raised his hand to the invader. He stopped hacking at the bark, then waved the chief out of the way. The chief would not leave. He reached toward the high limbs of the trees. He sang again, and in that moment, a gale blew out of the Gulf. The wind was so powerful it caught all of them by surprise. It shook one of the tallest trees that had been chopped but not felled. Suddenly, the tree swung back and forth. The chief did not move. He chanted, and watched as the tree hesitated then toppled over on top of the invaders, killing two of them instantly.

"The chief dropped his arms and lowered his head. The members of the tribe gathered around him. The invaders cried out, threw down their axes, and fled. The chief raised his voice as they climbed into their boats and sailed away. They understood the message of the trees. It happened without warning, the perpetrators caught by surprise. They had devastated a holy place and the home of the tribe, and they came to realize the awful consequences. Punishment was swift.

"It's an old story, Blanche, but the message is new all over again, that nothing good comes of the bad. It's truer today than ever before."

"And the girl on the beach? What do you think?"

"A warning? A harbinger."

Twenty-Six
The Pounding Wave

IT WAS THE SECOND MEETING AT THE TOWN HALL to discuss the development on the island, and this time Blanche was not going to let Langstrom get away with all the preening and dancing, and his posters and what not. She sprinted up the steps. The crowd was bigger this time. And their voices were loud.

Good.

Mayor Pat stood inside the door. "Blanche, I read your stories in the *Times*. You sure let 'em have it." She hobbled away before Blanche could say a word.

She supposed Pat was referring to the land development. Whose side was she on? She didn't put up with nonsense and lies, but Langstrom might have gotten to her all the same. It was hard to tell.

Blanche had followed up on a new study that claimed further development on the barrier keys would decimate migrating birds and their nests, leave barren stretches of over-populated beach where sea turtles had hatched, lay waste to sea grape, mangroves, and acres of trees and scrub palm that held the islands together. In one of her stories, she quoted Sara Fox of the Turtle Brigade: "We might as well cross turtles off our map if we don't get after it. They're (tourists, surveyors, seekers of property) tramping over buried eggs, despite the police tape we put up around the nests. And the extra lighting in condos and houses is leading the babies to roads instead of home to the moonlit Gulf."

Concrete and nature teetered in the fight over preservation, and islanders, overall, preferred nature. Clearly, the plans benefited a wealthy migration of two-legged snowbirds who had no stake in the island except as a temporary getaway from the bad weather up North. They were welcome, but destruction of the island was not.

Blanche held a copy of the newspaper, fanned herself, while she looked around the room, ever leery of Langstrom and company.

She had put Clint up to the idea for a series, and he'd approved it.

"Well, hi there, Miss Blanche."

She was so startled, she dropped the newspaper. He picked it up. The headline read: "Developer Plans Devastation on North End."

Langstrom's mouth tightened over each word as he read the headline. "Now, do you *really* think that's what we're planning?"

Blanche grabbed the newspaper back. "Thank you."

"For what?"

"For nothing."

They stared at each other, and if looks could kill, they would have both been dead.

"Mr. Langstrom!" It was the mayor. She stood over a pile of folders at a long table, waving in his direction. "We need you!"

"Like the plague," Blanche muttered. She stomped off, intent on finding Liza in the crowd.

It was déjà vu all over again. Except this meeting included a greater number of residents. The buzz rose a notch. Blanche had the emails, folded into a neat package of evidence in her bag. She smoothed her fingers over the crease in the paper. *This will be easy. No, this is not going to be easy.*

Liza was seated near the front row. She sparkled, as usual. Her top, a creamy lime green, said "Gin and Donuts for Breakfast" in sequins.

They hugged. "That's an unusual getup. Got any gin right now?"

"You could probably use a shot. I saw you talking to Cute Boy."

"He made some crack about the stories I wrote for the *Times*. Could it be my writing style?"

"For sure. He doesn't want 'devastation' pinned on him. Blanche, you better be careful. Maybe let Wade in on the act. Have him do some of these stories."

"Wade? He can't pour piss out of a boot, but he sure likes Cute Boy."

Liza's expression tightened into a frown. Or was that fear? "I'm getting so I look over my shoulder." She grabbed Blanche's hand.

Blanche squeezed back. "Me, too. Thanks for getting all these emails together, Liza. They're the bomb."

"Hope they don't explode in our faces."

The more they had looked into them, the more they saw that money had changed hands in odd ways, and supposedly there were more payouts to come. It wouldn't flow through Bob, or his office. But it was out there. *Where?*

Jack had been more evasive than ever. She couldn't get *jack* out of him. He wouldn't return her calls, except for the one: "I'm working on it, Bang. Stay out of it."

Same old thing. She needed to know about that flow of money. She needed an explanation, and she didn't care how busy he was. Somehow his new business and Bob's murder and Langstrom were all tied up together. Blanche worried about Jack all the while she wanted to shake him. *Some things never change.*

The mayor banged her knuckles on the table. "It's a pleasure to see you here tonight." It didn't look like it from the scowl on her face. She took in the room. Clearly, she had not expected the crowd. She looked like she was about to take an unsavory bite she did not want to chew.

"I'd like to *re*-introduce Sergi Langstrom. He is representing the interests of partners of a Chicago land development firm as many of you are so well aware." Her head popped around, searching for Langstrom, but she went on. "He has brought a draft of a plan to discuss in further detail, and he is willing to answer any questions you might have regarding the proposed development that…"

"Hey, we didn't ask for any development. *We* didn't ask for it, and we don't want it. That bunch of mansions will cut right through the north end and ruin our piers and beaches, not to mention all the baby turtles that'll not find their habby-tat." Sandy Burk sat next to Jess, who seemed to have an opposition group growing up around him. They buzzed and nodded. Sandy's sunburned face and faded shirt spoke volumes about where he spent his time and where his heart was planted.

Langstrom appeared, next to the mayor, and his smooth expression didn't show a hint of sympathy nor agreement. Instead of the formerly tousled appearance, his hair was neatly combed, and tonight he wore a tie, which was a poor choice. It put him in the Chicago-developer camp and made him stand out as the outsider he was. That was good. He'd knocked himself down a notch in the eyes of the islanders. *Was he that clueless? Didn't he know he did not belong here?*

"Sir?" Langstrom feigned interest.

"Sandy Burk, fisherman at large." The crowd laughed. Sandy wasn't much taller than Blanche although he was a large presence on the island, and he'd earned it. The guru of flounder fishing off the Reel 'n Eat pier, he was a fixture as had been his father and uncles before him.

"Mr. Burk, we are going to do everything possible *not* to disturb the environment of the island. You have my word."

At that, Sandy's red-blond eyebrows did a dance. "Is that right? You've said that before, and it just don't ring true. Sorry. Them surveyors been knockin' around, and they're very tight-lipped about what they be 'surveyin'.'"

"Well, let me assure you…"

"You can't guarantee nothin'. Not when you're knockin' down trees and pouring cement. Stands to reason somethin's gotta give here. You can't have it two ways to Sunday."

The humming in the crowd got louder. Reaction was solidly negative against Langstrom, positive for Sandy. Blanche was loving this. The last meeting had had no such love at all.

She felt for the emails. She and Liza had talked. Now was not the right time. A revelation would get lost in the melee. The islanders were having at Langstrom—pushing back hard, and she let it ride.

He paced around the table, his hands clasped behind his back. He stopped in front of the easels loaded with drawings of The Plan. "You see here? With the restoration of these native plantings, the island will be more in tune with nature than it was before."

"Tell it to Mother Nature. She has taken her course, sir, and you ain't doin' no good by changing her direction any more than you can change the wind."

This time Mary Gannon stood up. Liza and Blanche shot each other a look, and smiled.

Mary was a small force of nature herself, a whirligig of arms when she spoke, her hair a humidified cloud. "Here, here for Mother Nature! And for Sandy Burk." She twisted around to the neighbors. They nodded. She was not about to give the island to a bunch of Chicago developers. Her family had owned the Sand Dollar gift shop for more than fifty years, and she was a founding member of the preservation association. "We need to stand together! Many thanks to Blanche Murninghan for the stories in the *Times*. Put it out there, Blanche! Go get 'em!"

They were clapping. Several hands patted Blanche on the back. She felt warm, and alone. But Liza grinned at her, and whispered. "Way to go."

Blanche's face reddened under the scrutiny of hundreds of eyes, and she stole a look at Langstrom. He'd turned to stone.

Then Butch Cally, a produce trucker with groves in east Bradenton, stood up. "I like trees. We all like trees, Mr. Langstrom, but those ain't trees up there in that drawing. Those squares 'present mansions. Who's asking for those mansions? Is *that* Mother Nature calling? And do we have the roads and lines and whatnot to support all that construction?"

The mayor walked around the table toward Langstrom. They were a strange pair: The large, grey-haired woman, wide as she was tall, and Langstrom, who looked like he'd stepped out of *GQ*. He remained silent, his expression plastered with a look of innocence.

The mayor had the floor. "As a matter of fact, we do have the infrastructure."

Blanche could feel the words squash Mother Nature.

"Butch, those aren't mansions," Pat said. "Those are homes for islanders just like you."

"That so," Butch said. "All cheesy turquoise and pink like. Well, I'll just call up Victoria Secret, or whatever that gal's name is, and get me some jammies to go with. Mayor Pat, what kind of Kool-Aid you been drinkin'?"

That drew a hearty laugh from the crowd.

The mayor was undeterred. She puffed up like a large-breasted bird and ignored the interruption. "As for infrastructure, the town has done a number of studies and found that added tax revenue from the building, and the present plans in place for improvement of roads and sewers, will adequately support the project."

"Aw, baloney," said Sandy. "If you pardon me saying. For one thing, them roads and water system up there can't support all that building. You know it and I know it."

The mayor and Langstrom exchanged glances. They didn't move for an uncomfortable lapse. The mayor sat down, hard, and folded her hands. She fixed a stare across the room somewhere above the door.

Langstrom was quite ready to leap on his prey. Crafty and sleek, he walked toward the diagram, considered it, fist on chin, and moved around in front of the table so there was no barrier between him and the crowd. He smiled, and it was working.

"I can see how you'd say that," he said. The salesman. Calm as a sunny day. "In fact, I've been in the same boat, so to speak. I lived in northern Wisconsin. A beautiful little town called Wenthaven, named by the Dutch settlers who wrote back to the old country that they had 'gone home.'" He stopped and shook his head and chuckled. Blanche was seething. *Where is he going with this down-home stuff?*

"You couldn't see the sky for those pines, the lake so blue, the snow reflecting the sun," he said. He looked at the ceiling of the meeting room. Some in the crowd looked up, too, possibly expecting an apparition of clouds and pines.

Langstrom strolled among them: "It was—and is—a story book kind of place. Yes, it is still as beautiful as it ever was (pause) even with the development St. Mark Company brought to Wenthaven. Now we have Swiss chalets and ski runs, five-star restaurants and B&B's, and all of these are small businesses, no chains of any sort, and the locals have thrived. No yellow arches, blaring franchises, no, these are local people. Like you!" He pointed into the crowd, here and here, and there. "Most of my neighbors got financing through the development company. And let me tell you, Wenthaven is more beautiful than ever, with a new school and funds for paving the roads and fixing the sewers and the water lines. St. Mark—like straight out of the Bible—was the best thing that ever happened to Wenthaven. And I can say this because I was there. It's home."

Oh, my God. What is he going to do next? Part the Gulf? Throw down a tablet? She wanted to scream: *Go home.*

To Blanche's horror, Langstrom had dropped the "m" word again. Avoiding "murder" altogether and hinting at the availability of "money" for financing businesses and schools and roads. And then, the audacity of it all, he'd managed to include St. Mark, who would surely roll over in his grave at being smacked with The Plan. Blanche wasn't buying it, but she realized he knew how to move the crowd in the direction he wanted.

"What's this got to do with us? Swiss chalets and such?" Sandy Burk was on his feet again.

"Well, I know you don't want Swiss chalets." The group tittered. "Now, you tell me, Mr. Burk. What will development bring to Santa Maria? Just think about it a minute."

It was a friendly tone. They were humming, and the sound was far from music to Blanche's ears. She held the emails and then jammed them further into her bag. The timing was not right for the reveal. She and Liza exchanged a frown. An explanation would be lengthy, and they couldn't risk being shot down.

Liza nudged Blanche and shook her head. "We'll talk. Maybe come at them from a different angle?"

"Uh-huh. Funny he didn't mention the part of the plan that says they tear down the houses and the businesses."

Langstrom lingered at the door. A few islanders chatted him up. More than a little fawning going on over there. Blanche's stomach turned over.

All she could think about was the tearing down, the gouging, and the replacement that would create a fake, new Santa Maria. She had to keep fighting.

Twenty-Seven
A Fern
Called Blanche

ONE WAY TO REACH THE ISLANDERS WAS THROUGH THE PAGES of the *Island Times*. Blanche had been a full-time reporter but then went to part time. Clint, her editor, had tried to get her to stay on full time. A short, feisty dynamo, he'd hiked one foot up on her desk and said: "Hate to lose you. You're one damn good little digger." But she'd begun other writing projects, and she was enjoying her work at the historical preservation society. It kept her busy, and, fortunately, with Maeve's support she had been able to stay afloat and keep the cabin.

But now she had to get back in the newspaper game.

Blanche eventually found her way back to her small, wood-paneled desk in a dusty corner of the newspaper office near the window. She needed light, a shot at the island traffic in the small shopping center, the sound of gulls calling not far off the beach. The keys beneath her fingertips.

Blanche was a good "digger" all right, and she stayed with the story until she'd given it all she could. All that ferocity for covering news fueled her, especially now. She needed connections: the implications surrounding Bob's murder, the land development, and strange pieces of related information, some leading down blind alleys, others fitting nicely. She couldn't let it go.

She stood in front of Clint's desk, which had not been totally cleared in twenty years. She spied a Ronald Reagan headline or two. The newspapers—from all over the country—piled up, yellowing and curling with age, stacks of them in corners, like mushrooms in a forest of pages, books, pamphlets, old mail, and coffee cups. He was fond of using receipts and menus for bookmarks. She remembered if they wanted Chinese, they had to look inside a copy of *Lolita* in the "library."

She'd asked, "Why there, Clint?"

"Because we should feel guilty eating that stuff from Lo Ho Fat."

He did not take to suggestions for change. That was one of the many things she dearly loved about him on one hand, and on the other, it frustrated her. If Blanche mentioned the turnover to computers for desktop layout and publishing, the news of an increase in web-related reports and features, and the consequent, imminent demise of print newspapers around the world, she risked being thrown out the door.

"It's the thing, Clint. Technology. Innovation."

"It can come, and then, I wish it would go." He'd sighed. "Guess that's not going to happen."

"Print is on the down slope."

He didn't want to hear it. He was old school but supported his writers and found news and features (he called them feeeeee-chures) in the most unlikely places, sometimes before the news exploded. He saw complexity in the facets of events and brought news into context. Made it real, with the development of people and places who made the news. She learned from him to never leave a story without getting a lead to another.

"What's going on?" he said. He gave her that off-kilter smile. He held his breath. "Don't run off. I like what you've done so far with these land development folks. You need to keep digging."

"You know I will. The plan, and the murder. Possibly the worst stuff to hit us."

"Stay on the development side. I've got Wade working on the murder. Still waiting on details, but it doesn't sound good."

Wade. Blanche hoped she could avoid Wade. He had sharp eyes and used them to pretend he was looking into your soul when what Wade should have been doing was looking up the facts, and then checking and double checking what he was writing about. But he didn't. He was notorious for fudging the facts, and he seriously needed Clint's journalistic skills and advice.

"Wade? Why Wade?"

"Do you want me to manufacture a Pulitzer-prize winner for this assignment? You know we're short-staffed around here, unless, if I can believe my eyes, you are back full time. Now that would be real nice." Clint, still smiling, easing her in. Back to her desk. He looked over in the corner, in the window, Blanche's favorite spot that was being eaten up by a healthy fern with fuzzy tentacles. "I call the fern Blanche." He shrugged.

"Aw, Clint." She grinned, and then got down to business. "Listen, I've got something I want to run by you. Have you got time now?"

"For you. Of course." Clint drank the rest of what was in his coffee cup. Blanche shuddered to think. The viscose brown liquid had probably been sitting there for a day, if not a couple of days. He got up and pulled a couple of chairs around in front of his desk. Blanche opened her bag and withdrew copies of emails Bob had written and received before his murder.

"Liza and I were busy while Wilma blew around. Look here."

She carefully laid the stack of emails in front of him.

"What am I looking at? Some more of that goldarn web writing."

"Clint, it's not from outer space."

"Yes, it is." He pushed his glasses down from out of his bushy head of hair and studied the papers. Blanche sipped at a cup of water from the cooler and watched his expression. First he looked blasé, then his complexion started to change and soon he was red as a tomato.

"What was he up to? Looks like cash was changing hands. What's this Brecksall-Lam bunch? Aren't they the rascals who are behind that north end deal? They're into everything. Lawyers, trucking, development. They really have it covered, don't they?"

"How did you know about them?"

"Been bandied about." The island was a very small world, indeed.

"Langstrom. That hairball. He's tied up with them. Something else. My cousin Jack bought into their trucking division. I have to tread lightly here until I can get Jack on board. I want information, but I don't want to get him in trouble. As if he hasn't done enough of that already. But, really, I think he's an innocent party. He just signed the papers a while ago, and Bob had been dealing with them before that."

"Whoa," he said. "Maybe they wanted to get their foot in the door through the real estate angle. But it looks like Bob wasn't on the take. He gave all the money away."

"He was misled. Then when he told them he didn't want anything to do with demolition of the north end, they killed him." Just to say it made Blanche's throat constrict.

Clint studied Blanche, thinking, his long face solemn and expressionless, although he looked happy as hell. She was back.

"Blanche," he said softly. "Stay on it."

Sitting with Clint brought Blanche a flood of memory. Her grip tightened on her notebook, and all of a sudden, she wanted to be at the computer working on deadline.

Blanche stood up.

"I'm glad to see you."

She sat down.

"I want to stir it up, Clint. I really want to stir the hell out of it." She angled an arm on the desk, eyes fierce. "If it gets out that Bob was murdered over this land grab, and Langstrom is a phony front for this Brecksall outfit in Chicago, then we have the bastards. Plus, we can get support to deny building permits. The police chief has some of the emails, and he says he's following up." She frowned. "But you know Duncan. He acts like he's walking through Vaseline."

Clint stood up, a gnarled fist on the desk. The brows came together and dipped over a bulbous nose. "I'm thinkin'. Don't know why I'm thinkin' it. But those stories on the drug drops you wrote? Funny how all this bad stuff is blowing through right now. Seems like a real shit storm. Pardon the expression." Blanche had never heard him use an off-color word in the ten years she'd been at the paper. He was even something of a prude.

But now, Blanche could see the bloodhound in his eyes. "You know. It's funny how it all happens in threes, or multiples. I'll keep an eye out."

"You bet. There's trouble there, and county hasn't been able to nail the dealers."

That meant wearing out the shoe leather, or, in this case, the sandals. The worst a reporter could do was sit at the desk and call it in. Or misspell a name in an obit. Both crimes were cause for firing.

At least he didn't tell me to stay out of it.

"It's a long shot—a relation between the drops and the murder," he said. "But check it out. Tread carefully. And see if you can get more on Brecksall and Lam. For one, this'll lock 'em down real tight if they're behind Bob's murder. We need to get it right, from start to finish."

"You have my back." It wasn't a question.

"I can hear Maeve now. She'd kill me if she knew I was encouraging you to get mixed up in all this."

"Come on, Clint. Do you think I could possibly be at risk? Of murder? Again? Are they that stupid?"

"Yes. They are that stupid. Anyone who thinks they can get away with something like that is stupid. And desperate. Or worse. Just plain evil." The yellowed polyester shirt—with long sleeves— strained across his shoulders as he leaned on the desk. "I don't know, Blanche. Maybe I should get Wade to help you out."

"Dammit, Clint." All she could think of was Wade's heavy breathing and slurping when he drank coffee. The crumbs in his pathetic beard. He had all the finesse and interviewing skills of a bowling pin, and he looked like a large one. He was on assignment in Tampa. She hoped he'd stay there.

"All right, all right," he said. "Wouldn't do to bring him in now anyway."

"No, it wouldn't. Leave him in Tampa."

She grabbed her bag and the emails and rapped a good-bye on Clint's desk. He was already back behind his desk, typing away on his computer, circa 1990, which he grudgingly used for checking facts and writing some news items. She smiled. The layout and printing were all done by computer now—but she knew he still missed the industrial, greasy smell of newspaper ink. The wall of trays, the blocks of letters for setting up the lines of copy and headlines. His old Smith Corona sat on a pull-out shelf at his desk for whacking away at a story or two. It was the new millennium, and he wouldn't give up that typewriter.

She pushed through the bleary glass door of the *Island Times*, a tangle of loose ends clogging her brain, and ran smack into Sergi Langstrom.

Twenty-Eight
Piercing Blue Eyes

"How's your toe?" He didn't miss a beat.

"My toe is fine. How's the evil empire?"

"The what?" He feigned ignorance, and Blanche let it go. "Want to have coffee?"

The last thing in the world she'd planned to do today was have coffee with Sergi Langstrom. But, then, she always had it in the back of her head that they would meet up again. She needed to make the most of it.

What a stroke of luck.

"Sure. Why not. I could use a little jitters. There isn't enough of that going around."

Sergi laughed.

That's good. Soften him up. Or is he softening me up?

They fell into step and walked toward Peaches without even discussing where to go. He looked back at the newspaper office. She caught the glance. Her news stories about the impending "devastation" hung in the air between them. It was best she didn't bring them up.

"Haven't seen you around lately," she said. "Where you been?"

"Oh, you know. I'm around. Working on that 'empire.'" He flashed her a blinding set of whites.

Blanche looked away quickly, inhaled the hefty wake-up call of Peaches Mulligan's Guatemalan brew, the best coffee on the island. And with it, she regularly served up fresh bread, rolls, croissants, and cranberry muffins that were the rage of western Florida. Blue check curtains made the cafe homey. Oilcloth to match covered the square maple tables and seat cushions on the captain's chairs.

They settled in the window. *This is all business—I have to get down to business and dig.*

"Blanche." It sounded like he was starting a poem.

"Yes?" No blinking. No smiling. She waited. It was something she was taking a long time to learn, but she was learning. Like Gran said: *Open your mouth and tell all ye know.*

He stared at her, diddling with a muffin.

"You'd have liked my grandmother," she said, and then wished she hadn't said that. It seemed too personal to bring Gran into the conversation, but she would have been a big help. Blanche got most of her digging quality from Gran.

"Your grandmother?"

"Yes, she and her mother built and worked and lived in my cabin."

"Oh, I know the place. Is it yours?"

"Yes, mine and my cousin Jack's. I'd like to keep it that way." At the mention of Jack, his eyes flickered. Slightly, but a flicker just the same. She took a sip of coffee and nibbled on a muffin. Blanche didn't have an appetite, but she needed to do something with her hands, now that she had opened her mouth and put her foot into it. Along with a wad of crumbs.

"Well, I would hope so. It's a charming place."

He said "charming" like he was referring to toilet paper. He wanted to flush away all of the charming places on the island and replace them with McMansions. They'd make a fortune. At what cost? To whom? Blanche was getting angry thinking about it, and she was not good at covering it up.

"Really, Blanche, I hope you're not getting the wrong idea. We want to work with you and everyone who lives here. We don't want to ruin the island, which is the impression I think you are getting through some huge mistake on our part." He lowered his eyes. He had surprisingly long eyelashes. "We really want to work together." He leaned forward, elbows on the table. He'd pushed the coffee aside and looked directly at Blanche. "And those stories you wrote. Come on. Just not true."

She did not look away. "Not true, huh? I think the only thing around here that is pure fantasy is you and those plans. What you have in mind, given the presentations you made at the last two meetings, doesn't fit. Especially if the plan is to bulldoze the whole north end for those houses and that awful pink mall."

He sat back, sipped. Smiled.

Why is that smile so infuriating?

She attacked: "Who do you work for?"

"I work for myself. Don't we all?"

"Please don't be coy. This Brecksall and Lam outfit is behind the development plans, aren't they?"

"Well, yes, and I'm working with them, representing them, doing some of the leg work."

"How long have you been with them?"

"Why is that important?" Now he was on the defensive. Sergi cocked his head. "I saw you talking to that guy in the newspaper office. Is he a friend of yours?"

"Why?"

He leaned forward, his eyes so deep blue she felt like she was falling into the sky. "We could sure use some good press. About now."

"That is hardly my intention. I tell the truth. I work at the paper part time, and Clint is a good friend of mine."

"Sure hope you'll put in a good word for us." He looked doubtful.

"Did you know that Bob Blankenship had some dealings with Brecksall and Lam?"

"Really? I'd heard something about that. Lam wanted a local realtor contact down here, and he'd contacted Bob. It's terrible what happened."

"And you don't think your outfit had anything to do with it?"

"What? My God, I hope not." He looked genuinely shocked at the thought. To her, he didn't look like a murderer, but then often one didn't. "Why are you asking these questions? Are you working for the police chief? As well as the newspaper?" He said the last with a smile, dissolving the tense air that had blown up like a cold front between them.

She settled back and concentrated on delivering a level tone. "At the moment, I am a concerned citizen, and property owner. You haven't told me anything that is front-page. I want to know more about Brecksall and Lam, and you." She hoped the last didn't sound like a come-on, but she didn't care. If she could get him to talk, so much the better. She reminded herself to slow down.

Langstrom put his hand on the table, and he moved it subtly toward her.

What an odd bird. A handsome one, but odd.

"Oh, there isn't really much to tell. We're all just a bunch of hard-working Chicago guys who really like it down here in Florida. You know what I mean?"

She crossed her arms tightly against her middle. "No, I don't know what you mean. You're working directly against us, and what we are. A quiet, natural, lovely place. Your plans will destroy it."

"That is not the intention at all. If that's what you and everyone think, we sure aren't doing our job." He looked out the window.

He had a striking profile. Half Bradley Cooper, and half *David* of Florence. Didn't he say he was half Italian? Looks more northern….*Dang!* She forced herself to drop it.

"Blanche, I want this to work, for a lot of reasons. I would really like to get to know you better." Then the smile, the white teeth, the blue eyes, all converged on her, and she knew it was time to get the hell out of there.

"But, why? We are so different…"

"Well, vive la différence."

Mama mia.

"I hope you will come to see that we have more in common than you think," he said. "When Jack gets down here Wednesday, we should have dinner."

Wednesday! How does he know Jack is coming Wednesday?

She didn't trust herself to say another word. Her face was red hot, her temper on a low boil. Blanche picked up her bag and pushed her chair back. "Thanks for the coffee."

Langstrom stood up, mouth open to speak, but she was gone.

Twenty-Nine
Some Good Advice

BLANCHE HEADED BACK TOWARD THE CABIN with wings on her sandals. The running cleared Langstrom out of her head. For now. She needed to think.

The beach it is.

She was anxious to see the latest condition of the cabin. If Amos couldn't fix it before the next wave of goons arrived for the inspection, she'd be sunk.

The hurricane was hardly out of there, but Amos had already applied for permits to rebuild pronto, and that meant dealing with the local and state governments. He planned to use the footprint of the porch, but rebuilding in the beach zone required *special* permits. Special permits for a special place.

They needed some magic, and if anyone could work it, Amos could. First, local building inspector, Asa Clarkson, had to put his stamp on the cabin project. Blanche wondered which side of the land development battle he was on. He'd been at the second meeting to discuss the Brecksall-Lam development, and he hadn't said a word about the plans. There were people on the island who approved of the development plan—at the expense of Santa Maria. If he was a Brecksall-Lam supporter, he would give Amos hell about her permit. Another nudge at getting rid of the old, replacing it with the new and awful. This hurricane was especially ill-timed.

Worry rambled through Blanche's brain as she approached Tuna Street. She wondered about "the girl." When would she show up again? Blanche had searched the beach but never saw any sign of her. She had spoken presciently. She haunted Blanche. Her knowledge of the island, and of Blanche. That was even more bizarre. Blanche wanted Cappy to meet the girl, if that were possible. But would she go, if and when Blanche found her?

Blanche picked up a couple of boards lying near the foundation and stacked them where the stairs once were. The porch was still in a precarious condition with the second floor cantilevered over the southwest corner. But Amos had done a good job of propping it up with the two-by-fours. Blanche saw some evidence of chalk drawing on the concrete and a pile of empty soda cans in one corner. She'd call Amos tomorrow and find out about his progress.

The afternoon glistened. The sun threw a silver path across the Gulf, and soon it would turn gold. The birds were quiet, the day cooling off. Blanche contemplated taking a walk a little earlier than usual. She kicked off her sandals.

"Hello."

Blanche jumped. It was a soft sound, the source invisible. She scanned the beach. Of course, it had to be the girl, but she didn't see her anywhere. Blanche walked quietly toward the dune where they first met.

The girl stepped from behind a pine tree, blending into the sun and shadow. A dappled trick of the eye. Blanche might have missed her if she hadn't spoken. The dark eyes were striking. Her hair was again swept back from her face, a tight braid resting on her shoulder. She wore a faded outfit, but this time the shorts were yellow, the shirt, a loose, creamy animal skin of some kind. No shoes.

Her face glowed as if she held a secret she couldn't wait to tell Blanche.

"Hello yourself," said Blanche. "You scared the bejeezus out of me."

"What is this? Bejeezus?"

"I don't know." Blanche took a step closer. She was drawn to her as if they'd known each other forever, tied together in a love of the beach, the trees, and the birds. Two of a kind, and yet, different as the moon and the sun.

"Want to go down to the water? I was just about to take a walk," Blanche said.

"Yes, I like that." The girl extended one hand.

She had an odd way of speaking. There was that lilt of an accent but her phrasing was old-fashioned and direct. And most of what she said was in the present tense.

Blanche liked that. She often got right to the point herself. "Where did you come from?"

"I say it before. I live here."

"But surely you don't live on the beach, do you?"

"Sometimes. When it is necessary."

"What do you mean by that? Necessary?"

The girl laughed. "Again, you ask many, many questions. Right now, I am here, and I have a nice, quiet place. I will show you some time."

The girl rolled the shirt of skins into a neat bundle at the water's edge. She walked straight into the Gulf and started swimming into the sun. Blanche watched her as if she were sighting a strange sea creature.

Well, she is strange. But that's good.

Blanche waded into the surf up to her knees. She shuffled her feet flat against the sand, careful to alert sting rays to swim out of the way. She watched the girl, her golden arms rising with precision in graceful sweeps as she swam farther from shore. Blanche didn't have any desire to swim to Mexico. She stood and splashed, her fingers skimming the surface of the warm water. The girl's sleek black hair bobbed out of the Gulf as she came up for air. She turned then and waved at Blanche. Her teeth were startling white. She disappeared into the surf and popped up not two feet from Blanche.

"What's your name?"

"Haasi."

"Blanche."

"I know."

"You seem to know a lot."

"Only those who don't know anything act as if they know a lot," the girl said, splashing toward Blanche. "I know very little."

"OK." Blanche mulled that one over. She wasn't in the mood for a philosophical discussion, but if that's where they were going, then she'd be patient. And fascinated.

Haasi sat next to Blanche at the edge of the water. "Haasi," Blanche said. "That's unusual. What does it mean?"

"'Sun' in Miccosukee. My people also call me Hakla, which means 'hear.'"

"You have the perfect name."

Haasi smiled. "I listen for the bird and the fox, the alligators, and snakes."

A gull flew off, its call echoing down the beach.

They watched the rolling waves under a setting sun. It was calm today and the rhythm against the shore was easy and musical.

"You talked about listening the first time I met you."

Haasi turned to her then, her eyes a brilliant darkness. "It is what we must do."

"We?"

"We."

Blanche nodded. *Listen.* "To the sounds."

"Yes." The wind and sea grass crackled. Creatures skittered all around them. "Snakes make particular sounds when they hide in the grass. Especially before they attack. Human snakes, too."

"I think I know what you're talking about."

"Yes, I think you do. There are snakes. Everywhere."

Blanche considered this. "Now I've got snakes. Great. Developers, murderers, building inspectors with permits. And snakes."

"Yes," she said. "Listen, always listen, and it will give you clues. I will help you."

"To hear what?"

"Two-legged snakes."

"But where? Out here on the beach? Did you overhear a conversation, or see something in the paper? Haasi, did you go to one of those meetings?"

"All of it." Haasi smiled.

"Where are you getting this?"

"People don't notice me. I am small. And dark. That is an advantage. I have heard things that are not good. Some people want the money and the building and changes on the island. They are snakes; they do not care for the people who live here. Bob did not look where he stepped. He was not reckless, but he was a victim."

She turned to Haasi. "A victim! How do you know that?"

"I hear some things, but it is too early to tell. We will see. Soon."

"All right, OK. We need to figure out a few things. A murder and this development plan, for starters… I'm really sick of all this."

"Things will not be fine if you don't listen." Haasi sat ramrod straight, her legs in a bow. "And I don't mean with ears only. With eyes, with all the senses. Be aware." There was no lack of seriousness and determination about her. She was lean, every muscle taut and agile. She sprang up, and Blanche knew she would disappear. The girl had the movements of a swift bird, busy and focused one minute and gone the next.

"I will see you soon. I am around. And do not worry."

That was odd.

They really hadn't settled anything, except for one thing—an agreement that Blanche would "listen." She thought she was a good listener. But maybe not. She had to listen well as a journalist. When interviewing for a story, she noted what was necessary for the writing, and she needed to remember it. If she stopped to write it all down in the middle of an interview, she usually disrupted the flow of information from a source. She'd nearly perfected the tactic of repeating a key bit of information in her head over and over so that it would stick, even while she thought of a new question. A sort of multi-word tasking.

Blanche was good at it, and she was driven to get it right. She used memory tricks, she carried a notebook and a pen, and she'd developed a passable system of shorthand. And she listened. If she didn't, she didn't get the story. Lately, the journalism had come in handy.

The girl should know this. But Blanche knew she was talking about something else, something deeper. Whatever the girl was talking about was something that wasn't within Blanche's reach. Not yet anyway.

Blanche closed her eyes and listened to the sound of the waves, the shrieking of the gulls, the crackle of grass and palms as the wind played through them, and the hour got closer to sunset. She could hear the rain even before she felt it as it pattered toward her on the broad leaves of the sea grape. These were the lulling sounds, the music of the island. She sat still in the wet sand, and she listened.

Thirty
The Hard Heart
of Listening

LISTEN. IT WAS THE FIRST WORD BLANCHE THOUGHT OF when she woke up with a start.

Where am I?

Then she remembered. She was at Cappy's.

She checked the numbers on the digital clock and rolled over. It wasn't even five o'clock in the morning. She was groggy, snuggling back down into the huge feather bed. She had plenty of time before she had to get up, do errands, check the permits for the cabin—check with Liza and Duncan over some notes she'd taken after reading through those emails for the tenth time and fretting over Langstrom and his bunch of hairballs.

It wasn't too early for Cappy. It was his time to get up and get going. That was probably what she heard, the faint sounds of opening and closing and metal on metal at the back door. She punched the pillow and curled up under the covers. He was leaving to go fishing. She didn't know why he insisted on rising so early, but he said it was "God's hour and his, too." Not a soul was around at the slip where he moored his boat. He glided out into the Gulf early before the sun came up and then watched it slowly bring on another day. He preferred sunrise to sunset, which he viewed as the end of things; Cappy liked the beginnings.

She heard it again, a faint scraping sound. This was not Cappy. A chill ran through her. She wrestled with her thoughts at the edge of slumber, too anxious to move. She thought, it must be fronds against a back window, or an overzealous animal—feral cats roved the island and loved to nest in Cappy's clump of palm trees.

The scratching was not from a cat or a palm. Blanche stiffened. She sat up in bed and froze there in the dark. *This can't be.*

She crept out of bed and peered down the empty hall, the pictures on the wall reflecting shadows. It was quiet now, but she could hear her teeth grinding and she was shaking. She scooted behind the open bedroom door.

Tree branches and animals didn't make the same sound as metal on metal; tools did, knives did. She peeked around the door. Still nothing. She closed it softly and stood very still.

Listen.

Haasi's direction seemed clear now, and essential, given the fear that crept over her. She listened with both ears and her whole body. If listening was key, then listen she would do.

And talk.

She thought of her cellphone. Where the hell was it? She crawled quietly across the bedroom floor, feeling for her bag at the foot of the bed. Papers, books, pens, more notebooks, but no phone. She pawed through the mess, dumping it all into the deep pile of the rug. No luck. *Oh, great!* With a sinking feeling, she felt around on the floor. Her fingers roved the nightstand, knocked a glass of water over. She pulled her shorts off the chair, put them on, searching the pockets, but the phone was not there.

It was still quiet but for the beating in her chest. She breathed deeply, tried to calm down. Maybe it was just the hypersensitivity of the days. All of it building up and crashing down on her creating a flood of emotions. She was hearing things.

Well, whatever the sound, she wanted to find that cellphone and get out of that bedroom. If only to stand out on the back deck and breathe the early morning island air. She could just walk out the door, or not. *There is nothing wrong here.*

The scraping started up again. Now she knew. She had to get out of there, but there was no exit. The small windows were high, with screens. The hall to the front door ran past the back door, and whoever was there, would see her, even though it was dark. So dark, and maybe that would help. But how to get out? The house stood in a stand of trees, secluded, silent. The neighbors were back in Michigan. Blanche was alone, and for once in her life, she didn't like it.

She didn't dare move down the hall. Now she recognized the sound. The back door was aluminum, and it fit into an aluminum frame. Someone was prying open the door, and whoever it was worked quietly but not quietly enough. Still, the sound carried, and it made her sweat. All she could think about was that someone was trying to get in the back door, and there was nothing she could do about it.

She had to find that phone. There was a land line, but the receiver was missing. Maybe she'd carried it into the kitchen… or the bathroom? She couldn't remember. And then there it was on the floor next to the closet. She'd knocked it off at some point, and now she almost tripped over it. How had she missed it?

She grabbed the phone. It was dead. She stuck it on the cradle and prayed. She couldn't see a thing, but she tried anyway, punched in 911 from memory. Nothing. She had to hide. She quickly ran back in the corner behind the bedroom door. *No lock! And absolutely no luck!* That's when she saw the beam of light under the door, heard the boot hit the floor.

"Don't move." A strange, chilling male voice. Low and rusty. He banged the door open. She couldn't see him clearly, but he saw her behind the door, and he was quick. He shined the flashlight in her face. She still held the phone in her hand and thought fleetingly of hitting him over the head with it, but it was out of her hand and flung across the room before she knew it.

The latex gloves chafed her arm; he yanked her out of the corner in one swift move. "Nothing will happen if you shut up. If you don't, I'll break every tooth in your head."

Blanche had no trouble shutting up, paralyzed as she was with fear.

Nothing will happen? Plenty is happening.

And then, almost immediately, she was angry. "What the hell do you want?"

"You."

"Why?"

He was dragging her down the hall, through the kitchen and out the back door. Her feet danced an inch or so off the ground. This was not difficult for him since Blanche weighed all of 110 pounds, and he had a wiry strength that was formidable.

A white van was parked at the edge of the driveway in the pines and scrub, hidden from view. The side door was open. A dent there, she noticed. And then Blanche was thrust onto the floor of the van. He tied her feet and hands swiftly with thick rope and then closed the side door with a heart-wrenching slam. The last thing she saw before she was pitched into darkness was a flag and skull near the back window.

She was afraid to raise her head. She needed her bearings. She could feel the loopy carpet against her cheek. She smelled oil, like the van had been standing in a machine shop. Old, crusty carpeting scratched her skin. Her senses were raw, her mind racing with fear.

Listen.

She couldn't hear a thing, except the rumble of the engine under her. He'd left the van running. Where was he taking her?

He went around to the driver's side and climbed in. He put the van in gear, lurched backward, looking over his shoulder. Blanche managed to turn, prop herself upright. She leaned back in the shadows against a bucket and tools and rope.

They drove under a street light on Gulf Drive, and she got a look at his face. It was the same man she'd seen in the marina parking lot after Bob was murdered: young, smoking, lounging around, feigning no particular interest in his whereabouts. She was sure it was him.

Now, what the hell am I going to do with this bit of information?

Her fear grew and she used it. She was not about to let go. Maybe a good poke in the eyeball, or a well-placed kick. She'd have to find the right moment.

Truth was, she was helpless and just plain out-of-her-mind afraid.

"Where are you taking me? What do you want?" She surprised herself with the anger in her voice, surprised she could even find her voice.

"Shut the hell up."

So she did. She had to think. And, listen. She could practically hear Haasi in her head. As if that might get her out of this. She tried to sit up, scooting back on her rear end and using her bound hands to balance herself. The van rocketed along, swaying back and forth. Buckets and a shovel knocked into her.

The van was headed to the mainland. She could feel the familiar rhythm of the tires rolling over the surface of the bridge. She needed to keep her wits about her and figure a way out of this mess, and all the while, she wondered, *Why?* Why was he kidnapping her? She certainly didn't have any access to money, so ransom seemed ridiculous. She could only think this escapade had something to do with Bob, and that bunch in Chicago and the land development. What else could it mean? *If I ever get out of this, I'll have one hell of a story to tell. And then again, that may be part of the problem. Too many stories.*

Blanche closed her eyes. She forced herself to absorb it all, and remember. She needed details for the authorities to add to the latest sequence of events. Santa Maria had become a cesspool of murder, greed, drugs, and now kidnapping. Blanche couldn't tell which made her more furious.

The man wore the same blinding-white t-shirt as before; his hair was a distinctive cut and style, faded neatly into a square on his neck. He'd worn it long last time she saw him. His head was plastered with hair gel that smelled vaguely of musk with a cheap woodsy touch. Why anyone would want to smell like that was beyond Blanche, but she was not going to question him about his choice of hair gel. She just had to remember that he put it on his head. And, more importantly, she had to figure out what was in that head. That would be difficult: His eyes were a dead brown.

"No tunes?" *What is the matter with me?*

"I'm not going to say it again."

About thirty minutes later, the van stopped. Blanche strained to see out the window. They were parked at the foot of a crumbling old bridge that was now used as a dock for fishing. But there was no one fishing there. The place was deserted. The guy had parked in a remote area next to a stand of thick mangroves.

He got out and came around the side of the van. He slid the door open and untied the rope around her ankles. He lifted her out of the van and held her by the back of her shirt. She stood, her knees wobbling so much she could barely walk over the broken shell. It didn't help that she'd lost a sandal in the fracas.

Her feet bounced gingerly over the surface of the lot. Now she was shoeless. She didn't have to go far because it looked like the action was coming to her. Two men and a woman walked toward her across the parking area, out of the darkness, silhouetted against the palm trees and dawn sky.

She looked around at the thick growth edging the lot. The sound of waves lapped gently, an unlikely backdrop of calm against her wildly beating heart. There were plenty of places to hide, and then Blanche got a sick feeling. There were also plenty of places to bury people, dead or alive.

Thirty-One
Oh, Save Us from Hairballs

"THIS WON'T TAKE LONG," SAID THE WOMAN.

"What won't take long?" Blanche was looking for an opening that she could wedge some conversation into, some delay, so she could figure out how to talk them out of whatever awful thing they were planning. She wanted desperately to get the hell out of there.

"Our little talk." This time one of the men spoke. The driver had disappeared, but then she spotted him near the water. The red point of his cigarette glowed brighter when he dragged on it; his white t-shirt took shape in the dawn. An evil ghost. Blanche hadn't smoked in years, and suddenly she wanted a cigarette.

"OK. What do you want to talk about? The weather? The price of beans? Campaign finance reform?" The questions were ridiculous, but she was almost giddy with anxiety.

"We want to talk about you," he said.

"Me?" Barely a squeak. "What would you like to know?"

"For starters, why are you snooping around into that little situation that happened over near Sunny Sands?"

"I don't know what you mean. Bob and Liza are my friends. I always go over there and hang out."

Especially in hurricanes. Downloading emails about suspicious payoffs that probably led to murder.

"We think you do. And you've been writing for that newspaper, articles that we do not view as favorable to our project."

"Oh, that. That's nothing! Clint is an old friend. You know, he's always trying to get me to write a few features, an editorial here and there..." She rambled. "I used to work there. Full time. But now I don't." She felt a pang of guilt for getting Clint involved in the mix. She vowed to keep her yapper shut. Bob had been killed. This all seemed too worrisome. These people knew way too much about her comings and goings, and that wasn't good.

"This will stop," the woman said. "The snooping. And that newspaper job and those articles you've been writing up. We do not like the tone of your writing."

"You don't like my tone? What tone would you like me to use when you people come down here and start tearing up the place? Do you want me to be... fluffy? Sweet as cotton candy?"

Why can't I just shut the hell up?

But she couldn't stop. It was like they'd tripped a wire. The *tone* of this meeting did not bode well.

"Whoa, you're no cop. You're nobody making a lot of noise," said the taller man. They started to advance. For some stupid reason, Blanche started walking toward them. Then her feet turned to bricks. Or a brain cell kicked in. "We're telling you to back off. You're meddling where you shouldn't be," said the man, and then he stopped. "Then, maybe, it might be a good idea if you went back to that rag and started writing stories about the opportunity Breck… the development has to offer."

"That doesn't fit my style."

He took another step toward her. "Don't you have an old grandpappy? Who likes to go fishing early in the morning? It would be a shame if all he catches is a hole in his boat, say, nine miles out."

"You wouldn't dare. He has nothing to do with any of this."

"Well, you don't either, and now you've made it your business, and that's a bad business. For you."

Which, of course, gave Blanche all the more ammo. And determination. She reserved her energy for thought, which was pretty rattled at the moment. She bit her tongue.

The three of them talked softly. Were they deciding what to do with her? One of the men turned to Blanche. "You won't see us anymore," he said. They all folded their arms at once, like they'd rehearsed the scene. They were chillingly in tandem.

"What's that supposed to mean?" They were going to kill her, she just knew it.

"There seems to be no easy way to shut you up," the man said. "You've been around that place too long, too mixed up with all that preservation crap. Like I said, you are bad for business."

A bubble of anger rose up again, and it grew. If they were going to kill her, there was nothing she could do. But these hairballs— yes, it was the Corporation of Hairballs—were not going to stand there and dismiss her dreams, and Gran's and Cappy's—and those of the whole island, not the least of whom, Bob…. The world was full of them—stinking, puking hairballs, and Blanche was pissed.

"I don't know what you're talking about. I'm a news reporter. I've lived on that island all my life, and if you don't like it, or you want to take issue with the fact that I'd like to keep things the way they are out there, then that's too damn bad."

She thought she heard someone chuckle, but Blanche failed to see what was funny. The bubble had burst. She was scared again.

"Get back in the van." The smooth, cigarette-smoking driver was back.

He hurried her along. Here was this dance across the lot of crushed shell. He pulled her arm violently, hoisted her through the side door, and slammed it shut. At least her feet were untied. Free to go nowhere. But she considered this small advantage. She could walk away. Or sit there and wait. She had no alternative but to do the latter. He was still out there with her other captors, and she couldn't decipher what they were saying.

"Shhh."

Someone is shushing me? Really?

Blanche couldn't believe her ears. The talking outside the van had faded, but the sound inside was unmistakable. "They are going to take you down Palmetto on to the other side of the park where the mangrove is most thick."

Haasi!

"What the hell," she hissed. "What are you doing? How did you get in here?"

"Quiet. I will tell you later. When he parks the van down the road, and I believe he will, you and I will leave here."

"How do you propose we do that? Just tell him to let us off at the next stop?"

"You and I will wait until it is the right moment. When I say 'now' it will be *now*. Do you hear me? We are going out the back."

"Oh, great." Haasi gave her a poke in the ribs and disappeared amid the rubble. The van was a long one, crammed with a mess of barrels and buckets. Blanche decided it was an easy hideout for Haasi, but she couldn't figure how they were going to get out.

It was dawn, and Blanche could pick out more detail. The driver slid behind the wheel and the van roared to life. Blanche peered into the rear amid the junk, full nearly to the roof with buckets, a ladder, cans, tarps. A shovel. Blanche's eyes adjusted to the dim light. Haasi must be back there, crouching, so small she probably fit into one of those buckets. Blanche noticed the door in the back of the van—the would-be escape route.

The driver put one arm over the back of the bench seat. A sleeve of creepy tattoos snaked up his arm. He leaned toward the side mirror, then the rear view. Blanche was now certain it was the guy who'd hung around the crime scene, and it ground into her brain that he had to be the perpetrator. *The murderer.* She would be another notch. Business as usual. He didn't say a word, nor did he look at Blanche, but somehow she knew.

Then she jumped. Quick little fingers worked the ropes off her wrists. For someone who put so much stock in listening, she certainly was soundless. And invisible.

Blanche knew Haasi was there, somewhere, but it was more important that the driver didn't see her, or hear her. Blanche positioned herself upright to screen the back of the van, or tried to. She swayed and bucked with each turn. It was an older noisy model with a bad set of shocks, and it was giving Blanche a realignment of her vertebrae. She turned to see Haasi flatten herself against the carpeting and clear a path to the back door.

Blanche checked the rearview mirror. The malevolent expression of two black eyes concentrated on the road ahead, seemingly unaware of the untying of ropes and rearranging of the contents of the van.

She peered in the darkness for Haasi, but she was gone. Gone where?

And where were they headed now?

Blanche decided right then and there to let go of the fear. It was draining her acuity, and she had to be sharp. Clear her mind. If she knew one thing in her short association with Haasi, it was that she moved swiftly, and most likely she had a good lay of the land. Blanche had no thought as to how this would end, but the mix of fatigue and sheer terror was getting to her, and she had to let it go. She and Haasi would get out of this. Together.

The van rumbled, then stopped. They were parked somewhere out in the boondocks of Bradenton.

"Show time," said the driver.

"I do not think so." It was a whisper, and it came from the back of the van.

Blanche froze.

Thirty-Two
Sprint to a Finish

HE CLIMBED OUT OF THE VAN, AND BLANCHE SAW HIM FUMBLE with his cigarettes, patting his back pockets. For a light? His bad habit gave Haasi and Blanche precious seconds. For once, smoking was a good thing.

"Now."

The back door of the van flew open. Haasi's command came with a surprising hold on Blanche's wrist, and there was a clear field through the junk. Hands and ankles free, Blanche jumped out the back door behind Haasi, and they were gone. A sheer instinct for survival kicked in like a rocket.

Blanche found her legs as they raced away. Then they were in a tangle of mangrove. *Safe. Clawing through the jungle?*

They plunged deeper into the thick branches and waxy leaves and fought through the outgrowth. It caught them in a tight net, but they pushed out of it to the other side. The water was warm, almost pleasant at the swampy edge of the inlet. They stumbled through the limbs of the forest. Haasi ducked below the surface, and Blanche did the same. The world slid away, quiet and peaceful. She almost felt like staying there as the silky current carried them out of danger.

Maybe we've made it.

Blanche popped up and recognized where they were now—at a vast wasteland of scrub and growth south of Tampa Bay. She swam behind Haasi, around a bend, and onto a small outcropping of beach where they emerged and slipped on the rock-hard roots. Haasi danced over the mangroves like a hummingbird on the vine, guiding Blanche as they fled without looking back.

The roots were tightly woven, and the narrow limbs and dense leaves over the surface of the water were perfect cover for escape. Fish and other creatures that Blanche did not want to think about swam in and out of the tangle while she and Haasi wreaked havoc in the water world. If only these creatures knew what these large humans had created for themselves they'd be glad they were fish.

"Where are we going?"

Haasi put two fingers to her lips and shook her head, then signaled that they should swim. She led Blanche close to the shore where the water was shallow, and they glided off like otters along the bank.

The morning was overcast, but it was still early. Haasi kept her head down, barely above the water line, and she urged Blanche to do the same. They paddled through the grasses along the shore, hidden from all but the mullet and horseshoe crabs.

Blanche was exhausted, and grateful to Haasi for this crazy plan. They still had a long way to go, but she didn't want to think about it. She glanced back several times, terrified she'd see the driver. With a knife or a gun? But the growth was so thick that she couldn't see anything.

She didn't know how long they swam, or in what direction. The inlet surrounded by mangrove began to open wider, and the water became clearer as they left the murky area near their escape.

"The bay," Haasi said. One arm came up and pointed directly ahead. "Do you have your bearings?"

"Think so. We're north of the island nearer Tampa, aren't we? But I've never seen it from here." Blanche was out of breath, but she pushed ahead. Haasi must have read her mind. They paddled toward shelter of a small beach at the opening to the bay. Haasi splashed over to the narrow spit of land, and Blanche followed.

They collapsed against a wall of sand packed solid from the water digging into the shore. The cove formed a shell of protection. Blanche had never been so relieved, and thirsty. She pushed thoughts of the awful morning from her mind and turned her face to the day's first rays of sun. "Do you think we're safe?" She was wet, but warmth filled her bones. She wanted to hug Haasi, and she did. Haasi smiled.

"For now. But they are still out there. We will have to deal with them."

Blanche leaned back and closed her eyes. The humidity matched the temperature, so she would just stay wet and be glad they were both still alive.

"We will make it back to the island, and then you will have to hide," said Haasi.

"I can't just disappear. Cappy will be frantic, and those damn hairballs are still out there. I have to report this."

"Hairballs? What is this?"

"These are people—unsavory types with nothing more than eyes and hair. And no brains."

"Hmmm. I see. That is interesting. It seems there are many hairballs involved here."

Haasi scooted over to a large patch of tall grass and sat cross-legged. She motioned to Blanche to join her so they were out of plain view on the beach.

"First of all, Haasi, how did you ever get involved in this and, of all things, manage to hide in that van?"

"I told you. I listen. And I see. And I am with you. I am concerned for your safety." Haasi dusted the sand off her hands and looked around. "We can talk about all of these things at another time. We should move on."

But Blanche didn't move. "OK, but you were on the lookout at Cappy's. At five in the morning?"

"I planned to see you early. Your friend, the fine old fisherman, went out, and then I see this white van drive around. It stops in the dark. I want to warn you but it is too late. It all happens so fast. This man comes out of the van and is soon scraping at your door. It looks like he is trying to get in, and he should not be doing this. Then I see that he is dragging you along. You put up resistance, and that gives me time. I decide to move, to hide. To help you." She stopped then. Blanche leaned forward, hopeful she would tell her more. But Haasi straightened up. "It is simply a matter of common sense."

"You hid in the van?"

"Yes. It was easy. I am small, and the buckets big. And the van is extra big. I knew he would put you in there. Either that, or kill you in the house. I was ready."

Blanched shuddered to think what that meant, but she wouldn't have been surprised if Haasi was capable of producing a grenade or saber, or at least a sharp kitchen knife. She was inventive, and prescient to the point that Blanche was in awe of what she had accomplished in a couple of hours.

Haasi stared at the water, sadness etched around her eyes. "I wish I were faster, so that he does not remove you as he did. I am sorry, Blanche."

"Oh, Haasi. How could you know? How could anyone know?"

"That is the problem. We *should* know what these, as you say, hairballs are planning."

"How did we get out of the van?"

"Cloth. I put a cloth in the backdoor latch. I closed the door but not so tightly. I did this because I was certain he would lock the doors when he got in, and he did. You remember the click?"

"No."

"It is good to listen," she said. "I pushed it open when he stopped and got out to smoke. We were ready to leave then."

"Oh, you got that right. So ready."

"I'm thinking." She put an index finger on her chin and looked up. "It's good the back door of the van didn't fly open. Those buckets would have made a terrible noise. But, then, maybe that would have been good. It would have been another means of escape when he stopped to investigate."

Good lord. Blanche put her head against the wall of sand and let out a huge sigh. She turned to Haasi. "Thanks."

"No thanks is ever needed."

They dozed in the warm autumn sun. Blanche couldn't tell how long they sat there. Time didn't seem to have any edges. It just flowed out around her, like the bay.

Haasi sat upright with her hands raised to shoulder level, like she was praying. Blanche watched the concentration on Haasi's face, smooth and peaceful, completely removed from the disaster they had both escaped. She opened her eyes and smiled at Blanche.

"Are you rested? We must go."

"Go?" *Where? How?* Blanche stared out across the bay. But she had to go—get up and put one foot in front of the other, get on with it. It seemed like everywhere she stepped was disaster.

"We walk."

She dragged herself up and followed Haasi. She was dying of thirst, surrounded by salt water. It drove her mad, her vision blurry with fatigue and anxiety.

"How far?" She could see the bridge but the path was hidden, and it was difficult to determine distance.

"Do not worry."

Blanche's shoulders slumped. She felt near to falling down, but she fought it and picked her way along the trail. She had been all over the island and surrounding mainland up and down the coast. But the area looked different from a boat or car as compared to looking at it while trudging through the mangrove and swimming along the remote shore. After being kidnapped.

Haasi reminded Blanche of a tiger, creeping through the grass. Deliberate and sure. They had left behind a wide patch of thick growth, not only mangrove but scrub palms, dune grass and sprouting pines and live oak. It was so overgrown that light seemed to die within the wall of the dark green jungle.

Haasi nodded. "I think our trail is cold. We are not followed." She signaled Blanche, and the two trekked along the beach hugging a cliff of sand.

The Buccaneer Pass Bridge rose up in the distance. It connected the north end of the island with the bay side at the mainland.

"We are going there. It is the fastest way back. Let us be quick, and quiet."

It was the only way. They had to make it to that bridge. Swimming to the island was out of the question. The current and sharks would get them before the white van caught up.

Blanche could see freedom ahead—the bridge a link to safety—and it exhilarated her. But the van was out there. It wouldn't have turned around and gone back to wherever it came from, leaving them to run free through the mangrove. Her mind raced with the unknown possibilities. They were still in deep, even when, and if, they made it back.

"It's good the bridge is not so well-traveled at this hour. That's a consideration," said Blanche.

"This could be good, or it could be bad," said Haasi. "It is nice to get help. But for now, the plan is to stay together." Blanche did not question that. She longed to get back to the island, get dry, drink a large bottle of water, and about a gallon of hot coffee.

Haasi hardly seemed bothered at all. She blended with the dune grass. She even looked comfortable in her scant, faded clothes, despite their harrowing escape. Blanche drew a deep breath.

They picked their way over broken shell and driftwood. Blanche stumbled, but Haasi was light as a gull, barely leaving a track in the sand.

They arrived near the base of the bridge. Except for two cars off in the distance, there was no traffic. And, best of all, no van. The sun climbed higher.

Her thirst was huge, but they trudged on. Neither one wore shoes. Blanche's feet warmed to the concrete pathway approaching the bridge, but soon her soles were burning. Haasi reached the bridge, signaled, and started to dash over the span. It was hard to keep up. The girl was fast as a deer.

"Hurry. We should get out of view." Haasi called over her shoulder. She was nearing the other side.

Blanche was in the middle of the bridge when she heard the unmistakable rumble. She didn't want to believe it. *It can't be.* The white van pulled up alongside her.

Stick together. It was about the only rule Gran had for Jack and Blanche, and now she remembered it. *My God, Haasi had just repeated it.*

"Keep going, Blanche. Run. Keep up." Too late. Haasie was still shouting back at Blanche. She could hear her, but she couldn't see her. The van blocked her view, and so did desperation. She was caught. Again. The door of the van opened on the passenger's side. An arm reached out and grabbed Blanche, immobile with fear, gasping for breath.

Damn, this dude is strong!

She last saw a glimpse of Haasi on the other side, but it might as well have been the other side of the moon. Haasi's expression froze and her mouth formed an *O*, her arms outstretched.

Either the driver didn't know Haasi was close by, or he didn't care. Apparently, it was Blanche he was after.

The van sped off. It passed Haasi, ripping down the two-lane road before making a U-turn. Blanche hit a pile of buckets heaped on the carpet and tried to steady herself while the van rocked and shimmied.

She was fed up with this mode of transportation, tossed on to the oily old floor, but she tried not to think about it. The world would end soon enough. Surely this guy was heading off to some remote area to finish the job.

Haasi hid in plain sight behind pilings as she watched the van speed away. She managed to get a clear shot at the license plate number. And as it turned out, she had a very good memory.

Thirty-Three
Blanche-napped!

CHIEF DUNCAN WAS SITTING AT HIS DESK IN HIS OFFICE on Santa Maria. It wasn't a large desk, in fact, it barely accommodated all six foot four inches of him and 300 pounds. He filled the space, and he more than adequately filled the job of policing Santa Maria. Aloysius Duncan worked overtime to keep the peace and get along with his neighbors. He had once been an "island boy" himself, and he knew the value of keeping the kids off the streets and on the playing field. He coached, refereed when he could, and donated toward the cost of uniforms on behalf of the Manatee County Benevolent Association.

He was part of the fabric of the island and part of the county network, and Santa Maria was considered a plum outpost where nothing ever happened. Except when Blanche was concerned. First, those stories about the drug drops at Conchita. She'd stirred up a hornet's nest at the meeting, and later at the newspaper office with that reporting. Duncan wiped his forehead. Then this business with the murder. She was out for blood.

He sighed, and wondered about all that. Life on the island had changed. The drug drops were as yet unsolved. The murder of Bob Blankenship was the leading cause of his heartburn and of local concern. And the furor over the supposed impending land development added to his consternation. In the past week, he'd gotten a flood (along with the deluge of Hurricane Wilma) of threats, complaints from residents, calls about "right of eminent domain." Blanche had made it clear in the meeting that this right referred to the right of the rich to get richer. Even with the offer of "large sums" (undetermined, so far), most islanders wanted the Chicago folks gone and peace restored.

The state agency in Tallahassee called him about the hurricane damage, and he was getting a storm of calls about permitting for old and new construction. Most of the calls did not even involve the police chief, but people were upset, and when they were angry and upset, they went to the law. They knew they'd have the ear of Aloysius Duncan.

Of the seven piles of papers on the edge of his desk, he dunked most of it closest to the waste basket into the circular file. He chewed a Tums. The mushroom omelet at Peaches had been delicious but it wasn't sitting well. He couldn't do tomatoes any more, but he also couldn't drink coffee without frequent roiling pain and gaseous explosions. His wife, Emma, told him to knock off the coffee, that the dozen or so cups with double cream and four sugars he drank a day were causing the problem, but he couldn't do it. He needed his coffee. So he would suffer and buy more Tums.

Duncan made a few more phone calls to county about the murder. Nothing was shaking on that front with so little to go on. Blanche had her theory, but Blanche could find mischief in a box of cereal.

They were united on one front for sure. Bob had been a good friend, and they were bent on finding out who did it and why.

Blanche had given him a couple of leads—all of them pretty weak. But he needed to follow up. The piece of cellophane and that white van were intriguing. Yet, how could that go anywhere? The emails he'd picked up from Liza caused a glaze over his eyes that rivaled the indigestion from coffee and the omelet. He needed to get after Buzz for help deciphering those emails and get back to Liza. Soon.

As for Blanche, he had a real soft spot for the girl. Everybody had loved Maeve, but when the accident happened, and Maeve was suddenly mother to that tiny imp, the island also became Mother to Blanche. She couldn't go anywhere that a cookie or a sucker didn't appear, along with offers to babysit and promises to visit. Blanche had been an outgoing child, a dancer and singer— all too eager to belt out *Que Será* and *The Tennessee Waltz*, Maeve's favorites. Some of the light went out of Blanche when Maeve died, and her creativity had turned to writing. Blanche could not be consoled for quite some time. Her island family tried. He tried. To Duncan, she was his island daughter.

His mind was unsettled, and so was his stomach, but there was nothing wrong with his eyes. He was pawing through a stack of notes and messages when he looked up to see a bedraggled, but beautiful, tiny person standing in front of his desk. He didn't know where she had come from, but here she was. Her hair was shiny black and she wore faded jeans and a shredded t-shirt. At first he thought she was going to ask him for a donation. He was a soft touch for Girl Scout cookies and candy sold at the community center. But then he saw the look in her eyes. There was nothing sweet there. It riled him far more than his stomach.

"We have to hurry," she said. Haasi thrust a torn piece of paper at the police chief. "They have Blanche."

At first what she said did not register. "*What?*"

"I will explain, but we need to hurry. They kidnapped Blanche Murninghan. The hairballs. This is the license number of the white van. Call now."

"Now, see here…" But then he stopped. A mountain of urgency five feet tall stood before him. This was no joke. He needed no further coaxing. He pushed his chair back and picked up the radio. The message went out to the cars throughout the county. And then it crossed his mind. Better get it out statewide.

"…359XJM… Detain white van for questioning… suspect in kidnapping…inspect vehicle for white female, five feet, two inches, black curly hair. Name Blanche Murninghan."

Haasi was still standing in front of the chief's desk. She watched while he alerted officials. Her shoulders relaxed slightly, but she didn't move. "You have to find her. They want to kill her."

"All right now." He was on his feet, sputtering. "Suppose you tell me what exactly happened. You seem to know a lot about this here kidnapping."

And Haasi did. She told him. All of it. He had started pacing, and then fallen back into his chair. He was perfectly still, except for his eyebrows that jumped like caterpillars on fire.

It was almost four o'clock, and Cappy hadn't seen Blanche all day. The back door had strange scrapings on it, but sometimes Blanche locked herself out and had to jimmy her way back in. Still it didn't add up. Blanche always left a note. The bed was unmade, and Blanche always kept her space neat. He looked in the garbage can in the kitchen. No coffee grounds or orange peels, and Blanche dearly loved her coffee and fresh Valencias off the tree.

He called the cabin and her cellphone. They both went to voice mail. Was she inspecting the work, or lack of it? No answer. Cappy scratched his head, sank down in an arm chair. The tiny nerve endings in the back of his neck prickled, telling him this was not right.

She would have left a note. And she surely wouldn't move back until Amos gave her the all-clear. They were weeks away from completing the repairs. As the hour ticked on, he thought of the possibilities and none of them were plausible. He called again. She didn't answer her phone, and the neighbors hadn't seen her either. He began to worry.

Cappy didn't have much longer to think about it. Out the window of his kitchen, a blue light flashed by. A police car turned and cruised back around to his driveway. He got up and stared out the window. His phone rang.

It was Chief Duncan. "Now, Cap, don't be alarmed. I want you to come down here. Now. We have a report that Blanche was, well, picked up. Don't worry."

"Picked up?"

"We have every car in the county looking for her."

"Dunc, what are you talking about? What did she do?"

"Oh, no, no. It's not like that. Why don't you come over here and we can talk? We're on this, believe me. Anyway, as soon as you can. There's a team on the way over to check out your place. Don't touch anything."

An officer climbed out of the patrol car. It appeared that "the team" had arrived.

Duncan, Haasi, and Cappy met up in police headquarters.

Cappy knew who Haasi was even before she said a word. Blanche had described her perfectly, but he hadn't the faintest idea why she was standing in the police station. His mind was elsewhere, floating around Florida looking for Blanche. *Where can she be?*

Haasi took Cap's hand while Duncan shouted at Sergeant Reberton: "I don't care if there are a million white vans out there, you stop every goddamn one of them and check that license number. One of them has Blanche Murninghan captive. These people are dangerous as all hell. Find them." It was totally uncharacteristic of him, and totally called for.

Cappy's face was grey. Haasi guided him to a chair near the chief's desk. She thought about coffee, then settled for water from the cooler. She offered the cup of water. Cappy took it and felt a bond grip them.

"Why are you here. What do you know?" Cappy spoke softly. He needed his heart to stop beating so fast, he thought he'd explode.

"We will talk. Blanche and I are friends." It calmed him even while the chief shouted and slammed down the phone. He paced from the window and back over to where Cappy and Haasi were sitting.

"I don't know," Duncan muttered. Then he hefted himself onto the edge of the desk, knocking at least a day's worth of police briefings into the wastebasket. "We have to go over this again. Piece by piece. And, Haasi, you have to tell Cappy exactly what happened. I need to hear it again myself."

Cappy couldn't believe what he was hearing. Blanche had insisted on investigating the murder and the people behind the development plans. He'd tried to talk her out of it, and his instinct had been right. He wished it weren't.

"Blanche was looking into the murder and that land deal, and writing stories about all of it. Is that what this is all about?" Cappy already knew the answer.

"We think so. Haasi was on to them, then she saw the van in front of your house."

"I wish I'd known what this hairball was doing there. I should yell or call for help. Or something. But it was too late." She dropped her chin. "The man was quick. He went into your house and put Blanche in the van. In minutes."

Once Cappy had heard the story of the kidnapping, the escape, and the second kidnapping of Blanche on the bridge, he marveled at the ingenuity of the small girl, who at one point had saved Blanche—and probably would again with the license number of the van and the details of the ordeal.

"Thank you," said Cappy. But she could see he was near tears. "We have to get her back."

Haasi stood up then. "I can't sit here. I must go. I need to find Blanche."

"Now, look," said Duncan. "I think you've done enough."

"No."

Duncan sputtered. "Where can we find you? What's your address?"

"My address? That would be difficult. I don't have such a thing. But I will see you soon."

She was gone before either of the men could stop her. Duncan sat down hard, the chair protesting under his weight.

"I'm going home to see if your officers found anything." Cappy took another sip. He looked like he'd aged ten years in ten minutes. "Blanche left a lot of notes, and I think I should turn them over. They might be helpful. I'll worry about the consequences later, but I'm sure Blanche would agree that it would be best for you to have them."

"I'm sorry, Cappers."

"Don't be sorry. Find her. I'll be back, and then I'm not leaving until you do."

The chief picked up the radio again. "Well?" He yelled into the small black holes and broke the eardrum of whomever was on the other end of the line.

That's when the station door flew open and Liza Kramer burst in. "What the hell is going on? Peaches heard on the scanner that Blanche was abducted. It could only be Blanche. Who else around here is about five feet with black curly hair?"

Liza stood in front of the chief's desk and didn't seem to care one wit that he was talking to someone on the radio. Her hand kept beating the sequin seahorse stitched to the front of her sweater. She teetered on red patent high heels and put her hands on her hips. She didn't see Cappy. Her eyes bore a hole in the police chief.

"What are you doing about it? Should I get in my car and start driving around?" She waved her flame-red manicure in the air.

The police chief gestured with one stubby finger. "Just a minute. OK?"

Behind Liza came Peaches carrying a large bag of baked goods, which was evident from the aroma that flooded the office. Duncan had one eye on Liza and another on Peaches and the goodies.

"Peaches! Cranberry muffins. Energy. We need energy. And a miracle," said Liza. "Oh, my God, I don't believe this. I need a cigarette."

Peaches dropped the bag on Duncan's desk. A whoosh of freshly baked muffins sweetened the air. "I don't know what to make of this place anymore," said Peaches. "What are you doing to get her back?"

"Now, ladies, please. We're doing all we can."

"What is that?" Liza and Peaches, at once.

Duncan was still holding the squawking radio as he faced the two women.

"We have an all points. Everyone available is out there looking for her."

"It's been hours. She could be over the state line by now." Liza shouted. Her high heels clicked from one end of the office to the other.

Duncan adopted a calm tone. "Ladies, I think it best that you go home now. We will keep you informed."

Peaches hugged Liza and headed for the door. She gave Duncan a high five. Liza huffed at him. "I have to do *something*. I can't just *sit*." Liza, just sitting, was impossible; she was a human tornado.

"Well, when the time comes, soon, you can come over here and discuss those emails. I understand you and Blanche went over them together."

"I gave them to you last week, and you just ho-hummed."

"That wasn't my intent. Now, with this Blanche business, and Bob, and all, we need to dig deep into that correspondence. And whatever else you can tell me."

"You have a date."

"Harumf."

"We found a definite connection between Bob and Brecksall-Lam, those development people. And, now, come to find out Jack's working with them."

"*Jack?*"

"Yes, Jack. Our Jack. Blanche was worried that he might have gotten himself into trouble. She was waiting for word from him. He's supposed to come back soon. Now, sooner than ever."

"I need to call him," said Duncan, "and he better start talking."

Thirty-Four
Bird on the Fly

BLANCHE OPENED ONE EYE. SHE WAS HALF ASLEEP but not in bed. She was on hard ground, scratchy beneath her, but she couldn't move her head or keep her eyes open. Then terror grabbed her. She felt the scrub around her, and it was hot out there. Of course, it was hot. It was Florida, but it was too hot for October. It was October, wasn't it? She was so thirsty, she could hardly bear it. Her arms and legs wouldn't move. She lay there. She was floating, and there were small purple flowers in front of her eyes, but she just couldn't keep them open. She couldn't move at all.

She tried to listen. Someone had told her to listen. She tried hard, but it was so quiet. No birds or whistling pine trees. This was not the beach. Far from it. No soothing sand, gentle waves. Not even a frog or a cricket. Her fingernails dug into the soil, feeling for sand. She sifted some of it, and it soothed her. She drifted. She had no idea where she was going.

Cappy had hardly moved from the chair in Duncan's office all day.

The chief reassured him that nearly every white van in Florida had been stopped.

"Dunc, that would be about every other vehicle."

"We aim, but we don't always hit the mark," he said. "We're working across state lines now. Going to be a lot of pissed off painters and caterers getting pulled over." An enormous sigh escaped. "You best go home now and get some rest."

Cappy stood up and shook the chief's hand, looked him in the eye. "I'll be back. Probably with my sleeping bag."

Jack sat in the police chief's office. His head bent forward, tearing at his hair. "Tell me again what happened. I can't believe this."

"They found her notes among the stuff she left at Cappy's. That girl takes a lot of notes—the guy in the van, the day of the murder, her suspicions about those development people. Thank the good Lord she's got a knack for writing."

"Well, that's great. I told her to stay out of it."

"A lot of good that did."

Duncan got up and walked around the desk and sat atop it. He folded his hands and leaned toward Jack. "Now, just suppose you tell me all about this Brecksall-Lam bunch you're tied up with. And I mean *now*. Tell me."

Jack's head was bent, almost touching his hands folded between his knees. He looked up and his eyes were red, his clothes disheveled. He'd gotten the first flight to Sarasota and come directly to the Santa Maria police station. It was almost ten hours since Blanche's disappearance. Santa Maria was quaking with murder, destruction—and now kidnapping. The door to the station had been revolving as people came through offering food, coffee, time, and a lot of questions with no answers.

"I don't know where to begin."

"Come clean, Jack. There's more to this story. Blanche was right. She was on to something, and now she's paying for it."

"Bang. She's something else. Dunc, I'll tell you. In confidence." The two walked back to a small office off the kitchenette and closed the door. The chief crossed his arms. Jack sat down in one of the chairs, his face working, then he spat it out. "Brecksall and Lam are into drugs, big drugs, coming through Texas. I fell into it when I bought out their trucking division. I tried to back away from them, but it was too late."

"What the hell, Jack!"

"I'd say so. I've been leading a double life. I can't tell you what it's been like. I've been trying to figure a way out."

"Why didn't you go to the authorities?"

"I did."

"And?"

"I'm an informant. DEA is just about to blow the whole thing up. RICO, tax evasion, money laundering. And now, I bet, kidnapping. And they want me on board," he said. "My, God! Blanche!"

"Let me guess. The money laundering. Would that have anything to do with this fine little cast of Disney characters on the island?"

"Donald Duck, Mickey Mouse, and, mostly, Goofy." Both hands raked his spiky dark hair. "All of them. Pretty f-ed up."

"Great."

"If I'd told her what was happening, it might have been worse. But as it is, it couldn't be worse. She just doesn't let go." Jack left the tiny room and paced all around the office. His shirt hung out of his pants, and he looked like he was near tears. "We have to find her."

"No kidding." Duncan was back on the phone, and he had another one ringing. "Georgia State Police? Yeah, this is Duncan. What are they doing at the state line? Any developments?"

Jack leaned on every word, and none of it sounded good. He sank into a chair. He was going to kill Brecksall if he ever got his hands on him. Not only Brecksall, but others as well. There was a bad bunch involved, and it should never have come to this. They should have handled their business better, faster, safer. *How about legally?* Now this. If anything happened to Blanche, there would be hell to pay. He just hoped he wasn't too late.

He sat on the bed in the motel room, the phone glued to his ear. He rolled up a sleeve of his blue oxford pinpoint, drove a hand into the pocket of his pressed khakis. He was sweating, and the heat of the cellphone was making him crazy. All of these calls were driving him crazy. He had to keep switching phones, throwing out the old and picking up new ones. The bay was probably bubbling with the disease of these evil burners tossed into the depths. But he had to keep changing them out. It was important no one trace the calls.

"What are you talking about? I told you not to kill her." He sat, hunched over his knees, one hand covering his eyes. He got up and walked around the room.

"All right, you dumbass. Call me back. Yes, this number is good for a few more hours."

It wasn't a bad location, with the beach just off a private patio, but it was hardly five-star either. He picked up the remote absently and then dropped it on the brocade bedspread. Looked like Pauline Hemingway had been there. Yellow and red Spanish with fringe, and a faux crystal chandelier. *What they need in this place is central air!*

He didn't want to watch television, and he was sick of listening to these people, constantly tuning in and taking orders from the greedy bastards. He was stuck at one of the better island motels with a pool and Jacuzzi. All the comforts of home. But he wanted out of there. He wanted the money, and he wanted to be gone.

The phone rang again. "You dumped her where? Well, that's just great. Out there with the cattle and snakes. What is that? Fifty miles from St. Pete? Isn't that the old Wells ranch?"

He was pacing again. "What about the van? They won't find it then, and they won't find her. I'm tellin' you, I don't want to be tied up in it anymore."

Pause. More pacing. He picked up the remote again and switched on the news with the sound off. "I don't give a shit. I did my work down here, and now I want out. You're going to have to follow through, and it's probably best to let things settle in. Let them realize they shouldn't be trying to block the plans. Let time take its course. You never know, maybe a hurricane will blow the whole place off the map, and then won't you be happy."

There was a long pause. He stood still and listened to the sounds around him. "Wait a minute. I want to check outside." He went to the window, but he didn't see anyone there. The palm trees rustled and crackled, a bird sang out. He went back to his call.

"I gave you the numbers. Yeah, the Swiss account we opened. Get it right. Or else."

The two-legged snake had spoken, and that was all the bird listening at the window needed to hear. She flew away.

There was no word on Blanche's whereabouts. The white van they were looking for had not been spotted although thousands of white vans had been stopped, ransacked, the drivers questioned, traffic held up. Worry and frustration on the island mounted if the phone calls to Duncan could be any barometer. He had been at it all day with every patrol car and station in the state that he could recruit. Not a clue had turned up so far.

He needed sleep. But he couldn't go home and go to bed for the night. He had every county checking in. Sleep wasn't going to happen. But he was no good if he didn't at least try to get a nap.

He'd driven Jack back to Cappy's, and he hoped they were getting some rest. Cappy did not look well. Dunc was glad Jack was there, but his entanglement did nothing to soothe nerves. Everyone was frazzled, and still no word on Blanche.

Duncan took a hot shower and fell into bed. He couldn't eat anything except Tums. Emma was already snoring, and no question she'd been plenty tired, trekking back and forth to the station with sandwiches and coffee for him and all the islanders who hung around wanting to help. They were full of theories and, really, Duncan lamented, they were not any help at all. They were in the way. Duncan finally told them to go home. He had pulled out all the stops. He had more law enforcement on this than there was for the Lindbergh baby.

Clint Wilkinson at the *Island Times* had insisted on staying and listening to the police scanner and reading the blotter. He perused every lead that came in and drove the police chief to the edge: "This is not the time nor the place, Clint. You are going to have to go. We'll stay on it. I've got Sergeant Otom on it all night. He is going to wake me up and the entire island when he gets some word. Right now we have to get some rest."

Clint left in a huff but not before he reminded the police chief again to call him if he got word of Blanche's whereabouts. "And I'm not talking editorial here. I don't give a rat's ass about the story. I want her back," Clint said. "Blanche means the world to me. She's like a daughter..." His voice trailed off for fear of being a blubbering fool. He couldn't say another word. But at this point it didn't seem to matter. He was beside himself with worry, and he wasn't alone. Clint's comment hit home with Duncan: "Same here," he said, and turned away. They were supposed to be tough.

But deep down, Dunc was plenty worried. Blanche had been missing for at least a day, and the trail was stone cold.

The chief punched his pillow and tried to still the demons hurtling through his brain. He was almost asleep, despite the worry and gallon of coffee he'd consumed during the day, when the tapping started. A light sound at first, and then it got louder. He lifted his head and looked toward the window. A round shape was barely visible in the dark. A street light near his house cast some light, but he couldn't tell if it was a face. He thought he was hallucinating, which was highly possible, given his state of mind. He wasn't used to this. He was nearly sixty, and he wasn't a young stud football player full of it any more. The whole business was close to giving him cause for heart failure. Emma harping at him to plan retirement didn't help either.

He squinted in the darkness. The shape was still there, and this time the tapping was louder. He got out of bed and walked over to the window. It was a girl—a girl with black hair and eyes like a bird.

He glanced over at Emma, but she was still snoring. He opened the window. "My God, don't you ever sleep?"

"There will be time for that. Right now is not the time."

"What do you want now? And where have you been all day? We have more questions."

"Yes, there are always many questions and never any answers."

"Just a minute." The chief went for his pants and dragged them wearily over his knees. He went around to the backyard and started to call to the girl, but she was already there, standing in front of him with that straight back of hers and those piercing black eyes.

"I know where Blanche is and we must go. Now. I hope there is time."

"What are you talking about? How do you know?"

"I'll explain later. Do you know this Wells ranch, cattle and snakes, about fifty miles from St. Pete's? I think it is St. Petersburg."

"That sounds like the Roland Wellston ranch, owns half of Florida, and has a big spread out in the midlands in cattle country."

"Go. Now."

He didn't waste any time while he still prodded her with a few questions. She raised slim fingers. "Go." Within five minutes, he put his shoes and shirt on and got the car running with the girl in the back seat. There wasn't one single minute to lose, she insisted. Duncan remembered: Roland was long gone, and his ranch had become dead man's dump, if there ever was one.

Thirty-Five
Rose to the Rescue

SHE COULDN'T OPEN HER EYES, NOR HER MOUTH. Everything seemed glued shut, and she was shutting off. Like a light switch. Blanche wanted to laugh at that, but she couldn't laugh. It wasn't that funny anyway. It was strange is what it was. She was going away, but she hadn't packed anything. She didn't have shoes, or money. She couldn't feel her clothes. She could hardly feel the ground. It seemed like she was just plain numb, which was fine.

She blinked then. She couldn't feel, but she could see, even with her eyes shut. Someone stood not ten feet from her. Rose. Blanche tried to talk, but then she didn't need to.

What are you doing here, Mom?

She didn't speak, she just stood there and smiled at Blanche, and Blanche tried to smile back but, of course, she couldn't. She tried to open her eyes again, but she couldn't see very well, nor could she move her lips.

Rose was wearing a plaid dress, the one Blanche loved. They'd made a chocolate cake together in that old kitchen. The blue one with the red-striped wallpaper. Blanche's head barely came up to the counter, so her mother lifted her on to a small stool. Rose beat together the sugar and the eggs under the cabinet light, and she was laughing at Blanche with flour on her nose. Rose lifted the orange bowl and swept batter into pans. Rose hugged Blanche, getting flour on her brown canvas smock. She had been finger painting. Blanche wanted to hug her back, but she couldn't move her arms. She just lay there, watching and waiting for Rose to lift her again, and maybe she would.

It had been so hot in this place, boiling hot, in fact. She was boiling up. That was earlier, but now it was cool, and peaceful. She wanted Rose to talk to her, but she didn't say anything. She wouldn't go away either. She stood there looking at Blanche, and as long as she was there, Blanche felt like she couldn't go away either. She couldn't just leave her mother standing there, looking at her. She hadn't seen her in so long. How long was it? She was so glad to see her, and Blanche tried to tell her that, but there didn't seem to be any need. Rose knew Blanche was happy, and she wasn't in pain, just cool and peaceful there, lying on the sandy soil, among the purple flowers, waiting.

Blanche wanted to go with Rose. That was it. But Rose didn't want her to leave the spot. She wanted something else, and Blanche tried to figure out what it was but she couldn't break through. She couldn't think what it could be. What could be better than going with Rose? Blanche didn't know. She couldn't think anymore either.

She had to be still. And listen.

She couldn't help hearing it. At first, the sound was far away, and frightening. She couldn't get away from it. She couldn't see where it was. She just listened and didn't move. It wasn't a hurricane but it was as loud as one. Like a train but rhythmical. In cycles, or circles. Far away, clap, clap, clap. It came nearer. Maybe it would take her and Rose out of this place. It wasn't pleasant here anyway. She was more than ready to get out of there.

An enormous bird with wings covered the field where she was lying. Its wingspan darkened the area until it was the blackest dream she'd ever had, so dark and deep she just wanted to fall and keep on falling into it. Maybe the bird would scoop her up and save her or fly her around in the dream. But it was loud, the loudest bird. Not the sweet cawing or tweeting, like outside her porch. The bird no longer called sharply. It made a dense, dull sound. Whomp-whomp. A huge mouth that would eat her. Pick her up and carry her off.

Gusts of wind blew over her, and lights flashed on and off behind her eyelids. The dark was gone. The sound of the giant wings was terrifying, and closer. She heard shouting. Rose wouldn't shout like that.

But, then, Rose smiled, and she was gone.

Blanche didn't open her eyes as she lay in the bed, but that was all right. She could move her arms and legs, and that was something new. She couldn't do that before; she was glad she could do it now. A familiar voice was yelling in her ear: "Bang!"

She knew that voice. Jack.

"What are you doing here?" The question was almost a whisper, low and gravelly, and she wanted to know why he was yelling. She remembered a field with purple flowers, talking to her mother, and now she was here. And she thought of Haasi, sitting next to her through the dream that had lasted for days.

"You're in Bradenton Memorial, and you're alive." She felt a large thump next to her, she guessed it was on top of the bed. She wasn't on the ground anymore. She was clean, and the sheets felt smooth. She tried to keep her eyes open, and this time it worked, not very well, but she could see the outline of Jack's head next to her, pitched forward on the white sheet. He raised his head. He looked terrible, shocked even. His face was puffy and his eyes were rimmed red.

"Jack, you don't look so hot."

"Blanche, it's been almost five days. You almost died. You were so dehydrated; they thought you were a goner. Oh my God, Bang, I'm so glad you're back. It takes an awful lot… to kill a… Murninghan."

"That's a whole book."

Jack did not appear to be amused. He looked exhausted, but relief crept into his eyes.

"She's wide awake." A nurse stood in the doorway. She called down the hall then walked over to Blanche and picked up her hand. "Welcome back."

"Where have I been?"

The doctor was there, next to the nurse. The two buzzed hurriedly over Blanche's chart, and the doctor whisked out the door. Jack hadn't budged from his spot. He held on to Blanche's hand. "They drugged you and threw you out in that field. You've been delirious or sleeping for almost a week."

"All right. That's enough now." The nurse planted herself between Jack and Blanche. "Don't you think it's time for us to get a cup of coffee?" She was addressing Jack, but it didn't sound like a cozy invitation. She clearly wanted him out of there.

Jack called Cappy, who had been sitting next to Blanche all week. Cap had finally gone home to check on his house, take a shower, and eat something besides cafeteria food. Jack had worried about him. One patient in the hospital was enough.

Liza had been visiting, too, practically begging Blanche to get better, and Peaches came almost every day, bringing croissants and muffins, hoping the aroma would trigger a wake-up call. Many of her neighbors called, sent flowers, dropped by.

Blanche was happy to be back and on the mend, and grateful. She'd been mixed up in the murder investigation and in saving Tuna Street and the whole rest of it. This she remembered. As for her trip in the van that ended in a scrubby stretch of no-man's-land in the middle of Florida, it was all a vague recollection. It began with that hand reaching out of the passenger's side and grabbing her. She remembered Haasi's terrified expression, and the driver talking, and mercifully, that was about the end of it.

Where is Haasi? She lay back and dozed off.

There are the things I heard. I need to tell her to get ready.

She had this yearning to see her, and Rose. If it hadn't been for them, she'd probably be dead.

"Blanche." Haasi sat in a chair next to the hospital bed. She held Blanche's hand and patted it. Blanche opened her eyes. She tried to sit up.

"It's a mess."

"Yes, but you have started something that needs finishing. We are going to finish it."

"I'd just like to finish one night's sleep. Impossible in here. I need to get home." She started to lean forward and Haasi gently arranged the pillow behind her back. She smiled. The spunk appeared to be returning.

"Yes, you will leave here. That is a very good idea."

At that, Blanche swung her legs out of the bed and stood up. She wobbled some, one hand on the mattress. "I feel good. I just need some fresh air, and exercise."

"If you can, practice walking. Some breathing techniques. Exercise, cautiously, like you did before this happened."

Then Blanche got her bearings. "Haasi, I heard them. They're planning a major drug drop. A big one."

"What did you hear?"

"May be connected to Conchita Beach. I heard that goon on the radio, or phone, or something when he was driving me out. He thought he'd knocked me out with a shot of some kind, but I wasn't completely under."

"Well. That is a fit. I hear something is happening at the High

Tide. Jack and the DEA and Duncan are talking."

"How do you know all this?" But Blanche knew better than to expect an answer. Haasi smiled.

"I'll find out more," she said. Something in the way she said that made Blanche's spine stiffen. Like a shot of B vitamin, or adrenaline. She could feel her limbs kick in.

"I like the sound of that."

"I will return with an update."

"I suppose I could get up and walk out of here." She paced around the room and back to Haasi.

"Blanche, stay. For now. Get stronger."

"Murder. Lying and deceit and ruination of the island. The kidnapping." Blanche's eyes were bright and cheeks rosy. She did a tentative push-up against the wall, then five more.

Haasi put her hand on Blanche's shoulder. "Get rest. Promise."

Blanche reluctantly climbed into bed. *How can I be energized and tired at the same time?*

But she was exhausted. She'd suffered trauma. No doubt. There had been talk of the effects of "reversible coma" and possible "organ damage," but the worst worries and predictions proved false. Toxicology tests confirmed that Blanche had been drugged. It was the theory—though a weak one—that the drugs, which were as yet unidentified, had slowed her metabolism and may have been a factor in her survival. If she had tried to move, with no water and no protection beyond where she was left to die, Blanche might have spent what little strength she had and run out of time. Theories went back and forth.

Blanche knew she was just plain lucky. Heaven and earth were on her side. She had stayed alive with the unmistakable intervention of her mother and the girl with shining dark eyes. Rose had stood next to her in that deserted land and did not leave her until help came. She would always believe her mother saved her life by willing her to hang on. Haasi handled logistics on the ground. She'd led that search party directly to the field where they found Blanche. Comatose. The medics began treatment, and the hospital took over right after the helicopter landed on the roof of Bradenton Memorial.

The details were a blur. She floated into half-sleep, still a bit confused by all that had happened. But one thing was certain in the hazy hours. Blanche was not alone.

And now. A drug bust? Blanche opened her eyes. She looked around for Haasi, but she was gone. Blanche stretched her arms and legs, determined to rest up for the wild ride.

Thirty-Six
Meanwhile, Back at the Station

DUNCAN HAD BEEN VERY BUSY PUTTING PIECES TOGETHER. He held a report in his hand that conveniently fit the puzzle:

Authorities had found the van, abandoned, in a stand of mangroves near Tampa. In the back of it were women's shoes, both size five, one string sandal and the other a tennis shoe. The footwear was traced to Haasi and Blanche. The van was dusted for fingerprints and those findings were on the way to be matched with Blanche's cellophane wrapper.

Haasi appeared in the doorway to Duncan's office. She smiled at the chief and curled herself into a padded metal chair in front of his desk.

"You need more information. I went to that meeting in the town hall and I saw something was not right with that man. I was tracking him."

"What's that supposed to mean?"

"I am around. You know I overheard the man in the motel room, and I have seen him in many places."

Duncan produced Langstrom's photo, and Haasi nodded. "That is him. And, yes, he is very bad. His language, too. Not so good."

"Hmmm. He was at the Sun and Fun Resort here. Well, you know where he was staying."

"Yes, I overheard talk of where they put Blanche. And, oh, he wanted money put in a Swiss bank account."

"Now, isn't that interesting?" He was leaning back in his chair, the springs creaking under his weight. "Money. Keeps turning up."

"Yes, it is a bad root."

The chief sprang forward. "We are going to need more information, Haasi."

She uncurled herself from the chair and put both very small hands on his desk. "Oh, chief, you need much information, and help." Her dark eyes gleamed at him. He sat back and tented his fingers.

"We'll be in touch. We're closer. Not there yet, but definitely closer. You give that Blanche a big hug from her police chief."

Haasi produced a rare grin.

Duncan did not mention that Sergi had disappeared, and that Brecksall-Lam had taken no responsibility for the actions of a lawyer they hired to represent them. The latest comment from a spokesperson at the firm boiled down to this: "People may make odd decisions over which we have no control, nor liability."

Duncan told the person at Brecksall-Lam: "We'll see about *that*."

⚓

DEA was fully on board now, based on Jack's disclosure that

the trucking division for Brecksall was into drug-running. A peremptory raid of a delivery of unbelievably heavy leather hassocks to the Chicago warehouse confirmed it, and the sordid route was still being untangled. The company of Brecksall and Lam was circling the drain, for all Duncan could figure, but officially nothing had been proven. Their dealings were on hold while their books and employees were under investigation. And that included Jack and his newly acquired trucking division.

"Jack, what are you going to do now? What's the plan?" He sat in Duncan's office, his hands between his knees, looking somewhat like he'd been run over by one of his own trucks.

"They told me to hold tight, for now."

"Who?"

"DEA. I'm an informant, Dunc. Remember? Local island boy makes good." He didn't look good; he looked greyish instead of tannish. "We'll talk to the agent soon. Think you know him, Hank Miles."

"Sure do. Like him. But I prefer to go fishing with him—for fish, not drugs." Dunc sighed.

The chief got up and came around the desk to Jack. They were the only ones in the office, but he still whispered. "What the hell is happening, Jack? How? Just how did all this happen?"

"It's a long story. No, actually, a pretty short one. I took a long walk off a short pier. I thought I could cut corners; I needed a trucking division so bad for that new business, and, bingo, there it was. I can just hear Gran. You don't get somethin' for nuttin', and there really are no good short cuts."

"You got that right, son. We'll figure this out somehow. I'm not sure how, but we will. I'll keep you informed. Oh. But that's you, isn't it. The informant."

Jack gave him a rueful smile. "That's me."

Thirty-Seven
Bringing in the Feds

DEA AGENT HANK MILES WALKED INTO DUNCAN'S OFFICE a few days after Blanche woke up. He held a pile of notebooks, some of which belonged to Blanche. Duncan had shared some of the information, and Blanche was only too happy to get it out there to the authorities.

"The lady has a way with words," he said, looking up at Duncan. "We can identify the driver pretty well with this description. Did you get the prints back?"

"Not yet."

"I need to talk with her about the kidnapping," said Miles. He scratched his red beard and ran a hand through his straight black hair. They called him "Red" when his temper flared, which was not often. So far he'd been taking on this new assignment, cool and collected.

"Blanche just woke up a few days ago out of that near coma. The scumbags drugged her, dumped her on an old cattle ranch.

It's a damn miracle we got her back."

"Whew. You can bet on that. I know the place. We've uncovered a number of bodies out there, and when the animals get through with them…"

"All right, all right." Duncan didn't want the details. "You said you wanted to talk to Haasi? You'll just have to be patient. I can't get hold of her, but she'll show up."

She didn't have a phone. But she must have heard the call because there she was, standing in the doorway. She wore a bright yellow beaded shirt and a long braid neatly circled her head like a crown. Her sudden appearance startled the two men. Her eyes focused on them.

"I saw you arrive," she said to Miles. "I thought I would give you a moment with the chief." She walked in and sat in an armchair, crossing her legs that barely touched the floor.

Miles got up out of his slouch and shook her hand. "Pleased to meet you. I've heard a lot about you. Thanks for coming in. Let's talk." And Haasi did.

The driver as yet had not been apprehended, but every law enforcement agency had him on the blotter. He was not traced to the license number, but a witness had come forward, under a certain amount of pressure from the chief of Bonnam County and the Feds, and matched certain details of the van and the man to one Caribbean career criminal, a Dominique Placer, whose last name was Spanish for "pleasure." There was nothing pleasurable in Placer's background. A native of the Dominican Republic, of mixed French, Spanish and German extraction, Placer had somehow gotten himself into the USA and obtained citizenship. He moved to Chicago in his early twenties and involved himself with a remnant of the Chicago mob, a semi-extinct bunch of racketeers who had mostly been sent up under RICO—the Racketeer Influenced and Corrupt Organizations Act. He was the quintessential go-to for any crime on the agenda and would do anything for money. That meant killing, kidnapping, and confiscating that which did not belong to him. He was also tied up with drug smuggling, and that was one of the reasons Hank Miles had come to see Aloysius Duncan.

He and Miles sauntered over to Peaches. Duncan once more tried to digest an omelet he had a weakness for, and Miles made three blueberry-nut muffins disappear.

"We've got a couple of threads going here," said Duncan. "The killing, the kidnapping. And this drug business. Like a constant thorn in my shoe." The two sat back and looked at each other. "Lord, where did we go wrong."

"I don't think *we* is the operative word. We didn't do this, but we will figure it out." Miles finished off the crumbs.

"Bob's favorite," the chief added, stacking the litter of muffin wrappers. Peaches kept her eye on the handsome agent. She'd filled his coffee cup several times and brought him a cranberry-date muffin on the house, to top it all.

"Well, he had good taste." Then Miles frowned. "We need to get this sorted out, Dunc. A good place to start is with this hit man. He's going to open up a lot of doors if we can get him to open his mouth."

"Yeah. Well, first we have to find him."

"We're on it."

"What have you got planned down here?"

"A bust. We'll get into it later. We've already got agents in the field who are putting it together. But it's a big one. This one reaches from Honduras to San Antonio and up to Chicago. But the net is bigger. Jack Murninghan really stepped in it."

The omelet burned. Duncan popped a Tums and shook his head. "Jack. What do you know?"

"That trucking business. He went in full bore and didn't look where he was going, as far as we can tell. But now he's helping us out."

They got up and meandered back to the office. The two had known each other for years, and along with the talk of the criminals, they always got back to fishing stories and football. They liked each other even though they were supposed to be frictional counterparts, working in different fields of law. Miles hadn't had any official business on the island until now.

"Think there's any relation to the Conchita Beach drops?"

"Oh, yeah," said Miles.

They walked across the parking lot to the police department, which was no more than a squat white cinder block building on a canal near the marina. Emma had planted bougainvillea at the door and vinca and butterfly bushes under the windows, and the station had the cheery aspect of a fat lady all dressed up. Duncan called it home, at least ten hours a day lately. He opened the door for Miles.

"What I still don't get is why you call yourself the Drug Enforcement Administration. Are you administering the enforcement of drugs?"

Miles did not take the bait. "Ha Ha. That's funny, Al."

Duncan fell into his chair and put his elbows on the desk. "I don't like this business. I hope you're here until we sort this out."

"I am. And we will. Believe me."

Miles put his feet on an upended wastebasket and balanced a large coffee cup on his taut stomach. He played the air guitar while he considered the Santa Maria situation. If given a real guitar, police business would have sounded a lot better. He'd been accused of stealing the ghost of Robert Johnson, a soubriquet that Miles both appreciated and feared. It was hard to walk in another man's shoes, and sometimes it was a good idea. It was one of the reasons Miles was such a good DEA agent. He was skeptical and intuitive—with a good streak of empathy and humility. He was "down to earth," according to his friend, Duncan.

"Jack Murninghan is next on the agenda." Miles poured himself a cup of coffee and took a sip. He made a face at the bitter taste. "Dunc, why can't you make a decent cup of coffee?"

"What's that supposed to mean?"

Duncan ignored the remark about the coffee. He'd drink battery acid if it were presented in a foam cup. He pointed his finger at Miles. "Go talk to him."

"We need your help."

"Of course you do."

"I want to call him in, but I wanted to talk to you first. A courtesy, if you will. That trucking business he got himself tied into. They're into transportation for sure. Transporting heroin and cocaine, and we're not talking only Latin American gangs here and their willing customers in the US. The bigger picture is world-wide. From Afghanistan to Paris. We can't stop it, but we can slow it down, chuck a hole in it."

"Bring him in. We'll sit down."

"We also need to talk with the women, Blanche and Haasi. They had first-hand contact with some of these goons. Haasi's been helpful, but it's Blanche I want to talk to."

"For now, check out Blanche's notes. They've gotten us closer to Placer. Haasi is something of a bird. I never know where she's going to land, and when she does, look out. She has some uncanny insights and ways of finding out information."

"That's what I hear. Her info about this Sergi character is valuable. Let's also talk to Blanche. And Jack. He's the one with the trucks."

Thirty-Eight
A Bad Business

JACK AND AMOS WALKED DOWN TO THE WATER'S EDGE. They had been inspecting the work on the cabin porch, which government had called to an abrupt halt. Amos had shown the building inspector the plans to replace the porch floor with a different material than had previously existed, and Tallahassee surprised them with a demand for a $500 special permit to rebuild it. Amos had driven all the way to the capitol with the plans and the money. He wanted to firm it up quickly and get the place back in shape before "government" thought of something else. Jack was all for it.

"We always want 'government' to work in our favor, don't ya know," Amos said. They both had taken off their shoes and were ambling along the shore. A couple of dolphins gave them a playful show, not a care in the world.

"Well, I bet they roll out the permits like toilet paper to those land developers. They got the cash." Jack squinted out over the

Gulf. He field-stripped the cigarette and put the butt in his pocket.

"When you gonna quit?"

"When I can tie up this bundle of nerves and bury them in a hole somewhere."

"I hear you."

The two had gone to Manatee County High School together, but then, as is often the case, they didn't see each other for years. They hadn't hit forty yet, and they had both managed to turn out successful careers. Now it looked like Jack had hit a bump.

A walk on the beach was private with no ears to hear but their own. Jack didn't want to talk on the porch. It was a mess of timbers, rolls of screening, and a scatter of dusty chairs. The workmen lingered and they were none too tidy. They'd left a large bag of garbage and an ever-growing pyramid of soda cans and beer bottles. Amos was having a talk with them when Jack walked up. Alcohol had a way of screwing up building projects. Amos had already been down that road, and he didn't want to go back.

"What's going on?" Amos asked the question, and then laughed. So much had been going on, it was hard to know where to start.

"Most important, Blanche is better. They were worried about the trauma of the kidnapping, but apparently the physical side is under control. She's tough. She'll pull through."

"We're here for her. She seemed confused, but I would be, too." Amos had dropped by the hospital with flowers.

They both looked back at the cabin, its porch under construction, the second floor still propped up, but the project was coming along.

"It would be nice if she had a home to come home to."

Amos sighed. "Yeah, I hear you. This new permitting to rebuild is the hard part, but we got them this time around. The inspector wanted to condemn it, but I reasoned with them and proved it wasn't more than fifty percent gone. They bought it. I didn't tell Blanche."

"Well, don't. She's already out for blood."

"I know. I met him. He came after me looking for support for the land development. Talked of money. I hate to use the 'p' word. But I will. They were talking payoff to bamboozle the folks into thinking their buyout offers were good. No talk of the increased property taxes and the teardowns of the businesses and all the other stuff."

"They also tried to get Bob on board. Promised payoffs. They paid him off all right." Jack ran his fingers through his hair. "Jeez, I never should have gotten tied up with them. Looked so easy."

"You know what they say. It looks easy, look again. They wanted me to use my connections in Tallahassee and I told them no. I played dumb."

"*That* wasn't easy. Don't they know you've been building out here since you could hold a hammer?"

"Yeah. I deflected. Something wasn't right about them from the beginning," said Amos. "When I asked questions about the financial end of it, Langstrom was vague. At first, he didn't even want to give me Brecksall's address and phone number. Real cagey. He should have been more open about it. I think Blanche's instinct about the whole bunch was right on."

"I felt the same, but I went ahead and hooked up with them anyway. I was desperate to get stuff moving out of Texas to the Midwest, and they seemed only too willing to oblige. I didn't even finish all the paperwork—They said they'd take care of it. Now I see why. They have connections with what's left of that Chicago mob. Most of them got sent up, but the underground is alive and well and growing."

Amos looked at Jack. "Good God, how fast did you run from that?"

"Not fast enough. Langstrom held me off, said that was all a thing of the past. It's not. And right now we don't know how deep it goes."

They are about to move on Brecksall. Jack trusted Amos, but he changed the subject. "Have you seen Langstrom around? He disappeared just about the time Blanche was kidnapped. Do you know anything about the guy? Where'd he hang out, travel, stuff like that?"

"Not really. Haven't seen much of him lately," said Amos. "It's funny. He seemed so likable at first. We got to talking about sports, and apparently, he likes to ski. He got some kind of trophy out of college, was on a ski team and even tried out for the Olympics. I was impressed."

Jack remembered what Haasi said about Langstrom and a Swiss bank account. On the phone, he'd insisted on having money sent to such an account. That's probably where he was headed, Switzerland or the Austrian Alps, unless he stopped off in Vail. Ski resorts were one place to look.

"I think they could get them on RICO," said Jack. "Langstrom was complicit in the kidnapping, and attempted murder—and that's what they're calling it. He was partly the mastermind, and he must have called a lot of the shots. We have witnesses."

"Who?"

"Haasi. The girl is everywhere. And Blanche, of course, is deeply involved."

"He sure isn't much of a mastermind. That whole thing didn't go well for anyone. Blanche is traumatized and coming out of a coma, and let's face it, Langstrom was found out. You should be keeping a low profile, Jack."

"I've got protection now. I don't want it, but Duncan and the Feds insist. I hardly notice they're there, but they are. Blanche is being watched in the hospital, and she'll need it for a while. I can just hear her now, but maybe she'll be willing with all that's been going on, at least until this mess is straightened out."

"I wonder. Those guys parked in the sedan down the street aren't wearing bathing suits."

Jack glanced in that direction. "Very un-island-like behavior and dress, but so is a lot of other business going on around here." He turned to the Gulf horizon and watched a couple of pelicans hovering over a frilly wave. "Those guys got the right idea."

Thirty-Nine
Undercover Cousin

BLANCHE REMAINED IN THE HOSPITAL, and the doctor planned to keep her there for a few more days of observation. She continued to make a fast recovery, but she had little appetite. She could still taste the dust of an all-night stay out on the ranch, and she had a thirst that could not be quenched. Tests confirmed that she'd been given a street opiate of some kind—they couldn't name it—which caused weakness, blurred vision, disorientation, slower heart rate. If she hadn't been found by morning, she would have been dead of exposure and dehydration.

It was a miracle. The drug had worn off, but not the trauma and the nightmares. Lack of water and the cold had put her in a stupor. Rose had stayed until they came. She remembered this, and Haasi's frantic expression on the bridge.

She sat up on the pillows. Jack pulled a chair away from the wall and sat down next to the bed. "You are a sight."

"Well, thanks a lot. I'd like to see how you'd look after being dumped on the cold ground and left for dead."

"Awwww. Under the stars, amid the palms and wild flowers, with the aroma of dead cattle carcass in the air..." Then he leaned over and kissed her on the forehead.

Blanche made a weak attempt to punch him in the arm, but he dodged. "It's not all it's cracked up to be."

Jack had tears in his eyes. "You silly woman. Stick to the beach; stay off the ranch."

"I plan to." She stroked his hand. A machine beeped gently, a crisp white coat flashed past the doorway. "Haasi! Have you seen Haasi!"

"I'll say. You can't forget her once you've met her. But she sure makes herself scarce."

"She's always where she should be. She's remarkable." Blanche thought better of talking about the drug drop. For some reason, she thought Jack would not care to have her on board for those plans. She did not want to hear one more time, *Stay out of it.*

He had other news. "Haasi overheard Langstrom talking on the phone about where they left you out on that ranch, and then she went to Duncan. If it weren't for Haasi..." He put his head down.

"She's right here all the time, and one of these days we are going to celebrate. At the cabin. Do we still have a cabin?"

Jack stepped lightly. "Amos's working on it."

"How far away are we?"

"Not far." He hoped.

Blanche gestured toward the hallway where an officer sat on a chair with a newspaper. "What's up with that?"

"B, they tried to kill you. You're under protective watch. So am I. I'd say the whole damn island is under some kind of watch. If not a hurricane, a murder. I'm beginning to think it's safer in Chicago."

She gave him a wry smile and fell back on the pillow. "I wish we could be normal again."

"Not gonna happen. It's bumpy. We just have to get through it." His expression belied worry, and the effort to hold back information about the drug drop. Miles would be in the mix soon enough.

"I'd settle for getting out of here and going back to Cappy's. I need his cooking. Have you been staying at his place?"

"His place has been right here." He pointed to the spot next to her hospital bed. "He's been nominated for grandfather of the year. Everyone wants to adopt him."

"They can't have him. He's mine. But I'll share."

"Thanks. Guess you have to. I'll be at Cap's for a while. My business is on hold while we get some things settled down here. First on the list is you. Get well." He stood up and kissed her again on top of her head.

For Jack, being with Cappy relieved some of the anxiety. He couldn't sleep, so he was up at five with Caps at first light to fish with the nets and poles and lines, filling the coolers for fresh catch with bags of ice from Jess's. The arrangement returned Jack to happy days when the worst he could do was hook a pelican by accident and Cap showed him how to extricate the poor bird. Cap was all about basic business, everything in its proper place. Keep to the schedule, cook, eat, sleep. For Jack it was a little like being born again.

He wanted to make things right, and that was going to take time. His whole life was on hold and in need of repair, and, in particular, his trucking business. Fortunately, he wasn't a profligate spender, except for his penchant for exotic wheels and the occasional tailored suit which he thought nothing of wearing into the Gulf.

Jack spent most of the year on the road, but he was still attached to Blanche. He was determined to do what he could to get them out of this mess. He'd worried about her before, and now with the horrors of the kidnapping and all the other drama, he worried even more. He needed extra time to figure it out, and he wanted to be better family to Blanche. He'd shuffled off, leaving her with vague promises and warnings. When was that? Just a week or so ago? He should have stuck by her. Now he was more than willing to pay, and that meant time, not money. The business would be there when he got back—he hoped. He didn't want to lose it, but more so, he didn't want to lose Blanche. And then again, she might lose him. If the law found enough evidence to connect him to drug runners, it would take forever to dig himself out.

He didn't want to worry about that now. He had an appointment with the DEA, who wanted him to push further and give them more information on the Chicago business. It made him sweat just to think about it.

He was early for the appointment, and more jittery than ever, so what he needed was caffeine. He ducked into Peaches' cafe. He also wanted to thank her for all the muffins and love she'd showered on Blanche, who, of course, didn't eat any of it, but the nurses did and that was Peaches' plan. "Take good care of that baby," she wrote on one note that went with two dozen of her world-famous cranberry-lemon-walnut muffins.

Peaches wasn't there when Jack dropped by, but Sarah, her daughter, was behind the counter grinding coffee beans. Sarah was a younger, slimmer version of Peaches, with the same effusive and generous nature.

"Hi there," she said. Sarah's face lit up when she saw him. She'd always had a crush on Jack despite marrying the local football star.

"Hi there yourself," said Jack. "How's the fam?" They'd had a mild flirtation one prom season, but she'd really had her eye on the quarterback.

"Mine is just fine. I'm more concerned about yours. How's Blanche?"

"She's doing all right, thank you. Out of the coma and sitting up and already giving me hell. She wants to go home but the cabin needs a lot of work since Wilma. Have to rebuild. The second level was hanging by a beam."

"Life on the island. Although sometimes I wonder about this life. You know, Jack?"

"Yes, I do." They both glanced out of the restaurant window at the two Feds parked in a black sedan. They stuck out like two turkeys in an ice cream parlor. "Not exactly like old times."

Jack returned to the excellent aroma of the beans. He made a mental note to remind Duncan that he could get the good stuff across the street, that he didn't have to rely on the old urn that spit out used motor oil for "joe."

She handed him the paper cup with steaming French Roast. "On the house."

"You're the best. Take care, Sarah. And thank your mom, will you? You make the world go 'round with these muffins. The magic energy behind the Blanche cure."

"Oh go on." She laughed.

"See ya."

He sipped the coffee. The delay tactic had calmed him down some. He had a jaunty step on his way to the police station. For about one minute. The chief and Hank Miles were waiting. He slowed down, took each step with trepidation, wishing for it all to be over. If they could just clear up the business of illegal machinations at Brecksall, maybe they could solve the murder and go back to some semblance of peace. They had layers to work through. He could only hope.

Jack pushed open the door to the station, and it looked like fresh hell all over again.

"Now what?" he said.

"They found Langstrom," the chief said. He didn't even glance up at Jack. He had a radio in one hand, and a phone in the other. Hank Miles was pacing the office, talking on his cell. An officer was shouting to a clerk: "Well, get it. I don't care how. Just get it."

Another phone was ringing, but Jack couldn't tell where it was coming from. He wanted to go out and keep going.

But instead he took a seat and sipped his coffee. Miles was still talking, and no one was paying any attention to Jack, who looked at Duncan: "Well, good, that's good news. Now they can bring him in and question him, put it on the record."

Miles ended his phone conversation and looked over at Jack. "That is not possible."

"Why not?"

"Because they found him stuffed into a barrel floating in Tampa Bay."

"Dead? Langstrom's dead?"

"Very."

Jack started to sweat. He thought of Blanche. "I hope someone's over at that hospital watching Blanche."

"We're working on that. With Langstrom gone, we have to shift strategy. We need to chat, you and I."

"Well then."

"Come with me." Jack got up and followed Miles through the station to the small room set off to the side of a kitchenette. The door closed behind them with a resounding click.

The room was stark, the cinder block walls whitewashed. Two metal chairs and a long table on sturdy legs were positioned in the exact center of the room. Legal pads and pens lay on the table. A whiteboard stood in a corner with markers.

"We've got a deal for you, Jack. You cooperate, and we don't let the Feds take action against you."

"Whoa. What do you mean action? What the hell for? I'm already cooperating. You know that."

"Yeah, well, we need more. Your trucks have been running cocaine and heroin and God knows what all to the Midwest. The goods are loaded into that fake furniture you've been shipping, which is sent out from your warehouse to retail and then it goes to the street. We're talking millions, and not just from Latin

America. The shit is coming from Afghanistan by way of Europe to little old San Antone where your wheels sit and wait."

"I don't know what you're talking about. That last load of hassocks with the gold embossing cost a fortune."

"You bet. Do you know what was in those nice leather hassocks? Bricks and bricks, bags and bags. Of stuff."

"Fer chrissakes."

"You need Him, Jack, and you need us about now, too."

"I've known the Isaak brothers for years. I can't believe they'd be into that shit."

"They don't have to be. We don't know for sure that they are, but we aim to find out. There's always a loose link in the chain and we're going to find it, and we're going to test it. Maybe those boys know more than they're letting on. You need to nose around, and if you find anything out, you need to hand over the info."

Miles had been leaning on the table. He sat back casually, put his arms behind his head. He wore beat-up combat boots and a plaid western shirt with metal-rimmed buttons. His red beard was getting scraggly. He smoothed it, pulled a phone out of his breast pocket, and checked it. "They're calling about you. HQ. They want you to get on it, Jack. You and me."

"That's just great." His voice croaked. He'd opened a window and his whole life had flown out of it. What the hell was he going to do now? Cooperate, that's what. It was like taking a gut-wrenching gallon of medicine. He had to swallow it down and get rid of the disease. "I'll do whatever. I want Blanche to be safe. And I want out of this mess." He looked Miles directly in the eye. They had a deal.

"Thought you'd say that. You're smart. They've been using you. You need to get 'em. *We* need to get 'em."

"What's the deal with Langstrom? Do you have any idea why he turned up in the bay?"

"Allegedly, Langstrom knew too much. He screwed up the kidnapping, and he was working on screwing up the land development scheme. They wanted him gone, just like they want Blanche gone. That's why we've had someone over at that hospital. They don't care enough about you, Jack. Not yet. Let's keep it that way."

Jack wasn't confused anymore. Now he was pissed. He'd been used, and he was going to use whatever means to clean it up, protect Blanche, and get their lives back. He still couldn't figure how everything could go to hell so fast. But it did.

Forty
High Time
at the High Tide

THE HIGH TIDE BAR & GRILL WAS APTLY NAMED. Whatever the tide—in or out—a person could get very high at the High Tide any time. The locale was perfect. The restaurant-bar sat kitty-corner on a spit of sand and crushed shell off the narrow causeway on the main road between Santa Maria and the mainland. It had the grand view of Tampa Bay, convenience to all patrons, and a Jimmy-Buffet ambiance. A true Margaritaville if there ever was one.

The bar served a different two-for-the-price-of-one special every night from five to seven: margaritas, piña coladas, Irish whiskey, Bloody Mary's, screwdrivers, micheladas, all of it with generous shots of booze. The drunken snowbirds sat on the second-level deck of the restaurant and watched the sunset. If one guessed the exact time the sun went down, he or she got a free bottle of champagne to wash down the shrimp and snapper.

A lot of action went down with the drinks, seafood, and other goods.

If the patron didn't feel like drinking, there were other options to go along with the fish and chips and the breaded popcorn shrimp. Staff and patrons could pick their substance of choice: Tony Phelps, who was the entrepreneur, might offer a customer a trip to the kitchen where various stashes of cocaine, marijuana, and pills were available for purchase. The owner was happy to oblige, but, as they all knew, they had to be very careful. Word of mouth helped the business grow, but if Tony was double-crossed, there was hell to pay, and if rumors were true, hell had been paid off with the souls of several big mouths.

The older crowd was more or less a cover at the restaurant. They came and went, heavy and sunburned, gregarious and well-dressed, leaving large tips. The younger crowd, mostly regulars and a few visitors, were really the source of banner sales. They knew Tony, or someone who knew Tony, and they got into the back room for more than helpings of fish.

And this is where Miles and his DEA crew got into the act on the Florida end; the Chicago site was another project altogether.

At the Tide, while the boats mostly dropped off the shrimp and grouper, the seaplanes dropped off the drugs to other boats, and they moved fast. No one saw them in the dead of night. They swooped down to the bay some distance from the High Tide, sometimes dumping the parcels heavily wrapped in layers of plastic or meeting a boat, and then they swooped up into the air. Had a heavily boozed-up patron of the bar been watching, he or she would have thought a large pelican had flown in and out, the metal bird was so swift.

Jack's trucking company was a boon to the business. Unwittingly, he was a party to the continuing delivery of drugs between north and south. The Santa Maria location was hot. The development plan for the island and the drug action at High Tide were pieces of a puzzle, and it was no coincidence that the plan had settled near the High Tide. When the money started to flow from drug sales, the bulk of it had to go somewhere. Building a mall and a string of fancy condominiums and McMansions was a good place to launder it. Quaint little Santa Maria Island, populated with simple Florida folk, seemed like the perfect location to Sal Brecksall. Now he'd hit a bump with that damn reporter and the rest of them stirring up questions and trouble.

Miles and his DEA cronies had tracked commerce to the Santa Maria area, and they were set to go in. They'd known about the High Tide for a couple of years, but they'd never had enough. The Conchita Beach business was fairly new, and an indication of the expanding market. They had to do the ground work— the research, the questions, and they got to know the territory and the locals. It had taken many months to pinpoint the larger drops—and for Miles to get to be best buds with Tony Phelps.

Miles was not under any illusion. Too many people wanted drugs, hence, the demand brought suppliers. He was furious more wasn't done on that end—to end the need and desire for nose candy for wealthy playboys, and girls. He and the DEA were not going to end sales, not with so many stupid people out there. But he did mean to staunch the flow of this operation from Florida to Texas to Chicago. It was a big bite out of their ass. He would take it. If he could...

Soon after the meeting at Dunc's, Miles and Jack sat on bar stools at the High Tide, the cloying scent of piña colada and stale beer in the air, the bar top sticky. Smoke from the deck wafted in on the soft breeze, the bay between the island and the mainland stretched blue and calm under a mellow rose sky. They chased their whiskey with Heinekens.

They were careful not to get bombed; however, their intention was to give the appearance that they were two drunken yokels. Each had taken a trip to the deck to have a smoke, and to dump some of the booze in the lapping tide under the deck.

They ordered more of the two-fers. About an hour into their drinking, Jack's voice rose over the blender, the ice cubes, and the clink of beer bottles. "I told you that quarterback doesn't know his ass. Why they didn't put him last game is beyond stupid."

"You don't know what you're talking about." Miles wobbled. It was a convincing performance.

"Another NFL screw-up. Great. I suppose you think he has what it takes." Jack was yelling now, adding a sour note to the argument.

"Last call, gentlemen." Jim, the bartender, plunked the black pleather folder down between them. "Cash or credit. We take both."

"Huh? It's not even seven."

"You've had enough. Can't serve past your limit. My call. Sorry."

Miles dropped his head to his chest feigning bobble-headed drunkenness. Jack gave it a fine tune. He pretended to almost fall off the bar stool.

Tony came over. "Hey, man, how's it going?"

"Dunno." He was a plausible drunk, careful to keep it to wobbling and not looking Tony in the eye. He hadn't had quite enough alcohol to create a genuine, bleary look. He put on his sunglasses.

"Maybe you and Jack ought to knock it off for a while. Take a walk on the beach and come back later. Maybe even tomorrow. We're going to have a live band, Mercenary Blues Band. They're excellent, man. You'd love it, but not in the condition you're in."

"Excellent, excellent. Yeah, that's what we'll do. See y'all later," said Jack.

With that, the two of them slid off their stools. Miles left a hundred-dollar bill and managed to give Tony a sloppy high five.

Miles stumbled out the door. "Dude, he didn't even ask if we were driving." Jack was moving at a sober clip.

Tony was leaning on the bar, signaling Jim. "How much they drink?"

"At least five or six shots a piece. I finally cut them off."

"What numb nuts."

Miles couldn't know it, but it was exactly the reaction he wanted. He looked over the roof of the car at Jack. "Act One, and done. Hope he bought it. We're just a couple of dumb drunks." The two hustled off to see the chief.

Salvador Brecksall was the master of keeping a low profile. He'd acquired a slew of businesses for his Chicago operation, including trucking, real estate, medical devices, furniture imports. The business of drug running sort of fell into his lap when a friend needed packets of cocaine delivered to Chicago in gold-embossed leather hassocks through Turkey.

"Your distributors will love it," said the entrepreneurial exporter from Istanbul. He and Sal had met over Adana kebabs and belly dancing in Chicago, and Sal had not looked back. He bought in, but now he wanted to bow out. He needed to finish the lucrative run. He had his eye on a nice little stretch of beach front on Santa Maria, and although it looked like there had been a snag in the land development plans—that preening idiot Langstrom had not worked out—Sal was sure he could "persuade" the residents of Tuna Street to move out of the way and give a hard-working Chicago retiree his due. But first things first.

It was a warm October in the Chicago suburb of Bolingbrook, the gold and red leaves still attached to their black skeletons in the park, the musty smell of autumn hovering. Brecksall found Placer easily. The lanky fellow uncrossed his legs and stood. He dragged on his cigarette while he watched Brecksall lope toward him.

"Why we meet here," Placer said.

"What? You want the cocktail lounge at the Four Seasons? We

got trouble, and I don't want no ears, technological or otherwise."

"You don't say. That business with Langstrom? That development plan hit 'em down there like a bomb. A big stink bomb."

"You know we need to wash that coin. The land development was supposed to do it. I'm running out of dumps," said Brecksall. "Langstrom was supposed to be the face of The All New and Improved Money-Laundering Plan of Santa Maria." A fallen away Catholic, he made the sign of the cross nonetheless.

"Again. Just curious. Why'd you want him gone?"

"Too many demands. Annoying twerp. And he wanted a boatload for his lame services. Good work getting rid of him."

Placer lit another cigarette. He was wary of compliments, and of Brecksall. He'd learned not to trust anyone. Didn't hurt to get as much info as possible, then take the money and run. "It weren't easy. I had to take him out fast. Hate that squealing like a baby when they sees the gun. All of a sudden not such a tough guy anymore." Placer sat, crossed his legs, swung a boot back and forth. "Then I gets this oil drum, and he didn't quite fit…"

"Save it. It's done. That particular laundromat is on hold." Brecksall felt like he needed a shower. The park bench was warm from the sun, but he was near the boiling point. He just wanted to finish the operation and retire like that lousy ex-partner of his, Harry Lam, who slithered off the Florida and bought himself a gold Cadillac. He'd skimmed enough off the drug running, gotten away clean, and he didn't want to know more. Now he tootled over to the links every day on his golf cart and left the snow and the Chicago business behind. "Sal, you really ought to give it up," Harry had told his partner. "Think of your health."

Salvador wasn't thinking of his health at the moment. He was thinking about how he could get the last million out of the load from Afghanistan that finally was making its way up highway 65 in the back of Jack Murninghan's string of eighteen-wheelers. He wanted to be there in the warehouse to greet them when it all came in and was delivered to the hundred or so furniture stores. Fast. It seemed to take forever to get the shipments through and finally collect on the sales of the drugs. He had always been a patient man, but his patience was wearing as thin as the remaining strands upon his nearly bald head.

This nice pile of money would be his last gig. He'd done enough "laundry." Now, all he could think of was Tuna Street. The realtor said the owners didn't want to sell, but in Sal's world, everyone had a price. He'd keep at it until one or two of them sold. Maybe with a little pressure.

He'd already put the pressure on that girl, the journalist, and look how that worked out. It didn't.

"You made a mess with that girl. I wanted to be rid of her."

"Yeah, well, you can blame Langstrom and those goons you had down there. But it was all Sergi. What a prima donna. Told me to dump her, not kill her. Shouldn't have listened because now she's out there, and she may be able to ID me. I could still go after her."

"No. And have that police chief and all the rest of 'em after us? Too hot right now. Let's just get this done and get out. You have your orders. You need to be on Santa Maria for that drop. Going to be huge, and final."

"Final. Don't like that word. But I get you. We'll make it work, then I'm gone. Aruba or Seychelles. Abracadabra. Somewhere way the hell away."

"I'm going to meet you at the High Tide. You'll get the particulars later."

"When will I get paid?"

"Pronto."

Brecksall was relieved to hear that the hit man would be gone, out of his life. Fortunately, Placer never left a trace, even when he killed that realtor in broad daylight. Broke his neck. He'd do anything Brecksall asked, and do it quickly and clean. It made Brecksall queasy to know Placer would still be out there after the drop. But it couldn't happen any other way. He needed Placer for certain tasks, not the least of which was gathering up a pile of non-traceable cellphones. Placer was the go-between in this and in other things. He was slick, in and out with messages about incoming shipments, and very efficient at doing the leg work for deposits to the Cayman and Swiss accounts.

They were almost done. He didn't want to look over his shoulder. Sal didn't believe it, but he felt it—Placer could off him in a heartbeat—and it made him very antsy.

Sal climbed into his old Jaguar and sank back in the cracked leather seat. It comforted him, but only for a minute. He straightened his bow tie, looked in the rearview mirror and sighed. He raked a strand of greasy white hair off his forehead and started the car. He thought of the drop, and all that could go wrong. The Feds were poking around, but he and Lam had successfully unloaded the trucking division on Jack Murninghan. He could take the fall for that one. Brecksall had his overseas accounts and the balance was nice and fat. The spotlight was on Jack Murninghan, so while the light shined there, Brecksall planned to sneak off.

Hank Miles was good at coordinating details, but he couldn't be in two places at once. He'd studied military history, and he knew the value of the element of surprise. It made up mightily for the occasional screw-up. But there couldn't be any screw-ups here. The plan was to have the bust go off at the High Tide and in the warehouse of Brecksall and Lam in Chicago all at once.

Miles had been in on this type of operation before, but this one was his baby. He was ready.

Forty-One
The Girls Get Ready

BLANCHE WAS WELL-RESTED EVEN THOUGH THE HOSPITAL made her restless. Lingering in a hospital bed was not something she was used to, and she hoped she never had to do it again. Time had been lost in the investigation, and in the end, this side trip had done nothing but excite her curiosity and goad her to get to the bottom of the murder and this business with Langstrom and Jack's entanglement in the drug drop. She wanted out of the 'pital, as Jack called it, and she wanted to get on with it.

Haasi stood next to the bed. "The man. The hairball, you say. He is gone."

"Gone?" For a second Blanche entertained the notion that Langstrom and his development plan had vanished into the North. But Haasi's face told her otherwise.

"Very much. He is dead."

Blanche fell back on her pillow, the color drained from her face. She didn't like this news. For a number of reasons. She didn't wish this on Langstrom, and she was loath to think about yet another murder in connection with Santa Maria.

"How?"

"Not pleasant, but what is good about any of this? He met his end. He wanted you to be gone, Blanche. I am sorry for the death of another human being, but what he did to you was not human."

"*He* put me in here?" Her voice was barely a whisper.

"Yes, you can say it. I overheard him on the phone with the hairballs."

"Haasi, I've got to get out of here."

"This will happen."

The unmistakable click of Liza Kramer's heels echoed down the corridor. Blanche could hear her laugh. It seemed the afternoon sunlight got a bit brighter, the lilies in Blanche's bedside vase sat up. Liza whooshed through the doorway, her rose fragrance and blond curls and enormous bouquet of spring flowers in blue and orange tissue seemed to fill the room. Right behind her came a slender woman in a snug Chinese sheath printed with round white flowers on a red background, her hair a stylish short cap. She was carrying a small black bag.

Blanche opened her arms for a hug. Haasi smiled.

"Liza!" Blanche looked to Liza's companion and the black bag.

"Blanche, this is QiPi! I'm telling you, she is a savior."

QiPi bowed. "You are too kind."

"Qi, you helped me stop smoking, lose five pounds, and calmed me down some since Bob…," said Liza. Her hands flew to her cheeks, glowing with health and happiness. "Acupuncture, Blanche! It's wonderful!"

"Liza, you are the best friend anyone could ask for."

Dr. Haplewski walked in and took one look at Liza, QiPi, and the array of needles spread out on a linen cloth next to Blanche's bed. "What the ..."

"They're just visiting, doctor, and then they'll be going." Blanche sat up straight and smoothed the bed cover.

"No, we're not, not until you try this Blanche," said Liza. "Hello, Doctor." She batted her lashes and twisted a long gold chain from which dangled a tiny turquoise globe. QiPi remained calm and silent, hands folded, the picture of serenity.

"Hello, and good-bye, if you please," said the doctor. "You may not bring this in here."

"Why not? Acupuncture's been around for thousands of years, and it certainly can't hurt, you know, with anxiety and insomnia." Liza coaxed.

"And it can't help. Now, please, pack these things up." He spun on his heel and then gave Liza the laser eye. "Promise?" But he smiled. The poor man couldn't help it.

Blanche hunched her shoulders. Haasi said, "Maybe another time?"

"Oh, all right," said Liza. "But I've got to help. We need you, Blanche." She beseeched Haasi.

"Do not worry, Liza," said Haasi. "Thank you, Qi." She gave the slightest bow, so imperceptible Blanche did not catch it.

Blanche was about to leave the hospital, but only Haasi, Liza, and Blanche knew it. An escape, of sorts.

They were on a mission.

But first, Haasi and Liza paid Cappy a visit. The two women swept into his kitchen where Liza eyed the simmering bouillabaisse and then got down to business. "Cap, we need to get into Blanche's closet and bring her some things."

"Why? She's not leaving the hospital for several days," he said.

"Blanche wants to be ready when she leaves," said Haasi. "The doctor says she may leave soon, and she needs clothes. What she was wearing in the night time they found her is not suitable." It was a white lie, her first ever, and it pained her. Her intention was hidden; her words were the truth.

He motioned for them to follow to Blanche's room.

Liza chimed in. "You know, she's lost weight, but she's up and about walking. She wants to be properly dressed." She began throwing cosmetics into a bag though Blanche had few. Liza planned to add to the stash. They needed all the tools.

Cappy shrugged, and smiled. "Well, have at it. Completely foreign to me, but, I have to say, it's wonderful you are all like sisters to Blanche." Liza couldn't resist a quick hug, and then she got on with it. She handed Haasi a silk blouse and some creams.

Blanche was not a trendy dresser, but she had a basic assortment of things that tended to the colors of the sunset and island flowers. Haasi rummaged through the clothing. She and Blanche were the same size, and they were a striking pair. They were about to make the most of it.

Haasi headed back to the hospital with the clothes and make-up. It was a short bus ride off the island. She usually got a lift when she went to visit Blanche, but today, she didn't want any questions, especially about the bag of goodies she was sneaking into the hospital.

It was late afternoon by the time she arrived. Blanche was lying in bed, wide awake, watching the door. Haasi had studied the shift changes to the minute, and they had timed Blanche's escape for the precise interval when the nurses and other staff were running around, gossiping, updating each other and getting settled. Certain ones of them were more inclined to fritter, and Haasi had made a note of it. If someone wanted to die in the hospital, this was a good time to do it. No one would be poking around, bringing meds, and generally disturbing those who wanted to rest in peace.

Haasi was a familiar figure in the ward, and she wasn't stopped on her way to Blanche's room. On more than one occasion,

Haasi had visited Blanche when she wasn't supposed to be there, and she had always gotten around the posted security. It was amazing the places a tiny unassuming person could go; she was an underestimated presence, and for that, she and Blanche were forever grateful, and lucky.

She appeared next to Blanche. She was wearing a shift and lifting water bottles like barbells. She'd been forcing herself to eat more, exercise, and nap. She was ready. Enough with "one more test."

Haasi smiled. "Bring them on."

"Hey. You mean, bring it on?"

"No, I mean them. All of them."

Blanche dropped her arms and took the bag from Haasi. "Whatcha got?"

"All the colors I could find."

"Good. We need them. Been pretty dull lately."

Liza slipped into the room. She usually entered like she was leading a parade, but not today. She wore flats and a plain skirt and blouse. She put one finger to her lips, opened her purse, and withdrew several tubes and brushes. "Glamor time!"

"Oh yeah," said all three.

Haasi and Blanche were sitting on bar stools at the High Tide when Miles and Jack walked in the door. At first they didn't see the women, then Jack stopped. If he'd known Liza was planning to show up later, the scene would have been complete, and he would have exploded for sure. "What the…"

Miles said, "What's wrong? You look surprised. Or something worse."

"Something worse."

Miles followed Jack through the bar, and his eye landed on Blanche. She glowed, either because she was so sick of being sick, or the make-up session worked that well. It was probably a little of both. Miles had never met Blanche before, but, of course, he knew all about her. He'd read her notes. Jack had filled him in.

Jack walked over to his cousin, hugged her first, but then lit in: "What are you doing here? You're supposed to be in the hospital!"

"Well, I'm not."

"I can see that. Hank, this is my cousin, Blanche, and you know Haasi." Jack gave Haasi a hug, and Miles didn't take his eyes off Blanche's black curls and that grin. He ignored Jack who went right back to harassing Blanche for being an escapee. "I'll just bet the two of you are up to something."

Hank Miles nodded. He opened his mouth, but nothing came out. He took a step back behind Jack, the sweat beading down his spine. He studied the top of Blanche's head, and tried to think of something intelligent to say. There was something about that girl. He felt an arrow to the heart. But Blanche was busy haranguing Jack.

"Don't know what you're talking about," said Blanche. "It's perfectly legal for me to sit on this bar stool." She waved half a piña colada at him, and she was having a hard time covering up the fact that she found Hank Miles wildly attractive; the chemistry was evident. She wasn't shy or coquettish; it wasn't her way. She studied Hank's crooked grin and the hair that stood straight up like Irish wire, and his restless energy that she understood at once. Haasi poked her in the ribs. And then Jack started in again.

"You're supposed to be recuperating! *In the hospital!*"

"That has been done." Haasi leaned closer to Blanche and sat up straight, adjusting herself on the bar stool like it was her regular perch. It was the first time she'd ever sat on a bar stool. But it hardly seemed to matter. She seemed to be adapting, and she certainly looked the part. Her eyes were done up like Cleopatra's, heavily lined, accenting the winged shape. Liza's superb touch. Jack had seen Haasi many times since the kidnapping, but she had never been dressed in anything other than her usual island dress, which wasn't much. Tonight she wore an electric blue silk blouse and tight black pants. She crossed her legs and dangled one sandal up and down. She looked perfectly at home, and she was sipping a brown liquid in a very small glass.

This was the last place on earth Jack imagined he would ever find both of them.

Miles had one arm on the bar and was making an effort to be casual while he continued to stare at Blanche. She'd chosen to deck herself out in a tight red and yellow striped jersey sheath, which highlighted the contrast of her pale skin and dark hair. She appeared to be fully recovered from her ordeal. Though not happy to see her at the High Tide, Jack was awfully happy to see her looking so well while he wanted to grab her under his arm and whisk her out of there.

"Again, Bang. You're not answering. What are you doing here?"

"I'm recovering."

"What are you talking about?"

Haasi and Blanche looked at each other. They had an unspoken communication that was eerie. Jack recognized the ability: he and Blanche had always had the same connection.

Miles pushed off the bar. "Wait a minute."

"No, I don't think so. Too late for that. We know what's going on. Well, we know some of what's going on, and you are going to need all the help you can get." Haasi spoke calmly, and there was no dissuading her. She had been there—talking with Chief Duncan and Cappy, listening in at windows and conversations, asking unassuming questions—whatever it took. She knew most everyone on the island since her part in Blanche's rescue, and she'd become something of a celebrity though she shunned any credit for her participation. Clint wanted to interview her for the *Island Times*, but she declined. "We will have the interviews and stories later, and thank you," she'd told him when he finally tracked her down at Duncan's.

It didn't take a genius to figure out that Hank Miles and Jack and the authorities were planning something. They'd questioned Haasi, and she'd put it together and gotten back to Blanche. Haasi had lurked, and listened plenty. They knew about the drops at High Tide, and they were determined to pull all the loose ends together.

The weird thing was that most people who lived around Santa Maria knew about the drug sales, too, but there was never any way to stop it. Chief Duncan had tried to coordinate with other law enforcement, but the drug business continued, unabated. The right mix of law enforcement and follow-up had been missing. Until now.

Haasi and Blanche had come to want something more. They wanted revenge. These people were bent on destroying the island—and someone had killed Bob. Then the kidnapping. Blanche told Haasi the hairballs had threatened Cappy during the kidnapping. And this was the last thing that they would take from them. They would not touch a fine hair on Cappy's head.

The urge to make things right did not diminish; it simply burned brighter.

Blanche knew Dominique Placer was out there. The man conducted a hard, cold business. It needed to end. They would meet again, and they were planning accordingly. Placer was slick, but he had never met up with anyone like Haasi and Blanche.

Jack's eyes shot from Blanche to Haasi. He was frantic. "Blanche, you can't be here," he said. Miles had the same look of firm dismissal—mixed with concern and wonder—on his face.

"Well, we are here. And I'm thinking of ordering a hamburger. Would you like one?"

"No, I wouldn't, and neither would you. How'd you get over here? Do you want a ride to Cap's?"

"No, I said. We are going to have a nice time tonight, and I suggest you take care of yourself. You look stressed, Jack. Go about your business." With that, she turned to Haasi and they clinked glasses.

The bickering stopped abruptly when Tony Phelps walked in. He wore a bomber jacket and from the bulge under his arm, Jack knew he was carrying. Tony walked to the back room. Blanche took in the cold expression. Jack and Miles feigned interest in a ball game that was projected over the bar.

"A little warm for the jacket," Haasi murmured.

The night was going to be a hot one.

Forty-Two
Garbage Fish

SALVADOR BRECKSALL DID NOT WANT TO BE HERE for his last drop near the island, but it was a necessity. He might as well enjoy it. He drove his rented Mustang convertible over the bay bridge and marveled at the blend of sky and water. It was a diamond for the eye, a sparkling show of Mother Nature. He couldn't wait to get on with retirement and settle down here.

He still had his sights set on Tuna Street. And he was ready to pay whatever price to get a spot on the island. He had a tidy fortune. He'd been all about the money, and he hadn't cared much about how he got it. The drugs he flooded the streets with killed and ruined thousands, upon thousands, of people. But Sal was philosophical about his business dealings. "It's the people's choice. It's a free country." Surprisingly, he was all for legalization of marijuana because he assumed it would lead to more customers getting hooked on drugs. The leafy greens were his bread and butter, along with that sugar cocaine and heroin to top it all. What a feast. "People are so willing to go the banquet," he often said.

He'd argued with his former partner, Harry Lam: "Get the stuff legal. I pay Uncle Sam some tax. So what? He's happy, and I'm happy." He didn't consider the machinations of paying taxes and possibly having the IRS audit his books. It was moot now. He wanted out of the trade altogether. Harry had the right idea when he'd told Sal to take care of his health, and as a result, Sal surmised he would stop contributing to ruining the health of the others.

Besides, it was getting too risky.

Sal pulled into the Blue Dolphin motel in Bradenton Beach and checked in. He whistled while he walked. He would do this last run. Time was money, and a little side trip to Florida was nice, especially with the bad weather already up in Chicago. He eyed the small pool with rattan lounges and a Tiki bar where a gorgeous bikini-clad non-swimmer was sipping something fluorescent pink. "Ah, we don't have that in Bolingbrook. Not even close."

Sal ate grouper fingers at the Gulf Cafe, took a nap, and planned to head over to the High Tide. He wanted to get this show on the road. He had other things to do besides sitting in a bar and watching another drug drop.

Placer was at the ready. Somewhere. He couldn't risk being spotted, but Sal wasn't worried. The thug had a facility for covering his tracks. He needed to be careful. He could be recognized. Maybe by someone who had been in the vicinity of the parking lot the day Bob was found dead. Just the thought of the ruthless killer made Sal sweat, and he wanted to be rid of him, too.

He had other regrets. He sincerely wished Sergi had been better at his job, but the developer had been more interested in his paycheck than hyping up the money-laundering scheme and pulling off the kidnapping.

Of course, Sal and Placer knew nothing about the scheme Hank Miles, the DEA, and Chief Duncan had cooked up to greet the arrival of the seaplane, *Mephisto*. And he had no idea of Jack Murninghan's part in the drop. Sal was pretty much in the dark about a lot of the details. He would take the money, and run.

Sal sat with Tony in the back office at the High Tide. Several platters of greasy battered shrimp and grouper and empty beer bottles littered a side table. Sal had his feet on a chair. Tony had gone through the drop drill many times, and he felt one more run-through was necessary. Sal was twitchy and restless. He didn't seem to be tracking on the business at hand. And Placer, for all his worth, was MIA. "That bag of bones," said Sal. "Don't know where he got himself off to but he better show."

"Forget him. We don't have to do much," Tony said, "except watch that the business goes down nicely. We've got people."

"What does that mean? I've got people, too."

"I mean, you don't have to go swimming for the goods. I've got people who will drag the stuff under the dock into the boats and on to the trucks. You want to look?"

"Sure."

Tony got up and Sal followed him.

Miles waved at Tony as he walked through the bar with Sal. It was all Jack could do not to strangle Sal, but he pulled his baseball cap low and kept his head down out of sight.

Haasi and Blanche—and now Liza—had moved to a booth. Jack eyed them. They were up to something. He couldn't let it go. He had to get them out of there.

Minutes later, Miles called Jack out onto the deck. They fumbled over a pack of cigarettes and peered out over the bay. The evening was calm, a blue-black sky over water. A half-moon scattered light on the rippled surface of the bay.

They leaned on the deck rail, pretending their old drunken buddy routine. Their eyes shifted to Tony and Sal a short distance away. Miles could hear them with the listening device behind his left ear, and the conversation was being recorded. Tony had been bugged—in the lining of the leather of his favorite cigarette case.

He carried it with him all the time. It had taken Miles a long time to determine where and how to plant the thing, so small and flat it was no larger than a squashed bug. Miles was glad Tony was a chain smoker, and that he took the case everywhere.

"Well, how can you risk it? There are people around," said Sal.

"They clear out after one," said Tony. "Do you see a lot of people hanging around here in the middle of the week? We usually make the drop on a Tuesday, but we have to mix it up. Makes it nice to do it then. Sort it out, get paid, have the goods for sale by Friday night when it gets hopping."

Miles and Jack threw out just enough football terms to make anyone think this was a couple of semi-drunk guys arguing over stats. Miles hated smoking, but it was necessary in his line of work. He leaned on the deck rail, cupping the cigarette, occasionally jabbing the air with it.

"Hey, Miles, how you doin'?"

Miles acknowledged the bar owner with a nonchalant wave, and then he turned to offer Jack a cigarette and light it for him— his back to Tony and Sal.

"Street value. Mmmmm. Couple mil per this drop. Coke, heroin. Got Rick back on the *Mephisto*. Gonna be a nice one, this drop. Gonna be my payday," said Sal.

"You can count it already, Sal? You don't cut it with too much shit, do you? They know it. They're payin'."

"We aim to please. Ya know, I'm gonna miss the business. Been a good run and all. But I have to get out. I'm gettin' on, Ton."

Tony's face brightened at the mention that Sal was getting older. Tony could step up, get his end of the trade pumping, take more control of the business. There seemed to be no lessening of demand. The restaurant would go under before this business with the coke, heroin, and marijuana did.

Tony clamped his lips in sympathetic agreement and patted Sal on the back. "You got it. Been a good run, and we aim to keep runnin'. Those Conchita Beach drops won't end any time soon."

Miles pulled his ear, a signal to Jack to play it down. He continued a less animated discussion of Mike Ditka. "Oh, yeah." Miles slipped that in—between some generality about the '85 Bears and their latest quarterback.

They swigged the beer. They studied the horizon. A string of tiny lights like diamonds was lined up far away, the night fishing boats setting up to haul in the catch by morning. It was a clear night, perfect for a low-level flight over the barrier keys. A perfect night for a catch. They took deep, deep breaths.

Jack hunched his shoulders at Miles. It was almost impossible at this point to look casual, a guy enjoying the last of a late night at the bar. But he had to try.

Miles called it in. All clear. He did not use a phone—the beauty of new technology. He triggered the no-hands, no-phone call to other agents on the ground. Jack was supposed to retreat when the actual drop occurred, protect his cover. But he would be around. He planned to be part of this operation. Simple, fast, and clean.

His eye landed on Blanche and Haasi, both of them animated, sitting in a booth in the bar. And then he did a double take. Liza had joined them. A light shone down on them, laughing and talking. Concern hardened his features, but he seemed determined to stay focused.

"They're ready. Agents in place," said Miles. He still stared out at the bay, his hands folded on the railing. "Jack, you gotta lay low and get the women out of here."

"I'm workin' on that."

"Don't cause a scene. Let's play along for now. We might have to leave it the way it is and crank in extra protection for them." He spoke above a whisper, his eyes trained on the horizon.

"With all that's going on? They need to go." Jack bounced off the railing, but Miles held his arm. "Hey, how 'bout that new linebacker?" Miles's voice went up a notch. Jack sighed.

"Good thing Sal is here. He didn't see you but you can ID

the guy big time." Miles talked through his teeth, topped with a hearty laugh for cover. He still had a hold of Jack's arm.

"Just wish it would be over. What time is it?" Jack wiped sweat off his forehead though the night was a cool seventy.

"Almost game time."

Sal was expecting a shipment in Chicago the same night the *Mephisto* was to drop its load in the Florida bay. Miles couldn't believe the luck of the circumstances. Jack could place Sal at the scene of the crime in Florida, and agents in Chicago would follow up at the warehouse. If all went well, Sal was going to be cooked. Miles and the team had worked hard to catch the big fish, but they would settle for bringing in half a dozen other players, too, if it all worked out.

They had done everything they could to intercept the deal. Now, they had to wait. Miles had been on more than one raid, and each one was different, but one thread remained the same: greed and product. He was after the live fish he could throw in the tank. They were fish that swam for their lives. They were talking fish. Miles was hoping he'd catch some talking fish at High Tide, along with a sizable stash of product that would put all of them away for a long time.

They expected cocaine, heroin, and marijuana in the drop, but sometimes that bonanza didn't happen. Sometimes they got one supplier, and one product, out of the way, with a plan to go back for more. And sometimes they were just lucky to make a nice sweep of it. Miles was counting on the latter, according to his sources. Jack had snooped around at Brecksall-Lam, but came up with nothing. No one was talking about any illegal transport or investigation. At least, not yet.

Tony and Sal headed to the back office. Two o'clock was closing time on a weeknight. It was last call.

Miles field-stripped his cigarette and put it in his pocket. It was better than throwing it out where the birds and fish could choke on it. Wasn't that important? Apparently not, as Miles looked over the deck railing and saw dozens of cigarette butts down at the water's edge under the dock.

He also saw a row of motorboats, nice and shiny, of similar make. He'd been informed. The boats were ready to take on their cargo and race off to the trucks for distribution. He noted how they were anchored and also noted that they were pointed at the only means of outlet. They would have to cross the bay. All the possible trajectories had been researched, but Miles double-checked this with agents. They had located the trucks on the mainland side between Bradenton and Sarasota and scoped the territory. If the *Mephisto* didn't land at the High Tide and instead picked a random spot, the agents had to be ready to move and intercept at the receiving end.

All bases had been covered, but even the best plans had flaws. Miles had seen his share of screw-ups in his twelve years as a DEA agent, and their cost in time, money and personnel was an outrageous waste. They always happened because someone did not do the job.

Miles checked his watch. The plane was due over the bay near the High Tide between 2:15 and 2:30. It was a low-level flight plan, difficult to follow on radar. So far, the communication was that the *Mephisto* had one other scheduled drop and then would fly on to the High Tide. The plane would not be close to local water for more than sixty seconds; it would skim the surface, drop the product, and be gone.

The agents had worked out a plan of split-second timing to intercept the shipment, gather all the crooks, and get out of there. Miles had his end lined up. The shipment from the *Mephisto* would never make it to the trucks. At least, that was the plan.

Forty-Three
The Catch

BLANCHE, HAASI, AND LIZA SAT IN THE LARGE CORNER BOOTH at the High Tide, and they had company. Sal had decided to join them after Haasi engaged him in an earnest conversation about island history. She wove a tale of pirates, hurricanes, and sea creatures that had been spotted but not verified, and she encouraged him to drink. A lot.

Miles wanted the women gone, but it was too late. The flight was coming in soon, and Miles couldn't afford to create conflict. He'd have to call for back-up to keep the women clear. Jack had gotten Blanche off to the side and told her to get out of there, but she walked off.

Sal ordered round after round, and he got drunker and drunker. Tony came out of the back office once or twice and pulled Sal aside, but the party continued. Blanche had the idea that Tony preferred his comrades in the drug trade to remain sober, at least until after the drop. But Sal didn't seem the least bit worried. He talked about having a frolic on the beach with the girls the next day. Everything was going to be wonderful on this mini va-cay.

He didn't know who Blanche was. He'd removed himself from the politics of Santa Maria Island and left the machinations to Sergi Langstrom, R.I.P. But Blanche knew him—the one nosing around her property on Tuna Street. He'd called her "the island chick."

Blanche and Haasi took their drinks with them to the ladies' where they dumped most of the liquor into the toilet. They had to remain sober. They stood in front of the mirror, applying a bit of lipstick, washing their hands, and wringing them. Haasi murmured: "Sal must not remain sober. He must trip over himself and not think straight. He must be incapable of escape. He must be caught and go to jail where information will be forthcoming about his involvement."

"This island chick couldn't agree more," said Blanche, grinning.

They returned to the booth and were stunning and charming, full of intelligent conversation and brilliant history. Sal's flushed face was beaming. "Hey, Ton, these girls are a card. Come on over." But Ton waved and headed for his office.

Sal's head bobbled against the back of the booth. "You gals are the perfect tour guides," he said, eyeing the beautiful golden brown one. He didn't take his eyes off the cleavage that peeked from the V in her electric blue blouse.

Miles talked to the agents in the field through the device under his shirt, and Jack wore a stricken look. "Can't get them to leave," he said. Miles shook his head. Sal and Tony were on Miles's radar. It was going down fast.

It was almost two o'clock.

Blanche, Haasi, and Liza said good night to Sal with giggles and promises. Miles and Jack watched them leave.

"Whew!" said Jack.

Miles did not look convinced. "They really go?"

Sal moved to the parking lot. The women left the restaurant, but they did not head home. They scurried to the underside of the deck near the water's edge, and they kept an eye on their new "friend" who climbed into an SUV and sat there in the dark. They'd cooked up a few possible scenarios, and one of them involved a crook waiting inside a car. Liza planned to be the lookout in the parking lot.

Haasi was wearing tight pants which securely held a well-honed knife with a four-inch blade. Sal had tried to grope her on the way out of the bar, but she had gracefully put him off with a bare-faced lie. "Oh, there's time for that. I'll see you tomorrow, right?" The three women could hardly suppress a new round of the giggles. Blanche also carried a knife; she could feel the hilt against her rib. But she was reticent to use it. She was hardly as skilled as Haasi at wielding it. This Blanche had found out in a demonstration inside the hospital room when Haasi fashioned a pillow over the suspended television set and drew a face on it, which looked surprisingly like Dominique Placer. She proceeded to flip the weapon across the room with astounding accuracy.

Blanche had asked where she learned to handle a knife.

"It is something I know," she'd said.

"Well, shouldn't we all."

During the last days in the hospital, along with the vegetables and the push-ups, Blanche learned some basics with a knife. One of the first lessons Haasi taught her was to never let anyone know she was carrying one.

Tonight, they had a mission, and they decided it was better for Haasi to start off by herself. "Very small, and dark." Haasi grinned. It had gotten to be a joke because most of Haasi's recon was done in plain sight. She had an uncanny facility for fading into the background. She moved quickly. She was a woman who made the most of her talents.

Miles left the bar, but he didn't leave the grounds. The High Tide was built on stilts at the edge of the bay. A wide deck wrapped around the restaurant, and underneath, patrons pulled up in their boats. But now the patrons were gone. The owner had roped off a sort of phalanx of getaway boats.

Miles couldn't put it off any longer. He crept along the narrow beach from boat to boat with wire clippers and made sure they would not go anywhere. He'd left Jack on the deck above.

All along the shoreline, the mangroves grew in a thick tropical forest from the surface of the water to more than twenty feet in height. They grew fast and strong, and they were the guardians of holding the sand together. They were also excellent cover for the DEA agents who hid in the bayside jungle, waiting for the *Mephisto*.

The agents were in place, and so was Miles. And so were Haasi and Blanche. Liza had snuck off to the car to change and get in place.

While Miles was clipping the wires on each motorboat, Haasi was slipping around the underside of Sal's SUV slashing his tires. She would have to be quicker than Haasi was quick. The car would start to settle, and the drunken drug runner might get out to have a look. It took considerable strength for one so small, but Haasi was capable. Her arms were like cable, and she used her wrists like levers. Sal was grounded.

In under three minutes, Haasi was back under the stairs near the restaurant deck with Blanche. They watched the horizon, all but pitch black except for the sparkle on the water of a bit of moon and a few distant fishing boats.

Then he heard it: a slight buzzing like a bee caught in a jar.

They watched, and waited, and soon heard the plane as it smoothed out and got louder on the approach. Haasi and Blanche hid behind a clump of brush. Blanche was praying out loud that the creeps, or at least some of the creeps, would get caught.

"Well, look who's here." It was Miles. Jack had crept down from the deck and was right behind him. He was furious.

"Goddamit, Blanche, I thought you said you were leaving."

"Not a chance."

The plane was closer. They all ducked and focused on the water.

"Well, it's too late now," said Miles. "All of you shut the hell up. Stay out of the way, I mean it, and try not to get killed."

"Miles! We have to get them out of here," said Jack.

"Really? Are you going to drive them home? Now?"

"I don't think so," said Blanche. "And Sal isn't going to drive us home either. Or anywhere, for that matter." Blanche held up a knife, but Haasi gently put her hand on her arm and lowered it.

"What did you do? Kill them?" Jack was nearly shouting in a hoarse whisper.

"Tires," said Haasi.

Miles motioned to not talk at all.

If the plane weren't such a bird of horror, it would have been beautiful, the wings wide and reflecting the lights along the shore and the moon. Rick flew low and level, and appeared to be coming directly at the High Tide. Then he did a circle, like he was on a recon and just checking the scenery.

Miles stepped away, low to the ground, talking to the agents on his device. "Guy can fly."

"What's he doing?" Jack and the others watched as the pilot made another tight circle over the bay.

Miles was still on the phone. "Roger."

Haasi whispered to Blanche. "Who's Roger?"

Blanche laughed. Miles again motioned for silence. They sidled over to the edge of the mangroves and crouched near the water.

One dropped from the sky, then another, and then it was raining large brown parcels. The plane circled once and dropped several more. One of the agents shot at the plane. Another hit it in the tail section. It started to lose equilibrium, then it steadied and the pilot seemed to rev himself out of trouble. Another shot finished the job. The plane couldn't maintain its altitude, and it began its plummet into the bay. Blanche saw figures moving toward the water's edge, diving in, disappearing to rescue the doomed, and the drugs.

Tony ran down the steps of the High Tide, heading for the boats under the deck. Fortunately, he was alone. Blanche saw the boots clattering down the stairs and acted out of reflex. She came at him from behind the steps and tripped him, just as one of the agents appeared next to her.

Tony looked up, spread-eagle on the crushed shell. "What are you doing? I work here," he yelled.

"Yeah, man, I work here, too." The agent gathered the flailing arms into handcuffs and led him away. Tony's workers were cooling it in the walk-in refrigerator, but they didn't stay for long. Law enforcement ran from the mangroves, up the steps, covering the area inside and out.

Blanche retreated back under the stairs and saw something across the parking lot that sent a shiver through her. Clearly, it was a white van. *The guy likes white vans. Who'd a thought his taste could be so unwavering, and boring.* And then she saw Haasi, a small dark shape moving faster than a small deer. It was dark, but the moon and lights around the restaurant gave off enough to barely see. He came around the side of the van, his hair slicked back from a high forehead. He wore an immaculate white t-shirt, and his arms were well-muscled and tattooed. He started across the lot toward the boats for the pick-up. Looking for trouble.

He found it.

Placer pulled a knife from his belt. It glinted. He raised the weapon and was just about to drive it into the back of the moving camouflaged agent who crept ahead of him toward the boats. He was well-armed and well-trained, no doubt, but concentration and focus can be like blinders. The agent didn't hear Placer coming up behind him.

Placer was too late to his target. He had good reflexes, but it was not enough. Haasi drove her knife into his back, right below his shoulder. He let out an undisciplined scream. The agent turned and grabbed Placer's arm in mid-air. The knife was still in his hand, and one was in his back.

Blanche ran up. "Is he dead?"

"No," Haasi said. "Dead fish can't talk."

Duncan, and then more officers, and more, appeared. The ground had turned green in the dark with cops.

He was as mad as Jack had been. "What on God's earth are you doing here, Blanche? And you, too?"

"Never mind," Blanche said. "The red SUV in the parking lot. We slit Sal's tires, and he can't move. Sal's the guts of this operation. Liza is keeping an eye on him, but I think he's passed out in the front seat. We sort of had a few cocktails."

"My God, girl. What the hell are you talking about? You should be in the hospital."

"Can't we talk later, chief? Please? Go." Two officers headed that way, and Duncan was right behind.

Liza came clicking toward them in high heels and camouflage with glitter, her flame-tipped fingers waving at them. "Sal's on the loose. Got out the wedge I put in the door."

"How convenient. That's him," Blanche shouted.

Sal had taken off around the edge of the lot, and he was running for the boats.

It worked with Tony. Let's see if two is a charm.

She cut across the lot just as Sal ran past. It was dark at the scrub line, and she was praying she had good aim. She decided to duck and use her whole body. He tripped, and Blanche found herself under a bottom feeder.

She looked up through a tangle of black curls to see Liza, legs braced in a V, a pistol in her hand. "Wow, Blanche. Good work."

Duncan and his troops were clicking handcuffs on as many wrists as they could in the span of seconds. Liza trained the gun on them.

"Liza, for criminy sakes." It was Duncan. "Put that thing away."

"Sure." She tucked the gun into a holster on her chest, her legs wobbling. She dusted the sand off Blanche's shoulders.

Sal looked at Blanche. "You a cop?"

"Wouldn't you like to know. Do you have something to confess?"

He didn't answer. It was the fastest five minutes Blanche had ever lived through, but she was alive. She looked around. The agents had made fast work of cleaning up the place. The ambulances pulled away with a wet pilot, one wounded hit man, and a couple of Tony's handlers, plus Tony. The police wagons were full.

Forty-Four
One Big Happy Family

DUNCAN'S FACE WAS AN UNHEALTHY SHADE OF RED. "Goldarn it, Blanche." Haasi remained as placid as a deep lake on a calm day. Liza put on a Mona Lisa smile.

Blanche's eyes opened wide. "Well, aren't you glad no one ended up back in the hospital? Except for certain persons." With that, Blanche diffused the bomb that was Chief Duncan.

Hank Miles grinned. "I don't know what got into you girls."

"Nothing. It was always there," said Haasi.

They all looked at each other, and laughed.

It turned out that a lot of talking fish went to the tank that night. Sal was not suited to incarceration, so he was more than willing to fess up for better treatment. It was unlikely he would get out of jail for a long time, as with the rest of them. It was a marathon of talking bottom feeders.

The RICO laws proved to be handy in the several cases spread from Chicago to Florida to Texas. Anyone ordering a hit was as guilty as the one making the hit itself. Sal tried to squiggle out of it, but he had pretty much cooked himself on other charges as well. He had ordered the unloading of the shipment of drugs when the law swooped in. It was all recorded. He claimed to be storing imports on his property, but that went over like a wet leather hassock—about a thousand of which were found packed with cocaine in Sal's warehouse.

Dominique Placer was not going anywhere. He recovered from the knife wound—he had a long time ahead to sit and mend. He was put away on many charges, not the least of which was the kidnapping and attempted murder of Blanche. They were still trying to pin the murders of Bob and Sergi on Placer, and all bets were that it would happen. His fingerprints were a match, from van to cigarette wrapper. Blanche identified him as her kidnapper.

The basis of the development plan on Santa Maria had been to launder the drug money. Running their proceeds through the construction of a mall and mansions was a good way to hide the real business of the drug trade. Fortunately, for Santa Maria, the whole business collapsed with the raid at the High Tide. The land development was permanently on hold.

Blanche and Haasi sat at the round table on the porch at the cabin. Cappy was in the kitchen finishing gumbo and stuffing grouper, and they had fresh bread that Haasi baked. Blanche went into the kitchen and brought out the Tecate when Jack and Miles came in from the beach. Dinner was almost ready.

Duncan walked in. "I never seen so much paperwork. I hope the crooks don't come back because I can't take this."

Cappy picked up his iced tea and raised a glass. "Well, I think this is as good a time as any."

Blanche and Haasi both looked at each other.

"To the sister cousins," said Cappy.

Jack grinned. Miles looked confused. But Blanche and Haasi knew exactly what Cappy was talking about. In the past weeks, more than crime had come to light. The good also came out. Haasi revealed what Cappy had thought all along, since Blanche had come to him with the story of the Indian princess on the beach: Haasi was related to Blanche. They both claimed the same great grandmother.

"Fanny Ella was in love with the Indian chief. She had gone off with him, leaving Maeve with my people. I knew Maeve for many years. She never talked about her mother, but she knew the story.

"Maeve had a half-sister named Looci, meaning black-haired in Miccosukee. She went to the Withlacoochee River country, north of Tampa, near the springs. Many Miccosukee went there when Tampa started to grow," said Haasi. "She lived near the river and banyans and palms, moving among the hummocks in the Gulf, until the phosphate mining operations came in and destroyed the area. The dynamite scared the animals and ruined the water. Looci was my grandmother. My mother was Hakla, one who hears. The dynamiting and cracking in the earth killed her, but not before she sent me to the north to study."

Blanche had known, or suspected something. She'd felt a bond with Haasi from the day they met on the beach. For hours Haasi sat at Blanche's bedside in the hospital and made up stories. She talked about the Gull Egg, and Santa Maria, the natives and the Jacks. She kept it up until Blanche woke up. It was their secret.

Jack and Miles were uncustomarily quiet. Jack got up and gave Haasi a hug. "I guess that means we're cousins, too, right?"

"Well, this is sure one big, happy family." Miles raised his beer, and once again took up his favorite expression, which was a look of intense interest in Blanche.

The door burst open. The cabin had never been a place for formalities. There had been locks for a time, but now the welcome mat was out. Since the murders had been solved and the development plan had dissipated with the capture of the money-laundering drug runners, the sunny atmosphere had come back to the island.

Liza hurried through the door. "Yay! You're here!" yelled Blanche.

Liza set a large cherry pie on the counter and gave Blanche a hug. "I have great news. The state historical society has granted heritage status to Tuna Street, and also to the northern point. No razing or tampering, here or there, now or ever." She did a little dance and clapped her hands. She had several dance partners on that porch.

It was an odd announcement for a real estate broker, but Liza was not your average realtor. She cared about preserving island history, and Bob's legacy. Liza was finishing up for her broker's license, and then she intended to buy Sunny Sands from Bob's ex, who was only too glad to be rid of it. Liza's size sixes were planted firmly in the sand of Santa Maria.

"I just found out about it, Blanche. You'd put me down as a professional reference at the historical society. The announcement, officially, comes out next month. It wouldn't have happened, B, if you hadn't started it, and pushed them."

"Oh, Liza!" Blanche looked her old friend in the eye. "Here's to the pushers."

"Now, wait a minute." Cappy stopped handing out the beers, but they were laughing.

Blanche took Liza's arm and steered her toward Haasi. "And I'd like you to meet my sister-cousin, Haasi." It occurred to Blanche that she didn't know Haasi's last name. "Haasi?"

"Haasi Hakla nee Looci."

"Haasi Hakla nee Looci Murninghan," said Blanche. "More sisters than cousins."

"Well. Wow. I couldn't begin to sort *that* one out," said Liza. "But that's *great.*"

Cappy brought out the grouper stuffed with shrimp and set it on the table on the new porch—new lumber, floor, screens and windows, thanks to Amos Wiley. He'd made sure Blanche never knew what hit her.

Miles opened more beers. They ate and laughed and thanked God for huge favors. Blanche caught the rays of the sunset beyond the pines, the last of the pelicans and gulls cawing good night. It was indeed a good night and a good day coming.

Miles leaned back in the chair. "I guess we're just full of surprises today. I've got one myself. Duncan has agreed to hire me. I'm out of the DEA business, at least for now. I need some island time."

Cappy grinned.

"What are you grinning about?" Blanche said. "He'll just be hangin' around, eating us out of house and home."

"Well, that's fine with me," he said.

Blanche looked over at Miles, and smiled. "Ditto."

Acknowledgements

I WENT BACK TO THE SETTING OF MY MEMOIR, *The Last Cadillac*, to write this mystery, *Saving Tuna Street*, but I changed the name of the setting from Anna Maria Island to Santa Maria Island. I needed license; writers love license, all they can get. Then I took off in this new mystery series with my peripatetic character, Blanche Murninghan, who couldn't go anywhere without a lot of help:

Thank you, Marie Corbett, author of the memoir; January, who introduced me to Gillian Kendall, her excellent editor; and to Gretchen Hirsch, an insightful editor who is all about getting down to the bones.

To my editors at Light Messages Publishing—Thank you to the Turnbulls, Elizabeth and Betty and Wally, for taking on my story and making it better.

To my cousin, Charles J. Nau, a lawyer by trade and former English teacher at Notre Dame, thank you for your meticulous and often hilarious (thanks, I needed that) editing. A voracious reader, a discerner of truth, he went with me line by line down Tuna Street on our beloved island.

Many thanks to my sisters—Elizabeth Nau Montgomery, my first reader, who said I "nailed it" and, with that, gave me the boost I needed. To Patricia Nau Mertz, an inspiration, and Janet Nau Franck, for her unflagging generosity.

And, especially, to my grandmothers, who will always be with me: Elizabeth Nau Murninghan and Frances Ella Pike McLoughlin—You fill my heart and there you stay.

About the Author

NANCY NAU SULLIVAN BEGAN WRITING wavy lines at age six, thinking it was the beginning of her first novel. It wasn't. But she didn't stop writing: letters at first, then eight years of newspaper work in high school and college, in editorial posts at New York magazines, and for newspapers throughout the Midwest.

Nancy has a master's in journalism from Marquette University. She grew up outside Chicago but often visited Anna Maria Island, Florida. She returned there with her family and wrote an award-winning memoir *The Last Cadillac* (Walrus 2016) about the years she cared for her father while the kids were still at home, a harrowing adventure of travel, health issues, adolescent angst, with a hurricane thrown in for good measure.

The author has gone back to that setting for this first in her mystery series, *Saving Tuna Street*, creating the fictional Santa Maria Island home of Blanche "Bang" Murninghan. Blanche has feet of sand and will be off to Mexico, Ireland, and other parts for further mayhem in the series. But she always returns to Santa Maria Island.

Nancy, for the most part, lives in Northwest Indiana.

Follow Nancy:
www.nancynausullivan.com
@NauSullivan.